RANCHER'S DEADLY REUNION

BETH CORNELISON

MILLS & BOON

First Published in Great Britain 2018
by Mills & Boon, an imprint of HarperCollins*Publishers*
1 London Bridge Street, London, SE1 9GF

Rancher's Deadly Reunion © 2018 Beth Cornelison

ISBN: 978-0-263-26600-9

1018

MIX
Paper from
responsible sources
FSC™ C007454

This book is produced from independently certified FSC™ paper to ensure responsible forest management.

For more information visit: www.harpercollins.co.uk/green

Printed and bound in Spain
by CPI, Barcelona

To Jeffery—you make me proud every day!
All my love, Mom.

Prologue

The loud, frantic pounding on the front door at 1:00 a.m. boded ill. Pam Summers belted her bathrobe around her and started for the door. Her husband followed at a slower, groggier pace, while their four-month-old yellow Lab gamboled around the foyer and barked excitedly. When Pam looked through the peep-hole and saw who was there, she gasped at the young man's beleaguered appearance and snatched open the door.

"Brady? What are you doing here?" Pam studied her brother-in-law's disheveled clothes, slumped shoulders and bloodshot eyes with concern. His showing up on their doorstep at this late hour was unusual enough to elicit worry, but his appearance as he stood on their stoop spiked her distress through the roof. She clutched the lapels of her terry-cloth robe closed near her throat. "What is it? What's wrong?"

She heard her husband, Scott, walk up behind her, his slippers scuffing on the hardwood floor of the foyer. "Hey, little brother, what's— Damn! You look like hell."

"Can I come in?" Brady asked, his voice as rough as gravel.

Nerves jangling, Pam opened the door wider to let Brady into their Boyd Valley, Colorado, home. Kip, the puppy, ran out to the yard, while a warm, late-August breeze, redolent with the scents of cut grass and summer rain, followed Brady in. As for her brother-in-law, Brady reeked of beer and something harder.

"Is it Dad? Has something happened to Dad?" Scott asked as his brother staggered to the couch and dropped heavily onto the cushions.

"Nah, the old man's fine." Brady scrubbed a hand over his bleary face.

Scott frowned and wrinkled his nose. "You've been drinking. A lot by the looks and smell of it."

"Yeah, so what?"

"So…getting drunk is Dad's thing. I thought you knew better." He paused a beat. "Did you drive here?"

Brady said nothing and kept his eyes down.

"Damn it, Brady!" Scott barked, "You're not even legal yet. But driving while you're drunk…that's unacceptable. It's stupid and dangerous!"

Brady squeezed his eyes tightly shut and held his head. "I know."

Scott huffed his disgust. "You can sleep here tonight and go home tomorrow. Jeez, I thought you had more sense than to—"

"I asked Piper to marry me." Brady's announcement silenced Scott's tirade.

Pam settled on the love seat positioned catty-corner to the couch where Brady had slumped, dazed-looking. Scott eased down beside her, placing a warm hand on her knee.

"I'm guessing from your demeanor that she turned you down," Scott said.

"She's leavin'. Goin' to Boston for college. Didn't wanna be tied down to a good-for-nothin' ranch hand."

Pam blinked her surprise. "She said that? She called you *good-for-nothing*?"

"Didn't have to. It's kinda obvious. I mean, she's smart. Got a full scholarship to that fancy school out east. All I do is shovel horseshit and rustle cattle."

"Being a ranch hand doesn't make you good-for-nothing, Brady," Scott said. "This…feeling sorry for yourself bit isn't like you. I know you really like Piper, but people leave for college all the time."

"I don't *really like* her. I love her." Brady gave them a woeful look. "I *want* to marry her. But she turned me down. Flat. It's over."

Pam's heart ached for Scott's younger brother, but she could see Piper McCall's side, too. "I'm sorry you've been hurt, Brady, but Piper's leaving for college doesn't have to be the end of your relationship. Give her the space she needs to spread her wings. Eighteen *is* kinda young to get married. You both have plenty of time to—"

"What about the baby?" he muttered, his eyes filling with tears. "She thinks I only wanna marry 'cause of the baby. But…I love her. And not just 'cause of the baby like she thinks."

Scott exchanged a startled look with Pam, then asked cautiously, "What…baby?"

"Ours." He ducked his head and heaved a shuddering sigh. "Mine and Piper's. She's pregnant."

Something sharp and bitter pierced Pam's heart. She didn't want to resent anyone's pregnancy, but she couldn't help it. She and Scott had been trying for five years to have a baby—and failing. She worked hard to shove her pain down and focus on the issue at hand. "You…you're sure? She's sure?"

"Pretty sure. We didn't use protection a few weeks back." He glanced up with a guilty expression and raised a hand, "Stupid, I know. Don't lecture me. But we were caught up in the moment and—" He expelled a harsh breath. "She's been sick. She claimed she just had a stomach bug, but…" Brady shook his head, adding, "And every now and then, she just…puts her hand on her belly. Not her stomach but lower. I don't even think she realizes she's doing it, but I noticed. So she finally took a test and… I thought if we got married… I want to do the right thing for the baby."

Pam's stomach knotted, and her thoughts spun off in a hundred directions. Brady and his girlfriend had created a baby together by accident, when she and Scott couldn't have the one they craved so deeply. It wasn't fair. *It wasn't fair!* She shoved to her feet, putting a hand to her mouth and struggling to hold back the frustrated scream in her throat.

Scott sent her a worried look. He knew where her mind had gone. He was likely thinking the same thing but had to be brave in front of his brother.

"Brady, I'm sorry, man. I don't know what to say." Scott rubbed his hands on his sleep pants and divided a glance between her and his brother.

"I thought we had somethin'," Brady mumbled, his eyes blinking closed for a moment. He was about to pass out from the looks of it. "But she doesn't care. About me...or my baby..." He swiped at his face. "She can't get out of town fast enough. Don't think she wants to keep the baby...it'll mess up her college plans. That's all she talks about lately. Goin' off to that snotty school and leavin' Boyd Valley in the dust. Leavin' me in the dust."

Scott cast a side look to Pam. "Hon, I think Brady could use some coffee. Do you mind?"

She clenched her trembling hands, trying to hide their shaking. "I think he's beyond coffee. I'll get him a pillow and blanket so he can sleep it off."

She pivoted on her heel and stalked out of the living room and down the hall to the linen closet, fighting back tears. Brady had gotten a girl pregnant. Without even trying. By mistake. Pam swallowed hard. What would Piper McCall do with the baby? Keep it? Put it up for adoption? Abort it? Her gut clenched hard, churning with nausea at the idea of Piper getting rid of the baby. Scott's niece or nephew.

It wasn't fair! She swiped at a tear that tickled her cheek. Then stilled.

Scott's niece or nephew. His blood relation. An idea began to form, like a tickling at the nape of her neck. The tingling spread over her scalp as the idea grew stronger. Her heart thrashed in her chest, resolve solidifying.

She jolted when Scott touched her shoulder. "He's out."

"I want the baby," she said, barely a breath.

"I know. It's crazy. It's cruel fate that he—"

She spun to face her husband. "No. I want *that* baby.

Brady's baby is your family. If she's planning to give it up or is thinking she'll get rid of it…"

"Pam?"

She was starting to hyperventilate. Grabbing the front of her husband's T-shirt, she met his gaze with a pleading look. "We can call George in the morning. He has all kind of connections with adoption agencies around the country. I bet he knows people in Boston. That's who she'd contact, right?"

"Pam—"

She shook the fistful of his shirt. "Listen! Surely with this kind of head start, George can alert his people, find out what she plans to do with the baby, find out if she plans to give it away and pull whatever strings he has to to get the baby for us."

Scott didn't say anything for a moment, his expression sad but thoughtful. "If Brady knew we had his child, he'd—"

She shook her head vehemently. "*No.* We can't tell Brady. Piper can't know it's us trying to adopt. It'll be our secret. A closed adoption. If they knew it was their baby, it would be too hard, too complicated."

Scott wiped the tears she hadn't even realized she'd shed from her cheeks and kissed her forehead. "I know how much you're hurting, how much you want a baby. But I don't see how this would work. We'll adopt another—"

"It *can* work. We'll explain everything to George, and he'll make it work. He's the best adoption attorney out there. I know he can do this."

Scott was shaking his head, and she released him with a shove. "So you won't even try? We're talking about your niece or nephew! This was meant to be. I feel it!"

Scott ducked his head, his breathing heavy and quick. When he lifted his chin again and met her gaze, a spark of determination lit his eyes. "All right. I'll call George in the morning."

Chapter 1

Seven years later

Piper was leaving town. Ken Grainger watched the evidence play out on his computer screen. Thanks to the tracking program he'd installed on her computer on a weekend when the accounting office was abandoned, he could see everything she did on her work computer. Getting access to her personal laptop had been a bit harder, but he'd rather enjoyed the challenge. He was even able to access her laptop camera and watch her in her apartment. Well, as far as the camera angle allowed. But he'd caught a few glimpses of her walking through her living room in her towel last week, and he was still enjoying the fantasies that peek created for him.

He shoveled another spoonful of cereal in his mouth, then wiped dribbles of milk from his chin with his sleeve. He chewed and followed the movement of her cursor as she booked her flight for Denver.

Ken frowned. He knew she was from Colorado, but she typically didn't go back to her family's ranch except at Christmas and for a brief visit around Mother's Day. An October visit was unusual, and this break from her normal pattern didn't sit well with him. Why was she going now? What was he missing?

He grumbled a curse under his breath. He had to find a way to hack her new cell phone. He was missing so much valuable information by not being party to her texts and phone calls. Putting that kind of hacking in place would take a little more planning. Cunning.

He grinned as she typed in her credit card number to purchase the airline ticket. Challenge accepted. Piper was worth the effort and the expense involved. He would convince her, some way, that they were soul mates, destined to be together, and anyone who interfered with that destiny would pay the price.

Like Ron Sandburg had.

The dirtwad had tried to move in on his turf and had regretted it. He'd overheard Piper tell Elaine in the break room that the way Ron stared at her from his cubicle gave Piper the creeps. So after he'd seen Ron hitting on Piper at the coffee shop in the lobby of the office building, he'd made sure Ron Sandburg left Piper alone. Permanently.

The look of confusion in Ron's eyes, the instant of fear when Ron had known he was about to die, had been sweet payoff. A well-centered push on Ron's chest as he'd topped the long flight of stairs in his apartment building…and any threat Ron had posed to his plans with Piper went tumbling down.

Ken grinned to himself, relishing that victory.

Yes, he would come up with a way to add her new phone to his surveillance, he vowed as he hit Print Screen to make a hard copy of her flight schedule. He'd remedy this gap in his surveillance as soon as feasible.

But how? She kept her damn cell on her person all the time while she was at the office. He'd tried before to steal a peek at it, but she carried it in the pocket of the cardigan she wore year-round because the management kept the temperature of the office set to arctic.

Turning to his second screen, he navigated to the airline's reservation page and booked himself a ticket to Denver on the flight arriving just before Piper's. He wanted to be in place at the Denver airport to observe her arrival. Who would pick her up? Where would she go after arriving? The family ranch or a hotel?

He sloshed another bite of cereal into his mouth, irritated that he didn't know the nature of her trip. Had someone died? Was this a business meeting? He dismissed the idea of this trip being work-related with a brisk shake of his head. Surely if this was company travel, he'd have heard about it in staff meetings or seen something come through her work email. If he could—

He cut the thought off, seeing new activity on her laptop. Speaking of email…she was apparently writing one to—he leaned closer to the screen to see what she'd typed—Josh and Zane. Her brothers.

He set his now-soggy dinner aside and rolled his desk chair closer to the monitor where he followed her activity.

Hi guys, I just booked my flight out for Mom and Dad's anniversary party. Can one of you dolts find it in your hearts to pick me up and save me the cab fare in from

Denver? I arrive on the Wednesday before the party at 3:10 p.m. Love you both (despite your many flaws!) Ha ha! P.

An anniversary party, huh? He rubbed his jaw and considered that for a moment. On the surface, a family event seemed innocent enough, but…

Ken ground his back teeth together and stared at the monitor, as if he could read any hidden agenda into her return to her family's ranch. She had a good job, a good life here in Boston. She had *him* here in Boston, even if she hadn't yet realized what they could mean to each other. Maybe he was paranoid, but every time she went back to Colorado, he worried that she might decide she was missing something by not being close to her family. She talked fairly often about her brothers. He knew she and her brothers were triplets. Did she have some triplet bond with her brothers that might trump everything she had here in Boston?

Mentally, he bumped up the urgency to hack her cell phone before she left town in a couple weeks. He couldn't be sure how closely he'd be able to observe her once she got to Colorado, and he needed that additional link to her ASAP.

He went back to reserving a flight to Denver, then pulled up a list of motels near Boyd Valley, Colorado. Piper had said the town was small and rather remote, and the lack of lodging options in the town confirmed that. Two motels were listed within a twenty-five mile radius. One called The Mountaineer in Boyd Valley itself and a place called Catch-a-Wink in a community ten miles to the south. Next closest result was 56 miles away. He clicked the link for The Mountaineer's website and arrived at a rudimentary website that looked like it had been created as a junior high kid's school project. Jotting down the phone number for the office, he'd started tapping in the number on his cell phone. Activity on his monitor caught his attention. A quick reply from one of the brothers to her email.

Of course we'll pick you up, dummy. No prob. Can't wait to see your ugly mug! LOL! BTW, do you want to go in thirds on the cruise Josh and I are giving them as their gift? Have a good trip, Zane

"Mountaineer Inn. Can I help you?" asked the woman who answered his call.

"Yeah, you got any rooms left for later this month?"

"Absolutely. How many rooms do you need, and when will you be checking in?"

"Just one room." He only gave the lady from the motel half of his attention as he rattled off an alias. If Boyd Valley was as small as Piper said, it wouldn't do for her to catch wind of his presence there thanks to some town gossip.

"Can I pay cash for the room when I get there?"

"Yes, if you pay for the full stay on arrival." The lady from The Mountaineer went on to rattle off a spiel about their hot breakfast and something about local attractions, but he tuned her out.

Piper was replying to Zane's email.

Yes on the cruise. I already told Josh that. Not surprised Doofus forgot to tell you! :-) I'll give you a check when I get there. Excited! See you soon, P.

"Yeah," he muttered, hanging up on the lady at the motel. "We'll see you soon, bro."

Piper McCall entered the baggage claim area at Denver International Airport and scanned the crowd for a familiar face. Her brothers had assured her they would pick her up, but since then some question had come up about which of them it would be. Despite the long flight, she actually looked forward to the ride to the Double M Ranch. The hour-long drive would give her the chance to catch up on ranch and family news. She hadn't seen her identical twin brothers, the other two-thirds of the McCall triplets, since Christmas.

She missed the bond she'd had with her brothers. She might have felt a bit odd-woman-out growing up, but you didn't share a womb for nine months and not have a connection to your siblings.

"Piper!" a strong male voice called over the crowd noise, and she turned in the direction she'd heard her name. And froze.

The face she spotted by the luggage carts was definitely someone from the ranch. But not one of her brothers.

Brady Summers.

Son of their foreman. Her first love. And her first lover.

Her mouth dried. Why did it have to be Brady?

He raised a hand to make sure she'd seen him, and she bobbed a stiff nod of acknowledgment. Her gut somersaulting, she wove through the milling passengers and airport personnel toward Brady.

She silently cursed her mother, who had, no doubt, set this up. She'd have to explain to her mother, again, that she and Brady were over. Kaput. History. Time to stop throwing them together, believing that the old spark would reignite, and the McCalls and Summerses would live happily ever after.

She exhaled a cleansing breath. Okay, so her mother didn't know the whole truth about what had happened between Piper and Brady. Probably for the best. Piper shuddered internally at the notion of what her mother might do if she knew the whole story, the whole, checkered past between her and the foreman's son.

Brady doffed his cowboy hat as Piper approached and gave her his charming, lopsided grin. "Hey there. Good flight?"

"Average." She heard the slight falter in her voice, the flutter that matched her staggering heartbeat.

Damn it, why did he have to look so good to her even after all these years? Better even. His youthful face had matured with a stronger jawline, sharper angles to his cheekbones and more rugged overall appeal. Brady's eyes were the same piercing green, though, and the smile that tugged at his lips had the same power to tie her insides in giddy knots. His gaze held hers as he greeted her, and she felt his stare to her marrow. Could he see how he still affected her? How the mere sight of him turned her insides to goo?

Steeling herself, Piper surreptitiously wiped her sweaty palms on the seat of her jeans.

"Welcome home." He reached for the backpack she had draped on one shoulder, and she shrugged away.

"I can get this. I have two suitcases coming, though. Carousel 3."

He lifted a shoulder. "All right."

She jerked a nod and turned to search the lit signs for the carousel.

"Piper?"

She glanced back at him. *Please don't make this harder than it already is.*

His gaze dropped to a boy standing slightly behind him. The boy was playing with a small windup fire truck, rolling the toy up the side of a trash can. "Connor, c'mere. I want you to meet someone."

Connor glanced up, staring at Piper for a moment, his eyes the same clear green as a Rocky Mountain lake. The same green as Brady's eyes. Air backed up in her lungs. If her life had gone differently...

Connor scuttled to Brady's side, jerking her from the dangerous path of what-ifs.

"Piper, this is Connor. My nephew."

The breath she'd been holding left her in a gush. *His nephew.* Of course. Relief made her knees tremble, but on the heels of that release came the stark reminder of why his nephew was with him.

Brady's brother and sister-in-law were killed in a bad traffic accident on Interstate 70, her mother had said in a phone call a few months back. When had that been? January? February? The couple had left custody of their son to Brady, a move that still puzzled her. Pam had family, sisters with children who'd surely have been better equipped to care for the little boy.

She worked to hide her dismay over the couple's deaths from the boy.

"Connor, this is Josh and Zane's sister, Piper. Can you tell her *hello*?"

The boy stepped forward with a shy smile and stuck his hand out. "Hello. I'm Connor. Nice to meet you."

A smile bloomed on her face, and she took the small proffered hand. Crouching to the boy's level and letting her backpack slip to the floor, she said, "Pleased to meet you, Connor. You have wonderful manners."

He twitched a crooked grin and shrugged. "Yeah. I know."

She snorted a laugh before she could muffle it. Glancing up at Brady, she added, "And so humble."

He grinned and flipped up his palm. "He's a work in progress."

Piper sandwiched Connor's hand between hers in a warm clasp. "How old are you, Connor?"

"Six." His face brightened. "I had a cowboy birthday party."

Piper chuckled. "Cowboys, huh? Like your uncle?"

"And Grampa. He's foreman at the Double M!"

Piper matched the boy's enthusiastic expression. "I know! Guess what? I've known your Grampa since before I was your age."

Connor tipped his head and gave her a skeptical frown. "Really?"

"The Double M is my family's ranch. I grew up there."

He nodded sagely. "Like Josh and Zane."

She tapped his nose. "Bingo. They're my brothers. We're triplets. We were all born the same day."

"And Brady?" Connor's green eyes widened. "He grew up at the Double M, too. Like my daddy. 'Cept… Mama and Daddy died. So now Brady's my daddy."

Piper's smile drooped, and her throat clogged painfully as if she'd swallowed a jagged stone. She angled her gaze to Brady and nodded. "Right. And Brady. I knew Brady and your dad growing up." Drawing deep breath to regain her composure, she pushed to her feet. "Wanna help me get my suitcases?"

She tousled Connor's sandy-brown hair, the same color as Brady's—

She determinedly cut the thought off as she hiked

her backpack onto her shoulder again. Not Brady's. Like Scott's. But even that wasn't right, she thought as she set off toward the luggage carousel.

She cast a side-glance at Brady as they made their way through the crowd, allowing herself to conjure a painful memory from the first summer she'd been home from college. The trip that summer had been the first time she'd returned to Colorado since breaking up with Brady and setting out for Boston, for independence, for her fresh start. That first year had been the toughest year of her life, and seeing Brady after eleven months away from home and family had been gut-wrenching.

In a stiff conversation with Brady in the stables, an accidental meeting she'd barely made it through without crying, she'd asked all the polite questions.

"How's your dad?"

"Dad is Dad. Same as always."

"And Scott?"

"Good. He and Pam adopted a baby."

Piper remembered the stabbing pain in her heart and how she'd forced a quivering smile. *"Wow. That's great. Tell them congratulations from me."*

Connor wasn't Scott's biological son, so the similarities she saw between Connor and Brady were just coincidence. Or some misplaced wishful thinking. Or her head playing the heart-wrenching what-if game again.

Brady placed a callus-roughened hand on Connor's head, lightly ruffling the boy's silky hair, as they waited beside carousel 3 for the belt to start moving. "What do your suitcases look like?"

"Plain black like a thousand others." She set her backpack at her feet and rubbed her aching shoulder.

"One has a red luggage tag, and I tied a little blue ribbon on the other."

He nodded. "Got it."

"So…you drew the short straw, huh?" she asked without looking at him. She pretended to be intently watching the crowd and the shadowed maw where her flight's cargo would soon appear.

"Pardon?"

"To come get me. You pulled the short straw?"

"Actually, I volunteered."

She cut a side-glance at him and met his piercing gaze. "You did?"

"Yeah. I thought Connor would get a kick outta seeing the airplanes, the terminal. Oh, before we leave, I've promised him we can get a cinnamon pretzel at Auntie Anne's."

A loud warning beep blared from a speaker just above their heads, interrupting any reply. He wasn't here for her. He was here for Connor…and a cinnamon pretzel. She wasn't sure how that made her feel. Relief? Disappointment? And why did it matter to her?

The conveyor belt started rolling, and someone with an oversize duffel bag on his arm pushed past Piper, knocking her into Brady. She tripped over her backpack, lost her balance and landed against him with an *oof*, her hands splayed on his chest and her nose in the V of his open collar.

Brady wrapped his arm around her waist to steady her as she regained her footing, and heat flashed through her. From his taut body, from embarrassment…and from a kick of lust she couldn't quell. As she righted herself, she drew a deep, calming breath and immediately regretted it.

Brady smelled so good. And familiar. A sexy combination of soap, hay and male warmth that took her back to hours spent in his arms. Naked. Inquisitive. Bursting with young love and rampant teenage desire.

Piper shifted her grip from his chest to his arms, trying to wiggle free of his hold. "I'm good. You can let go."

But he didn't.

After a couple of strained seconds, she glanced up to repeat herself. Maybe he hadn't heard her in the din and bustle of the airport. When she met his eyes, her voice stuck in her throat. The intensity of his gaze left no question that his thoughts had followed a similar track to hers. Motes of longing swirled through the green depths and tangled with shadows of regret. His mouth looked soft, but his jaw muscles flexed and tightened with restraint. He wanted to kiss her. She recognized that look well, and so did the muscles in her belly that quickened and the nerves in her lips that tingled with the memory of his kisses. How easy it would be to push up on her toes and steal the kiss his eyes promised.

Instead, she forced her throat to loosen enough to wheeze. "I'm okay. L-let go."

Slowly, his arm slipped away, even though his stare held hers for several more painful heartbeats. Despite her assurances to Brady that she could stand alone, her knees trembled as she stepped back, threatening to give out.

Pull it together, McCall! This moony, love-sick calf act will not help you get through the week and back to Boston with your heart intact. With the steely determination that had helped her survive her freshman year, keeping her grades up while she battled morning sickness and a broken heart, she shoved aside the jittery sparks dancing through her and put some starch in her spine.

"That one?" a young voice asked, and she felt a tug on her shirt. She glanced down at Brady's nephew and found him pointing behind her. "That one has blue string."

Blue string…suitcase…airport. Piper blinked several times, bringing her surroundings back into focus. For just a moment, she'd lost track of the rest of the world. Being with Brady had a way of narrowing her scope to just the two of them.

"Grab it, buddy." Brady stepped past her, a guiding hand on Connor's shoulder.

The little boy scuttled forward through the crowd with his uncle at his heels. When Connor grabbed the huge suitcase's handle and struggled to drag it off the conveyor belt, Brady added a helping hand. After the bag thunked to the floor, Brady stepped back, letting his nephew raise the handle and roll the suitcase through the crowd.

Piper shook the tension from her hands and arms and blew out a puff of air, gathering some semblance of composure. Pasting on a smile for Connor, she reached for the oversized suitcase as he dragged it to her feet. "Need some help?"

"I got it," Connor said and grunted. "Sheesh! How many clothes did you bring? That's heavy!"

"Oh, that's not clothes. That's my bag of rocks."

Connor frowned for a second before twisting his mouth in a crooked grin. "You're teasing!"

She flashed a playful grin and shrugged. "Maybe. Maybe not."

Brady approached with her other suitcase in tow and asked, "Is this it?"

She nodded. "Thanks. I think that's everything."

"All right then." Brady dug his keys from his pocket and bounced them once in his hand. "Let's go home."

Piper's stomach swooped. *Home.* Once upon a time, she'd called the Double M Ranch home. But she had a new life now in Boston. She'd found the independence she'd been looking for when she went to college, but that independence had come at a cost. She'd lost the close family connections she'd taken for granted growing up. She'd stayed away from the ranch for most of the last seven years. Her freshman year, she'd hidden herself at college to protect the secret she carried, afraid of her family's reaction, running from Brady and from a future that couldn't be. She'd flogged herself with regret and guilt. Each year that followed, she allowed herself brief visits, but kept mostly to the main house, avoiding the stable and cattle pens at times she knew Brady would be there.

"Wait!" Connor cried as they started for the parking garage. "Don't forget my pretzel!"

"Oh, right," Brady said, giving his head a shake and patting Connor on the back. "Sorry, buddy. Now let's see. Where is Auntie Anne's?"

A review of the airport map in the lobby showed the only Auntie Anne's was past the security gates.

"Sorry, buddy. They won't let us go to the part of the airport where the pretzel store is without a ticket," Brady told his nephew and ruffled the boy's hair.

"Where do we get a ticket?" Connor asked.

"We don't. Not today."

Connor wrinkled his nose in protest. "How come? You said I could have a pretzel!"

"I know. I'm sorry." The look on Brady's face said everything he didn't. How much he hated letting his nephew down. How hard he was thinking about a way to make it up to Connor. Piper sent Brady a sympathetic smile and tapped Connor on the shoulder.

"You know what? I've been craving a big chocolate ice cream cone for hours. What do you say we stop for ice cream on the way home instead?"

Connor looked unconvinced at first, but when Piper batted her eyelashes and clasped her hands under her chin with a "Please?" the boy nodded. "Is that okay, Uncle Brady? Can we get Piper some ice cream?"

"That we can, Con." He gave her a wink of thanks, and the moment of conspiratorial connection wrapped around her like a hug, warmth burrowing to her core. As they made their way out of the airport, Piper tried to rein in the soft emotions that tugged at her. She didn't want to let her guard down around Brady or share private smiles that would chip away at her protective walls. Even after seven years, she was clearly still vulnerable to Brady's lopsided grin and soft-spoken charm, and she was thankful for the buffer and distraction Connor would provide on the drive back to the ranch.

With Connor struggling valiantly to roll one of her heavy suitcases, they strolled down the long aisle of the parking deck until they reached Brady's mud-speckled pickup truck. After Connor scrambled up onto the back seat of the extended cab F-150, he seized Piper's hand and tugged. "Sit with me, Piper!"

"Well, I—"

"Pleeeeeease?"

The light green, puppy-dog eyes that beseeched her were impossible to turn down. She glanced at Brady, who only chuckled as he slid behind the steering wheel.

"Sure. Why not?" she said.

Closing the front door and glad for the excuse to

move to the back seat, she climbed in next to Brady's nephew, waved her hand blithely and in a nasal voice, said, "Home, James."

Connor wrinkled his nose. "James? His name's Brady!"

"Not when he's our chauffeur," she said, wagging a finger, her voice still pinched and snooty.

Connor caught on to her joke and gave a belly laugh. Mimicking her hoity-toity tone, he said, "Drive us home, James!"

Brady loosed an indelicate snort, then returned, "Righty-o, Sir Snoodlepants."

Connor's peals of laughter filled Piper with an odd warmth, and she couldn't stop the giggles that bubbled up.

"Hey, Piper," Connor asked as they backed out of the parking space, "how do you stop an elephant from charging?"

She cut a glance to Brady, whose cheek dimpled as he grinned. "I don't know. How?"

"Take away her credit card!" Connor's eyes lit as he delivered the punch line, and Piper found herself chuckling at the boy's delight. She didn't have much experience around children. Most of her friends were either unmarried or putting off starting a family while they launched their careers. Yet Brady had had fatherhood handed to him under difficult circumstances. The notion made her chest tighten. If she hadn't gotten the scholarship that took her to Boston College, how would her life have been different? Could she and Brady have made their relationship work? Could they have been parents to—

She nipped off the thought before it fully formed. *Don't go there.*

Focusing her attention on Brady's nephew, she asked, "Do you know what an elephant's favorite vegetable is?"

He shook his head.

"Squash!"

"Squash!" Connor repeated with another hardy laugh. "Did you hear that, Brady? *Squash!*"

"Afraid so, little man."

Connor continued to entertain her with riddles as they drove out of the airport and merged onto the highway.

She mentally thanked Connor for providing an excuse not to make awkward conversation with Brady. The boy's invitation to ride in the back seat with him also gave her the opportunity to study Brady's profile covertly, to drink in the subtle changes in his face without him knowing.

"Do you know any more jokes?" Connor asked, his cheeks flushed and eyes bright with his amusement.

Piper scoured her memory for one of the lame riddles she and her brothers had told each other years ago. "What is black and white and red all over?"

"A zebra with a sun burn!" Connor shouted, clearly pleased with himself.

The boy's mirth elicited an answering chuckle from her. The music of Connor's giggles fed her soul. Laughing loosened the knots of tension that had kinked inside her the moment she spotted Brady across the airport lobby. More than that, goofing around with the little boy was a release she'd needed from the pressures and worries of her sixty-hour-a-week job and a few high-maintenance friends in Boston.

When was the last time she'd allowed herself to be silly? To laugh with the kind of carefree abandon that

Connor enjoyed? Not that she didn't share light moments with her friends and coworkers in Boston. She did. But with Connor there was no agenda, no drama. Just a little boy enjoying bad puns and simple irony.

Connor delivered the punch line of a joke she realized she'd missed as she was musing, but she groaned and grinned as if she'd been paying attention. As he started another riddle, Piper had the odd sensation of being watched. She'd experienced the prickling sensation at the back of her neck frequently over the past few months, so she knew the unsettling feeling well. Her gaze flew to the driver's seat, and she found Brady staring at her via the rearview mirror. His gaze locked with hers, a strange, unreadable expression sculpting his face. The odd look held a note of intimacy, but also an edgy curiosity. Was it wariness? Fear? What did Brady have to fear from her? She didn't have long to analyze his expression before his attention darted back to the road.

Connor, too, had fallen oddly quiet, eyeing them, then turning his gaze out the window and shifting restlessly in his booster seat. The boy's brow beetled, and he said, "Uncle Brady, is this the road where Mama and Daddy died?"

Piper stilled, and a cold sorrow sliced through her.

Brady's hand tightened around the steering wheel, and he again glanced in the rearview mirror, this time to study his nephew. "Yeah, it is." He paused, then added, "But not this part. Their accident happened the other direction from the big city."

"Oh," was all Connor replied, still staring out the window.

Piper rubbed her thumb over the knuckles of her opposite hand, keeping a concerned gaze on Connor and regretting the lost conviviality. How was the boy handling the death of his parents? Knowing the challenge Brady had faced, taking custody of a newly orphaned boy while dealing with his own grief over Scott and Pam's deaths filled her with a new respect for her longtime friend. Brady had dealt with a lot more obligations and hardships than other men his age, even when he and Piper been involved as teenagers. The loss of his mother and his father's heavy drinking had meant he'd had to grow up fast and take on more family responsibility, especially after Scott married and moved out of town.

"Connor?" Brady said softly. "You all right, buddy?"

The boy heaved a mature-sounding sigh. "Yeah." Then, "I miss them."

Brady nodded. "Me, too, buddy."

Piper tightened her fists in her lap, hurting for Connor, for Brady. Scott and Pam had only been gone nine months. Their deaths had to still be a raw and confusing subject for Connor.

After another minute or two of strained silence in the truck, Piper searched for another joke to tell, a distracting question to redirect Connor's thoughts and lighten the mood. Or was that even the right move? Should she follow Brady's lead and let Connor work through this moment on his own? All she knew was that her heart hurt for the little boy, and her instinct was to do something, anything, to put a smile back on his face. But what did she know about parenting?

While she was debating, Connor said, "Hey, Piper?"

"Yes, sweetie?"

"What do you call a wet bear?"

She released the breath she held and flashed a warm smile at the boy. "I don't know."

"A drizzily bear." He shot her a quick grin, then turned back to his window, falling quiet again. "My dad told me that one."

"That's a good one," she said and patted his knobby knee.

Connor twisted his mouth and wrinkled his nose. "My mom and dad died in a car accident."

Her grip on his knee tightened. "I know, sweetie. I'm so sorry."

"I live with Uncle Brady and Grampa now. At the Double M."

Piper nodded. "Do you like the ranch?"

His face brightened a bit. "It smells bad 'cause of all the animal poop, but you get used to it."

She couldn't help but snort a chuckle at the boy's bluntness. Having grown up on the ranch, she'd never really noticed or cared about the odors that accompanied all the animals. For her, the scents of oiled leather and freshly cut alfalfa were sweeter than roses.

"Riding horses and helping Uncle Brady with the cows is fun," Connor added.

"Well, I've been away from the ranch for a lot of months, so my riding may be rusty." She tipped her head and gave the boy a dubious frown. "Would you help me with my horse while I'm visiting this week?"

Connor sat taller and grinned. "Sure! I'm good at saddling and riding." He glanced to his uncle, adding, "Aren't I, Brady?"

"You are, little man. That you are." Brady sent Connor a proud grin as he met his nephew's gaze in the mirror. "When we get home, Grampa will have dinner waiting, so I want you to go straight back to the house and wash up. Okay?"

"Y'sir."

Home. Piper turned her attention to the scenery passing outside her window. She'd been so absorbed in Connor that she'd not realized how close they were getting to the Double M. The beef-cattle ranch had been in her family for three generations. She'd grown up around muddy boots, bleating calves and horse tails swishing away flies. Her parents and brothers still lived on and worked the ranch, and someday she'd inherit one third of the Double M.

But was the ranch still her home? She'd been gone seven years. Seven eventful years. She'd done a lot of growing up since she left the Double M. She'd earned her degree in finance, gotten her first nine-to-five job with a finance company, set herself up in an apartment that she'd decorated to her taste.

And she'd made the toughest decisions of her life to give birth to, then give away, Brady's baby.

She swallowed hard and pressed her hand to her stomach. The memory always caused a guilty roil in her gut. She'd made the best decision she could as a scared eighteen-year-old, but that didn't mean she didn't constantly second-guess herself.

As Brady took an unexpected exit from the interstate, Piper glanced up, confused. "Where are you going?"

He angled his head toward her. "Ice cream. Remember?"

Connor sat taller, and his face brightened. "Yay! I'm gonna get chocolate, too, Piper!"

"One scoop, buddy. And you have to promise to eat your vegetables at dinner," Brady said, one eyebrow arched.

She shook her head slightly. When had Brady turned into such a…a…*parent*?

The answer came to her, and her stomach curled in on itself. She really had no appetite for ice cream. No desire to extend the awkwardness between her and Brady. She only wanted to get to the ranch and decompress after her flight, unwind the tension that had coiled in her the instant she'd spotted Brady. But she'd be damned if she'd be party to disappointing Connor, a boy whose world had been so thoroughly devastated in recent months. For Connor's sake, she'd paste on a smile, eat a chocolate ice cream cone and endure a few more taut minutes playing nice with the one man who still had the power to break her heart.

Ken didn't recognize the cowboy who'd met Piper at the airport. Nor did he know anything about the little boy. The guy wasn't one of her brothers. He'd seen the pictures of them she had on her desk at the office…and stored in her laptop. Irritation crawled through him. He didn't like the idea that Piper had people in her life that he didn't have at least a little information on.

Whoever the guy was, Piper had seemed startled to see him. She'd been cool and standoffish at first, but when that klutz with his big duffel had knocked her into the cowboy, he had been quick to catch her, slow to release her. Piper and the cowboy had shared a look that hinted at a history together. A history that might not be completely in the past. Something hot and not-yet smothered.

Hatred had burned his gut, and he'd wanted to charge across the airport and grab the randy cowboy by the throat. He'd vibrated with the urge to tear up the mystery rancher and leave no question that Piper was *his*.

But doing so would blow his cover, would mean

leaving the concealed post he'd staked out ahead of Piper's arrival. It was too soon to let her know he was here, that he'd come to Colorado to be with her, to prove to her that they belonged together.

Now, from the rental car he'd had waiting in the short-term parking lot since his arrival two hours ahead of Piper, he followed the cowboy's pickup truck from a cautious distance, across the plain at the foot of the Rocky Mountains where crops, pastures and farms dotted the landscape.

Not wanting to be noticed, he hung back when the truck left the interstate, waited impatiently while they stopped for ice cream, then continued following from a distance as they headed northeast on a state road. He managed to keep Piper and the cowboy in sight until they turned in at a gravel driveway. Ken slowed as he drove past the rutted road the pickup had taken and studied a crude, stripped-log entry arch. Hanging from the top of the arch, a sun-aged wooden sign greeted people with *Welcome to the Double M.*

He paused long enough to search for GPS coordinates with his phone, planning to use satellite images to scope out the terrain tonight from his motel room. He had a cell signal, but it was mediocre at best. He grunted his disgust. Why would anyone in their right mind want to live out here in the middle of nowhere with a bunch of smelly cows? He could give Piper so much more than this!

He shook his head. No, not *could*...he *would* give Piper more. He *would* show her their destinies were locked, intertwined. He would save her from this dirt hole in the middle of Nothing, Colorado. He'd even take her away from Boston, if needed. They'd find a place where no one could find them, no one could distract her, no one could interfere with his plans for the future with Piper. *His* Piper. His soul mate.

He'd make it happen. And just like he'd eliminated Ron Sandburg, he'd get rid of anything or anyone who stood in his way.

Chapter 2

A menagerie of people, dogs and horses filled the ranch yard as Brady pulled to a stop near her parents' house. Her mother was the first to reach her as she clambered from the back seat of Brady's truck, and Melissa McCall wrapped Piper into a tight hug, while Ace and Checkers, the family's blue heelers, circled happily with their tails thumping against her legs. Brady silently unloaded her suitcases and climbed back on the front seat without a word.

Her brothers appeared from the stable and took turns lifting Piper off the ground as they greeted her with bear hugs.

"Your dad is out in the north pasture, but he texted me to say he'd seen you arrive and would be in soon," her mother said.

Piper nodded and watched Brady drive his truck to the foreman's house across the ranch yard, where he'd lived with his father his whole life. He parked under a large tree and helped Connor out.

The little boy gave a wave to her, which she returned, before he ran inside with an awkward six-year-old's gait.

"That Connor is such a sweet kid," her mother said, putting an arm around Piper's shoulders and walking her into the house. Zane and Josh each grabbed a suitcase and followed.

Piper swung her backpack onto the bed she'd slept in for eighteen years, then cast a gaze around her childhood bedroom. Her mother had changed little about the decor since Piper had left for college seven years earlier, and the familiar pink-and-gray chevron pattern of the curtains, the 4-H ribbons and high-school rodeo trophies on her bookshelf, and the ragged stuffed rabbit, nestled with the throw pillows on her bed, flooded her with a nostalgia that tugged in her chest.

"Jeez, Piper, did you leave anything in Boston? You're only gonna be here a week. You needed two suitcases for seven days?" Josh griped as he tossed her suitcase onto the bed next to the backpack.

"Plus a backpack," Zane added as he brought her second piece of luggage into the room and dropped it on the floor at the foot of her dresser.

"Hey, careful with that! My laptop's in there," she said, frowning at Zane. "And yes, I need two suitcases. I brought work clothes and boots for helping in the stable or pens, nicer things for dinner or going to town, and dressy stuff, shoes and makeup for Mom and Dad's party."

Josh snorted and shook his head. "Whatever. Glad I'm not a girl. I like to travel light."

"Is *travel light* code for *not change your underwear*?" she said with a smirk.

Josh faked a belly laugh. "Oh, sister dear, you are a riot!" She play-punched his arm, and Josh caught her wrist, pulling her into another bear hug. "It's good to have you and your hundred-pound luggage home again, Pipsqueak."

She hugged him back, then turned to give Zane a similar squeeze. "I missed you two lugs."

"Of course, you did," Josh replied, ruffling her hair, which he knew good and well she hated.

Though her brothers were technically identical twins, each had developed a look that matched their individual personalities. Zane, the oldest by three minutes, was also the studious and more responsible one. He kept his raven hair cut short and his square jaw clean-shaven. He'd made marginally better grades than Josh or Piper, primarily because he'd applied himself more diligently.

She yanked away from Josh's manhandling and scowled at him. "Jerk." She knocked his black Stetson off his head, a retaliation which she knew would irritate him, and gave him a triumphant grin.

Josh, who'd been the more athletic and adventurous twin from the get-go, wore his hair past his ears and often neglected to shave for a day or two at a time, leaving him with a scruffy shadow of a beard. Their mother claimed Josh was part wild stallion, hard to tame, and he had seemed pleased to live up to the reputation. Both had piercing blue eyes that made girls swoon, and they were happy to take advantage of that benefit. Piper had envied her brothers' blue eyes, her own being a lackluster shade of gray.

Josh swatted at Piper with his hat as he picked it up, and Zane snorted a laugh at her expense.

"Well, some things never change," said their mother from the doorway with an eye-roll for their shenanigans. "You two leave your sister alone and let her unpack in peace. I'm sure she's tired after traveling all day."

The family cat, a brown and black Maine coon mix named Zeke, trotted in and hopped up on her bed to sniff her suitcase. She reached over to pat the feline, glad to see the family pet after months away. She really needed to rethink the apartment she was in with the no-pets rule, she decided. She scratched Zeke on the cheek, the chin, then stroked his back, finishing with a scritch at the base of his tail. Zeke ate up the attention, tilting his head this way and that, encouraging her to continue.

"Can I get you something to eat, honey?" her mother asked. "Or maybe a glass of lemonade? Dinner's not for another hour, and I'm sure you must be famished."

"Actually, Brady, Connor and I had ice cream on the way home from the airport. But lemonade sounds great. The airplane air really dried me out." She grabbed her throat and stuck out her tongue as if dying of thirst.

Giving a *mrrp* of protest when she stopped petting him, Zeke climbed on the suitcase and rolled over to show the long, silky hair of his belly. Piper couldn't resist plowing her fingers into the thick, super-soft fur and giving Zeke a belly rub. "Good boy, Zeke. I missed you, too. I bet these mean ole boys ignore you, don't they?"

Their mother smiled as she said, "Zeke lets us know when he wants attention. Believe me!" Turning to leave, her mother crooked a finger, motioning to Zane and

Josh. "Let's go, boys. Back in a minute with your lemonade."

Zane lifted a wave as he turned for the door. "Later, then."

"No, don't go. I don't need quiet to unpack," Piper said, stopping him with a hand on his arm. "In fact, I'd love to hear what you've been up to. What's the gossip in town?"

"Gossip? How the hell should I know?" Zane said. "We don't keep up with all that he-said-she-said, who's-doing-who crap."

Piper pulled a face. "You know what I mean. What's happening around here? How's the ranch?"

Zane and Josh exchanged worrisome looks.

Josh rubbed a hand on his scruffy chin. "Honestly, not so good."

"What?" she said, sitting heavily on the edge of her bed. Zeke nipped at her wrist, demanding more pats, and she stroked the cat's head while focusing on her brothers. "What's wrong?"

"Man, don't dump it on her now," Zane said. "She just got here."

"Dump what on me?" She divided a wide-eyed glance between her brothers, her pulse kicking into high gear. "Tell me, 'cause my imagination is going to fill in the blank with the worst possible scenarios if you leave me hanging."

"We're planning a family meeting after dinner." Zane put a placating hand on her shoulder. "We'll tell you then."

She shrugged Zane's hand off and shifted toward Josh. "Tell me, Josh. Give me the bullet points at least."

Josh shoved his hands in his pockets and sent Zane a defiant look. "She has a right to know."

Zane only sighed.

"What!" She was ready to clobber them both if someone didn't end her suspense.

"We're in pretty bad financial straits. We've had a couple turns of bad luck, had some investments go sour and..." Josh took off his hat and raked fingers through his shaggy black hair. "Thing is, we need to find a new income source or we could go under."

Piper let her jaw drop and her shoulders sag in shock. She narrowed a hard stare on Josh, then cut a querying glance to Zane for confirmation. "*Go under*? As in lose the ranch? Have to sell?"

Zane raised a hand. "It's not time to panic yet." He shot Josh a dark glare. "Tactful, man. Way to go."

"No point in sugarcoating it." Josh beat his hand against his Stetson and leaned back against the wall. "The truth is the truth. We've had a series of bad years, topped off by accidents and hard luck, and it's taken a toll."

Acid burned her gut and backed up in her throat. In all the years she'd been in Boston, she'd never considered the possibility that someday the ranch wouldn't be here, that her childhood home and her family's way of life could disappear. "Wh-what kind of accidents?"

Josh crossed his arms over his chest. "Well, this summer we lost a lot of cattle when one of the ponds in the west pasture got tainted with pesticides."

She furrowed her brow, perplexed. "How did that happen? We don't use pesticides in the pastures."

"Vandalism, most likely," Zane said.

"Vandalism!" She goggled at Zane. "Did you find out who did it? Were they charged?"

"We may never know." Josh's face was dark with disgust. "Not like there were security cameras out there to catch the perp. No cans left around with fingerprints. No reports of the same happening to other farmers."

"What about tire tracks or footprints or...or..."

Zane was shaking his head. "Nada. The ground was too hard thanks to the dry spell in July."

"That's horrible! How many head did we lose?"

The tap of footsteps heralded their mother's return before she appeared in Piper's doorway with a glass in her hand. "Here you go, sweetheart. I—" Melissa McCall stopped short, sending a frown to her sons. "I told you two to skedaddle and let her unpack." Her scowl softened when she looked from her sons to Piper and back again. "Good grief. What's wrong? Why the long faces?"

"They were telling me about the financial troubles the ranch has had. And the poisoning of the west-pasture pond."

Their mother pinched her mouth tight in irritation. "Why are you two burdening her with this? She's only been home five minutes!"

"Don't blame them, Mom. I asked. A better question might be why didn't anyone tell me about the trouble the ranch has been having sooner?" She pinned an accusing look on her mother, then shared the glare with her brothers.

"Oh, honey, I didn't want to worry you when there was nothing you could do about any of it. The ranch business is—"

"Still my business," she interrupted.

"Is it?" Zane asked. The bitter edge in his voice surprised her. "Your absence over the last few years would say otherwise. I don't remember you being here while we were sweating through vaccinations and branding or losing sleep over how to make the books balance."

"Zane!" Their mother stepped into her bedroom and set her glass of lemonade down on her dresser with a thump. "That's enough!"

He rolled a palm up, his jaw remaining set. "I'm just saying…she chose to move away and not be a part of the nitty gritty of running the ranch. Family is supposed to come first, and it bothers me to know she can turn her back on us so easily."

"Bro," Josh said in a hushed tone, "chill."

Piper raised a hand to Josh. "No, that's okay."

"It's not okay, Piper. I'm sorry he was so rude to you," Melissa said.

She shook her head again. "No, I'm a big girl. If that's how he feels…" She shifted on the bed to face Zane, tucking a foot under her. "Nothing about leaving my family for Boston was easy, Zane. My staying away has nothing to do with my love of the ranch or my family. It's…complicated. But the last time I checked, I'm still a McCall. I'm still one-third heir to the ranch… eventually." She cut a wry grin to her mother. "No rush, Mom. Just saying." Then to Zane, "Just because I chose to accept a scholarship and pursue a career in Boston doesn't mean I don't care about the ranch. Especially if the future of the ranch itself is at stake. This ranch is in my blood, same as yours. Don't shut me out."

Zane rubbed the back of his neck and sighed. "Here's the thing, Piper. And don't take this the wrong way because, well…you know I love you, right? I'd do anything for you."

She hummed her disagreement and twitched a corner of her mouth at him. "Except clean the bathroom, as I recall."

Zane matched her teasing grin. "Okay, there are exceptions, but…when it counts, I'd die for you."

Josh clapped a hand to his heart, his expression melodramatic. "Same here, sister. In a heartbeat."

She tossed a throw pillow at Josh. With a withering glance to Zane, she said, "I'm touched. Why do I hear a *but* coming?"

"But..." Zane said.

She tapped the tip of her nose and sent Josh a wink. "Called it."

"But…" Zane continued, nonplussed by his siblings, "I see no reason to keep you in the loop if you're not here on the frontlines, putting in sweat equity every day the way we are."

Zane's bluntness punched Piper like a cattle prod to the gut. She grabbed a fistful of chenille bedspread and squeezed while she swallowed her pain and worked to hide her hurt from the three pairs of eyes studying her. She lifted a shoulder and forced a tight grin. "Love you, too, bro."

"Way to win her over before we lay out our proposal," Josh muttered.

"What proposal?" she asked.

Zane and Josh exchanged one of their twin-telepathy glances. After a moment, Josh bobbed a quick nod and said, "We'll fill you in tonight. Zane and I want to have a family meeting after supper to talk about some ideas we have for the ranch."

"Am I invited?" Piper asked, giving Zane a churlish look.

"Don't be a brat." He hooked an arm loosely around her neck and dragged her in for a knuckle noogie to the top of her head. "Of course you are. You're family, right?"

Wiggling to her feet and free of his grasp, she swatted at him and straightened her hair. "Am I, Mr. Sweat Equity? Am I allowed an opinion?"

He easily caught one of her hands as she batted at him and drew her into a hug. "Sure, as long as it agrees with mine."

"Okay then, my opinions and I will be there." She returned his hug, savoring the sense of calm and security that flowed through her after the strained ride from the airport. Her brothers had always protected her growing up, and she'd missed having them close by while she faced the challenges of her life in Boston. Too soon, her brother backed out of the embrace—because heaven forbid he appear too emotional or affectionate!—and, reluctantly, she released Zane. His crooked smile asked silently, *Are we good?*

She nodded and returned a *we're good* half grin.

Josh quickly took his brother's place, giving her a quick squeeze before shuffling toward the door. "Welcome home, Pipsqueak."

"Thanks, Doofus."

"Ditto," Zane said.

Their mother stood back to let her sons pass, and she smiled warmly at Piper. "It *is* good to have you home, honey. Oh, I've missed you!" Her mother stroked her hair and kissed her forehead before following the guys out. "Let me know if you need anything."

A sudden, unexpected wallop of emotion surged up in Piper's throat, making a verbal reply impossible. Instead, she blinked back tears and gave her mother a nod and a smile.

Turning toward her suitcases on the bed, she dashed away the moisture that stung her eyes and swallowed against the knot that choked her. Why was she so weepy about this trip to the ranch? She hadn't been this sentimental and fragile even on her first trip back after her freshman year at BC. After the physical, mental and emotional upheaval of the longest year of her life. After having Brady's baby, surviving finals week while purging all the pregnancy hormones from her system, and coming to grips with the idea she'd never again see the face of the tiny life she'd created—and given away.

She'd prayed that whole first trip that no one would read the truth of what she'd done in her eyes…and that Brady wouldn't learn how she'd deceived him about the fate of their baby. No, she hadn't lied to him, she'd told herself, but letting him live with his mistaken beliefs that she'd miscarried still gnawed at her conscience. Yes, that trip back to the Double M had been colossally difficult, but she'd survived it and visits since then with a stiff upper lip. And she had to do the same now.

Certainly the shock of seeing Brady at the airport had worn down her defenses. As had the poignant introduction to his nephew and the reminder of Scott and Pam's tragic deaths. Add to that the stressful month at work where the company had lost the Regal, Inc. account, one of their most important clients, and had reps from the corporate office breathing down her neck. And the freak accident that had killed the guy that worked in the cubicle across from her. Ron had been a nice enough guy, if a bit forward at times, and his bizarre death a couple weeks back had shaken the office staff. Then to be greeted with the news that the Double M could go under was the pickax blow to the thin shell that had held her intact in recent weeks.

With a cleansing breath, she shoved at Zeke's backside to scoot him off her suitcase where he'd settled. "Time to unpack, fuzzball. Move it." Another push roused the large cat, who stood and stretched. When she unzipped the top of the luggage, the noise intrigued Zeke. With his ears pointed forward and a quick head cock to the side, he bicycled his paws on the suitcase as if digging up whatever prey inside had made the rasping sound. The cat's antics tickled Piper, and the laugh that bubbled up in her helped staunch the rising tears. "You goofball," she said, lifting the Maine coon into her arms for a snuggle. Immediately the feline's chest rumbled and he head-butted her chin, returning the affection. "I missed you, too, fuzzball."

After a moment, Piper set Zeke on the floor and pulled her favorite blue jeans from the suitcase along with her well-worn cowboy boots and started for the closet. Then paused. Turning back to the bed, she stripped out of the slacks and blouse she'd worn on the airplane. As the clothes fell to the floor, she kicked them aside and pulled on the jeans, a T-shirt and her boots, welcoming the comfortable fit like an old friend.

Seeing Brady at the airport had been an unsettling surprise, but it was behind her. For the rest of her trip, she resolved, squaring her shoulders, she would survive by avoiding Brady the same way she had on previous visits. She'd help her family sort through the difficulties the ranch was facing, would celebrate her parents' anniversary and would be back to Boston in a week. And everything would return to normal.

Yes. Normal. Normal was good. The status quo was safe.

Her strategy seemed sound. Logical. Achievable.

So why did her plan leave her feeling so empty?

Brady couldn't sit still. He paced from the kitchen table in the house he shared with his father to the picture window in their living room. He gazed out at the

Double M Ranch yard to the tree where Connor was playing on a tire swing while the boy's dog, Kip, sniffed around the yard, and he heaved a sigh. Ever since picking up Piper at the airport he'd been restless.

Of course, he knew the source of his restlessness. Piper's visit had the potential to blow his world apart.

Or not.

The situation could play out in so many different ways. And if experience had taught him anything, it was that life had a way of unfolding in completely unexpected directions. You couldn't prepare for all the strange twists and possible scenarios fate had in store. That unpredictability was at the root of his uneasiness. Because his first and most important priority was protecting Connor.

He knew Piper would never intentionally hurt Connor. But Brady, of all people, knew that good intentions could still backfire. He'd let Piper rip his heart out again, relive the agony he'd known when she'd left him behind for Boston, if he could spare Connor even a little pain. The poor kid was already dealing with the loss of his parents. The boy was vulnerable, and Brady had to keep his guard up.

He heard the back door open and close, followed by the familiar scuff of feet and weary grunt as his father came in at the end of the day and shucked his work boots in the mudroom. "Brady?"

"In here." He shuffled back to the kitchen to greet his dad.

"You're back from the airport already?"

"Yeah. Plane was on time. We got back a few minutes ago." Brady propped a hip against the counter and jabbed his fingertips in his front pockets.

Roy Summers gave a small nod. "And how is Piper?"

"Fine." *Still beautiful. And witty. And determined to deny the feelings that are so clearly just beneath the surface of our broken relationship.*

His father stopped at the sink to wash his hands. "She met Connor?"

"Yep."

"And?"

"And what?" he asked irritably.

Roy frowned as he dried his hands on a dishcloth, then yanked open the refrigerator. He selected a beer and popped the tab on the can. "Jeez, never mind."

"What do you want me to say? They met. Connor charmed her with his jokes. We stopped for ice cream. Connor and Piper had chocolate fudge. I had butter pecan. Anything else you want to know?"

His father took a long drink of his beer and gave Brady a sour stare. "Nope. Not a thing."

Shoving away from the counter, Brady stalked across the worn linoleum floor to move Connor's school backpack from the table to a hook by the mud-room. With his back still to his father, he said softly, "Sorry. I'm just…edgy."

"Welp," his dad said, pausing to take another sip, "best get yourself pulled together before this evening. Zane stopped me on the way in from the stable to ask us to join the family at the main house tonight for some kind of meeting."

Brady faced his father and narrowed a dubious look at him. "A meeting? About what? Why does he want us there?"

"He didn't say. Just that he'd like us to come. He wanted our input on some business or other about the ranch."

Brady scratched his cheek while a wary curiosity

warred with the logistics of attending the mysterious summit. "What do I do with Connor?"

His question earned a slight hitch of his father's shoulder as Roy settled in his favorite living room chair. "Don't know. Bring him. Or ask Helen if she'll keep an eye on him for a bit."

Helen Shaw had been a cook at the ranch for the last five years and the girlfriend of ranch hand Dave Giblan for the last two years. She'd flirted with Brady when she first arrived, but he'd let her know, as kindly as he could, that his heart belonged to someone else. Maybe that had been a mistake. Helen was great. She was everything you could want in a girlfriend and potential spouse. Except that she wasn't Piper.

At the time, he'd still hoped that Piper would come around and realize they were meant to be together. But in every subsequent visit from Boston, Piper had been increasingly distant, more evasive, more guarded around him. Brady knew he should move on, find someone else to build a life with, but his heart was stubborn. Setting aside his feelings for Piper wasn't easy, and just a glimpse of her when she was home for the holidays or stilted pleasantries when they crossed paths in the stable or ranch yard was enough to rekindle his hope.

And then Zane had agreed when Brady volunteered to pick Piper up from the airport today. He'd spent more time with her this afternoon than in all the years since their breakup combined. When she'd stumbled into his arms at the luggage carousel, the urge to kiss her had smacked him hard, shaken him to the marrow. If she hadn't pulled away when she did, he'd have given the kiss her eyes had asked for…because her face had said she still wanted him. The sexy catch in her breath had been the same telltale signal of her desire that he'd learned when they made out in high school.

But then, damn it, she'd raised the shield she'd used for the last seven years to keep him at bay. The shift in her body language had said clearly that nothing had changed for her. She had closed the book on him and moved on.

Fine, he told himself, pulling out his cell phone to text Helen about babysitting. *Message received, Piper.* He was no glutton for punishment.

And yet… Brady knew he was sitting on a landmine. He had a moral responsibility to deal with the situation and correct all the wrongs that had been done in the past. He gritted his back teeth as resentment curled through him. All of his life he tried to do the right thing—for his father, for Piper and now for Connor. For all his best efforts, he'd gotten nothing but heartache, frustration and the burden of untangling the messes other people dropped in his lap.

He sent his text to Helen, and as he stashed his phone in his back pocket again, he hitched his chin toward his father's beer. "If we're meeting with the family tonight on ranch business, then maybe you should lay off the booze. At least until after the meeting."

His father responded with a surly look and another pull of his beer. Then with a grunt of fatigue, his father shoved himself off the stuffed chair and carried his can to the sink. After pouring the rest of the beer down the sink, he sent a dark look to Brady. "There. Happy?"

Brady swallowed the bitter retort that rose on his tongue. He'd only be happy when he no longer had to retrieve his old man from bars where he'd gotten too drunk to drive home. And when he no longer had to cover for his father around the ranch on mornings when

Roy was sleeping off a bender. His father had always been a heavy drinker, but this year, since Scott and Pam's deaths, Roy had crawled deeper into the bottle.

Roy moved to the refrigerator and sent Brady a hooded glare over the open door. "What's for supper?"

Brady scrubbed his hands on his face and shook his head. "Hadn't gotten that far. There's leftover soup. Guess I'll make Connor a sandwich to go with that. What time is this meeting we've been asked to attend?"

"Seven." His dad, the foreman at the Double M for the last twenty-eight years and a hand before that, bore all the signs of a life in the sun, a career of hard work and heavy drinking. Tanned, leathery skin with heavy creases around the eyes made him look older than he was, and his thinning brown hair bore a permanent crease from his sweat-stained Stetson.

Was that what he had in store? Brady wondered. Aging prematurely and finding his only solace to a lonely life in the bottom of a bottle? He loved ranching, loved fresh air and the wind in his face. He even loved the Double M as if it belonged to his own family. He appreciated and respected the McCalls, but he dreamed, too, of having his own place someday. He wanted to build a prosperous cattle ranch that he could leave to Connor. Maybe there was still a chance he'd find a way to go to veterinary school. He supposed it was getting time to make some decisions. Some hard choices. Having Connor in the mix now, along with his concerns about his father's drinking, complicated things. He needed a steady income, a place for Connor to feel he had roots and stability for a while longer.

Of course, he'd also always thought he'd settle down and raise a family with a woman who shared his passion for the outdoors, animals and hard work. In his mind's eye, ever since he'd stolen his first kiss from her behind the bunkhouse when they were twelve years old, that woman had always had Piper's glossy dark hair and gray eyes. Her willowy body and full lips. Her sunny smile and contagious laugh.

After the last seven years of receiving the cold shoulder and distance from her, he really needed to let that vision go. Folding his cards and moving on was the smart thing to do. He knew that. But how did he walk away when he'd so recently been dealt the ace he now held?

No, he'd keep his seat awhile longer and play out the hand. Piper was worth one last chance.

Chapter 3

That evening after dinner, Piper walked into the den with Josh and eyed the available seats for the family meeting. Spying her father's big, comfy recliner, she headed for it. As did Josh. Realizing his destination, she quickened her step, as did he, until they were racing for the prized seat. They arrived from opposite angles at the same time and end up in a tangled, laughing pile that made the chair rock and creak.

Their father came in carrying a glass of lemonade and sized up the situation with a wry grin. "Joshua," he said, lifting Zeke the cat off the couch and patting the cushion, "I've got a place saved for you right here." Michael waved a hand, telling him to vacate the recliner. "Vamoose."

Josh feigned affront. "Why me?"

"'Cause she's prettier, and I like her more," their dad deadpanned.

"Ha!" she gloated and shoved at her brother's shoulder. "You heard him, Doofus. Move it!"

As Josh shoved to his feet, two new arrivals to the den caught her attention. Brady and his father. Piper's heart slammed against her ribs, and she grabbed the back of Josh's shirt, tugging him close enough to whisper in his ear. "What are they doing here? I thought this was a family meeting."

"It is," he said, straightening his shirt where she'd mussed it up. "But since they are key to the running of the ranch, we thought they would give us useful input."

"Roy, Brady, thanks for coming," her father said, offering his hand to their foreman to shake. "Come in. Have a seat."

Piper avoided eye contact with Brady as he walked past her, sidestepping Zeke, who'd flopped on the floor and rolled on his back to stretch. Brady took the love seat across from her. But Roy Summers stopped in front of her with a lopsided smile. "Piper, it's good to see you, darlin'."

She stood and gave Brady's father a hug. "You, too, Roy. How have you been?"

He heaved a sigh that smelled of beer. "Honestly? Not so good. It's been a hard year."

She bit her bottom lip and tightened her hug. "I bet it has. I'm so sorry about Scott and Pam."

He pulled free of her embrace with a stiff nod. "Thanks."

Pausing to rub Zeke's belly, Roy moved to take his seat on the sofa next to Josh and Zane, and when Piper turned to reclaim the recliner, she found her father had stolen it. Her father gave her an unrepentant grin, and she grunted her protest. "Dad!"

Josh chortled as she searched the remaining seats

for an empty spot. Her mother was in her favorite arm-chair, which meant the last seat left was the other half of the narrow love seat. Next to Brady. Schooling her expression to hide her dismay, she sank onto the cushions, trying not to brush against Brady.

"All right, boys," her father said, turning up his palms as he divided a glance between Zane and Josh. "We're all here. What is this about?"

"Yeah, um…" Josh rubbed his hands on his thighs as his eyes met his twin's gaze. "Zane and I have come up with an idea for the ranch that we think will add enough revenue to help pull us out of the financial crunch we're feeling."

Piper's stomach clenched anew at the idea that the family business—their home and way of life—could be facing a crisis large enough to threaten their future. Beside her, Brady settled back on the love seat, adjusting his position in such a way that his elbow poked her upper arm. She tried to ignore the casual contact. She needed to focus on what her brothers were saying and not on her seatmate. She bent over and snapped her fingers near her ankles, hoping to entice Zeke to come to her. The cat raised his head and looked her way but refused to answer her summons. She'd have to find another distraction from Brady's proximity. Sending the Maine coon a thanks-for-nothing glare, she readjusted her position, trying to appear relaxed while staying as far to her side of the seat as possible.

"In looking for new sources of income, we knew that in order to make any new ventures a success, we needed to look at areas we were already skilled in," Zane added.

"Besides the cattle business, the thing Zane and I know best is adventure sports. Rock climbing, white water rafting, rappelling and the like." Josh's expression grew animated as he named the high-adrenaline activities he and Zane had mastered in the nearby Rocky Mountains.

"So we thought we could share that knowledge, that love of adrenaline, with others," Zane said, picking up the explanation in a seamless back and forth of input, the twins practically finishing each other's sentences.

Brady shifted his position on the love seat, resting his arm along the back. Piper sensed more than saw the move, and her skin prickled with an awareness of his arm so near her shoulders. She could tell he'd recently showered. The crisp scent of his soap mingled with a more woodsy aroma of deodorant or other body product, teasing her nose...and her imagination. She struggled to focus on what her brothers were saying instead of the body heat and sultry scents that radiated from her seatmate. She sat taller, keeping her back stiff as she perched at the front of the cushion in order to avoid touching him. Even the thought of his arm brushing the back of her neck sent distracting ripples of disquiet dancing along her nerves.

"We can renovate the bunkhouse to lodge paying guests," Zane continued, "and take people out to Grandpa's tract of land on hiking, camping and adventure-sports outings."

"Sorta like a dude ranch but with the focus being the sports and extra activities. An adventure ranch." Josh paused briefly, casting his gaze around the room, clearly gauging his family's reaction. "We'll show people stuff about the ranch, riding horses and working with the cattle, but the highlight will be a camping and hiking trip where we rock climb, raft, zip-line... whatever."

Zane picked up the thread, his eyes alight with a fiery passion for the idea. "The point being to give adventure seekers the chance to do the kind of stuff they come to the mountains to do in combination with the ranch experience."

Piper caught her brothers' excitement, knowing they wouldn't have brought this idea to the family without having a plan to make it work. Zane, the workhorse and responsible one of the triplets, would have addressed the details, at least.

Their father knitted his brow. "Have you looked into the cost of liability insurance for something like this? Start-up costs? The advertising expense to get people to come?"

"We've done preliminary inquiries with a few insurance companies and have drawn up a list of start-up costs." Zane paused for a beat, leaning down to idly scratch Zeke's ears as the cat rubbed against his legs. Glancing up from the cat, Piper's brother pulled his mouth into a moue of regret. "Getting the ball rolling will be costly, but Josh and I can take out a business loan—"

Their mother made a soft sound of displeasure.

Zane gave their mother a quick, we'll-be-okay grin and continued, "And we'll do the lion's share of the work in order to keep the cost of salaries to a minimum."

"Our plan is not to go full-scale right off the bat," Josh jumped in. "We'll do smaller, more manageable trips at first while we figure out what works and where we need to make changes." He faced their father and included Roy with a glance and a nod. "We don't want to cause any trouble with the cattle operations or burden anyone with unmanageable workloads."

"Of course, we'd love to have any help or expertise you want to offer," Zane said, "and we'll pay any ranch staff that contributes time and skills to the effort."

"What time frame are you looking at? When do you hope to have your first guests take one of these trips?" Roy asked.

Her brothers exchanged a look, and Josh said, "We'd love to get this off the ground as soon as possible. We'll start the renovation work on the bunkhouse this month and shoot for our first trip in the spring. Around April?"

A meditative silence fell over the group as their parents and Roy, judging by their expressions, mulled over the idea and formulated more questions. Piper hazarded a quick side-glance to Brady, and as if he felt her gaze, he angled his head to meet her eyes. Her pulse stuttered, and a warmth stole through her. To hide her reaction to him, which she feared showed on her face, she pasted on a grin and turned to her brothers.

"I love the idea! It makes sense, considering we aren't using the bunkhouse now. It uses your talents and passion for outdoor recreation in a profitable way. And vacation ranches are very popular. I read an article in the airline magazine—not this trip but one I took for business a couple months ago—that talked about how popular adventure sports are becoming." She knew she was prattling, filling the silence and hoping everyone would credit the flush in her cheeks and at her neck to excitement for the plan rather than Brady's unsettling proximity.

Zane and Josh beamed, and after exchanging a brief but meaningful look, Josh said, "I'm glad you think so, because we have a proposal for you."

Piper blinked her surprise. "For me?"

Zane nodded and scooted to the edge of the sofa as

he leaned toward her, hands on his knees. "We want you on our team."

She chuckled warily. "I am. I just said I was behind you, that I liked the idea."

"No, not behind us. Beside us. A joint effort," Zane clarified.

She tipped her head in query. "You want me to invest in the start-up? I...guess I could give you—"

"Not your money," Josh interrupted, then flipping up a palm, "Well, maybe some money. Down the road. But right now what we are asking is for you to work with us. To be part of this."

Piper's heartbeat thundered against her ribs. "I don't unders—"

"Move back home, Piper. Be our accountant, our bookkeeper, office manager..."

When Josh paused, Zane added, "Be our partner. We want you to do this thing with us. You're the third part of the McCall Trouble Trio. And we want you to be one third of the whole venture, expenses, profits, duties. We want your talent, your education, your experience with finance. Not just for the adventure ranch but to help save the Double M."

Her heart swelled hearing her brothers ask her to join them. To be included. To be wanted and needed by them. Her throat tightened with the same damn emotions that had ambushed her earlier in her bedroom.

Josh reached for her hand and squeezed it. "You belong *here*, Piper. Not in Boston."

Frowning, she pulled her hand back. "Excuse me! I like my life in Boston. I have a good job and friends and—" She cut herself off with a disgruntled huff.

Stunned by her brothers' request, she flopped back on the love seat, heedless of how doing so meant

Brady's arm was now draped close to her shoulders, his warm forearm pressed to her nape. Flattered as she was by their proposal—Josh's Boston comment aside—the notion of leaving Boston and moving back to the ranch was daunting. Giving up her income, giving up the little apartment that she'd decorated to fit her style, giving up her friends…could she do that?

But coming back to the Double M would mean being near her roots, her family.

And being near Brady, she realized, her heart shuddering to a stop. She sucked in a sharp breath as her pulse now lurched to a gallop, and she became acutely aware of the heat of Brady's arm against her neck, the weight of his penetrating gaze. The sensation of a thousand champagne bubbles bursting tingled in her belly and skittered from her neck to her fingertips. She swallowed hard and, knowing all eyes were on her, waiting for her response, she forced her tongue to work.

"I…don't know. I'm honored that you asked. Truly, it means a lot to me that you want me to be part of this…"

"Of course we want you, Pipsqueak. You're a Mc-Call. This ranch is as much your legacy as ours." Zane flashed her a gentle smile. "In fact, you could say it's your duty, your family obligation to help save the ranch."

Josh smirked and tipped his head toward his brother as if to say, *Yeah. What he said.*

"Boys, don't guilt-trip her. Being part of the family doesn't come with strings attached," their mother fussed. "Piper, dear, I know you love your life in Boston, and moving home to be part of the boys' venture is a big decision. Don't let them pressure you."

She nodded, then shook her head, not really knowing what she wanted to convey. Her hands were shaking, and her thoughts spun like a dust devil. "I have to think about it. I just don't know…"

"Can you give us an answer before you go home next week?" Josh asked.

"Joshua, your mother just said not to pressure her." Their dad arched an eyebrow at the twins. "You just hit her with this. Give her breathing room."

She flashed her dad a smile of thanks and fell silent again, thinking, stewing…and trying to suppress her body's sensitivity to the man beside her. His every subtle movement or heavy breath, each side-glance or faint whiff of his scent managed to scatter her thoughts and throw all of her senses into a tizzy.

Finally, she said, "I need more detail. How far have you gotten working out fees and expenses, insurance, construction, logistics? There's a million little things that could trip you up if you don't have a well-thought-out plan."

"I have to say," Roy said quietly, "I agree with Piper."

Zane and Josh were nodding.

"Of course," Josh said. He launched into a deeper discussion of how the trips would be planned, how they would convert and upgrade the bunkhouse, and the contractors they'd talked to about rigging up a zip-line on the scenic property in the foothills of the Rockies that the family had inherited from the triplets' grandfather. The adventure tours was the perfect use for the property that couldn't be sold thanks to their grandfather's wily will stipulations and bequests.

Zane took over when questions turned to financing, liability and staffing.

Piper had to admit, her brothers had given the idea

a lot of thought, and their passion for the project was a vibrant, breathing presence in the room.

"Wow," Piper muttered, when Zane finished speaking and cast his glance around the room.

"I'm proud of you, boys," their father said. "You've put a lot of work in this, and I believe the idea has merit."

Melissa said nothing, but the shine in her eyes and the wide smile she gave her sons spoke plenty.

Zane glanced toward the love seat. "Well, Piper?"

"It's a lot to consider, dork." She gave him a wry grin. "Give me a chance to process."

"Any other questions?" Josh asked, shifting an expectant gaze from face to face.

"Brady," Zane said after a few beats, breaking the silence, "you haven't said anything."

Brady grew still, then sitting forward and splaying his legs slightly, he propped his forearms on his thighs and pressed his fingertips against each other. His change of position meant his leg touched hers from knee to hip, and it took all her composure not to jerk away as if burned. But the heat of his body penetrated to her marrow and flowed deep into the dark spaces where she'd tried for years to lock away her memories of him, of young love and what could have been.

"Not sure it's my place to weigh in," Brady replied, and the low rumble of his voice vibrated in her chest, in her soul.

"We wouldn't have asked you here if we didn't value your opinion. You know ranching as well as anyone in the room, and you've gone rock climbing and rafting with us out at Grandpa's property. We're hoping you'll be on our staff, help us get up and running."

She held her breath, waiting for Brady's reply, thinking of what it would mean to live close to him again, see him daily, if she accepted her brothers' request. The thumping in her chest that echoed like a drumbeat in her ears had to be loud enough for Brady to hear. She balled her hands in her lap and fought to calm her ragged nerves. She'd come so far in her healing, in making a fresh start for herself. Or so she'd thought.

And now her brothers, whom she loved deeply and shared a special triplet bond with, wanted her to move back to Colorado. To be a part of a new and exciting project, part of saving the family ranch. To be *included* in a venture, a closely held dream for themselves and the family business. What would she have given in high school to have felt that kind of inclusion, to have believed she was as important to the ranch as her brothers?

Brady lifted a shoulder and said simply, "I like it. I'm behind you whatever you decide."

"Great! Thanks, man," Zane said while Josh beamed with relief. "Maybe you could help us persuade Piper, then?"

She shot a glare toward Zane that went ignored.

Brady turned his face to study her profile, and a prickly flush started on her neck and crept to her cheeks, sinking to her soul.

When he spoke, his voice was hushed, tinged with a note of sadness that arrowed to her heart. "I'm not sure I have any influence with her anymore. Can't say I ever really did, truth be told."

She met his piercing green gaze, and a fist of regret and grief clamped around her throat. "That's not true," she whispered for only him to hear.

"You sure about that?" he said, his voice pitched low to match hers. "I remember things differently."

She drew and expelled a ragged breath. "This isn't the time or place."

"I agree."

She tore her gaze away from his, masking her hurt and discomfort from her family with a trembling half smile and lift of her chin.

Brady was undeterred, whispering, "But since you seem to want to avoid me, we've never had another opportunity."

"Stop," she growled under her breath.

He heaved a weary sigh, and his shoulders slumped as he dropped his focus to his boots. "Later then."

Later? No. Not if she could help it. She was so tempted to get back on a plane and flee the ranch for the safety of Boston, the safety of distance from Brady. But she'd come for her parents' anniversary celebration, and she refused to leave before the weekend party. Standing up her parents, disappointing them was unthinkable.

The awkward expressions her family wore told her the exchange with Brady had not gone unnoted. Josh scratched his chin and rolled his eyes, while Zane clapped his hands together once and said, "Well, that's the plan. Any other ideas or questions before we call it a night?"

Roy rose from his seat and jammed his hands in his back pockets. "If you guys want me to take a look at that business plan with you, especially as it relates to the activities happening on the ranch premises, the bunkhouse renovation and so forth, give me a holler. I'm glad to help where I can."

Josh stepped forward to shake Roy's hand. "Thanks. We appreciate that."

Piper's mother and father also stood and approached the twins, and Brady used the moment to lean closer, his breath warm against her ear. "We need to talk."

Piper shoved to her feet and sent him a quelling glare. "No, we don't." Then softening her tone and digging for a tight smile, she added, "Thanks again for getting me at the airport today. Tell Connor I said good night."

"Piper—" He reached for her hand, and she jolted at the warm scrape of his callused palm closing around her fingers.

"Good night, Brady," she said firmly, although she heard the telltale crack in her tone. Pulling free of his grasp, she clutched her now-tingling hand to her chest and rushed from the den.

Her brothers had given her so much to consider, possibilities that she'd once longed for with her whole heart. If she'd felt she had a place here at the ranch after high school, would she have followed the same path, made the same choices she had back then?

Regret was a bitter pill, and she knew second-guessing herself served no purpose. For seven years she'd dealt with the hard choices she'd made. She'd not looked back. Yet in only a few hours of being back at her family's ranch this trip, her world had been upended. She couldn't deny a part of her longed to move back to the Double M. What a cherished honor it would be to take an active role in saving the ranch, her family legacy.

But was she strong enough to have Brady in her life again? Leaving him in the past had been hard enough. The past needed to stay buried. Because if Brady became a regular part of her life again, the walls she'd built to protect her heart would come crumbling down.

* * *

From his position at the top of a ridge, Ken squinted through his telephoto lens and brought the Double M Ranch buildings into focus. Figuring out which one was the main house, where Piper would be staying, was easy enough. The main house was the biggest building and had a long front porch with rocking chairs, a river-rock chimney and large windows that glowed with warm golden light. Through process of elimination, he would figure out soon enough which window was Piper's bedroom.

As he studied the house, two men emerged through the front door and shuffled across the ranch yard toward a house nearer the stables. Several dogs yipped and raced around, following the men.

Damn it! The presence of dogs meant he'd have to be extra careful when he approached the buildings. Dogs were living security alarms. From his vantage point, one appeared to be a yellow Labrador retriever, and the other two were medium-sized black-and-white dogs with big pointy ears. Ken lowered the lens for a minute, thinking. What were those dogs called? Shepherds? No, blue heelers. Smart dogs, he'd heard. Sighing his frustration, he made a note on his pad to figure the mutts into the equation, then raised the high-powered lens again, snapping pictures.

Zooming in on the faces of the cowboys, he discovered one was older, maybe fifty or sixty years, and the other was the guy that had driven Piper from the airport that afternoon. The guy who'd been too familiar with her, held her too long when she'd stumbled, watched her too closely when she hadn't known he was looking. But Ken had seen it all, and he didn't need a crystal ball to know this guy meant trouble.

The younger cowboy with too much interest in Piper had to be dealt with.

Ken clenched his teeth and lowered the camera with the powerful lens. Piper belonged to *him*, and if anyone or anything posed a threat to the future he had planned for them, Ken swore that threat would be eliminated.

Chapter 4

Early the next morning, Piper headed to the stable to visit her favorite mare, Hazel. Her freshman year of high school, Piper had been with Hazel's mother for the late-night delivery of the dapple-gray filly, and Piper had bonded quickly with the new addition to the stable. She hoped that a brisk ride out on the ranch property would help clear her head and give her the perspective she needed while weighing the choices her brothers had laid at her feet the night before. Ace and Checkers raced out to greet her, barking and wagging their tails. A third dog, a yellow Lab that she didn't know, trotted up as well and put her massive paws on Piper's chest, seeking attention.

She pushed the dog's feet to the ground but bent to rub her soft ears. "Good morning to you, too. Ace, Checkers, who's your friend?"

"Ruff!" Ace's body wiggled as much as his tail did

as he circled her feet, waiting impatiently for his turn to get patted. Once each canine had been acknowledged, Piper continued to the stable, a lift in her spirits thanks to the unconditional affection and exuberance of the dogs.

Male voices greeted her as she stepped into the dimly lit stable, and she paused by the door, listening for a moment. She recognized Roy's husky voice, followed by a young one that had to be Connor's.

"Like that?" Connor asked.

"Not quite so much. Remember we don't want him to overeat. It could make him sick."

"And fat!"

As she followed the exchange between the grandfather and grandson, Piper grinned and picked out a bit and reins from the ones hanging on the wall by the main alley door.

"Well, yeah. That, too. But colic is the main thing we gotta watch out for."

"When he can't poop?"

"That's right."

Connor chuckled, and Roy said, "Hey now. Colic ain't no laughing matter, Con. I've seen horses die from it."

She'd started down the row of stalls, stroking the nose of any horse that had poked its head out to greet her, when a third voice joined the first two.

"About time for you to head to the bus, buddy. Don't want to be late for school." *Brady.*

"Aw, man!" the boy whined.

She stopped in her tracks, suddenly glad she hadn't announced her presence. Maybe she could turn and quietly sneak back out...

"Hey, Piper!" Connor called down the alley.

She scrunched her face in defeat, then putting on a warm smile of greeting, she turned to face the little boy whose small boots thumped as he trotted down the center aisle to her. "Hey yourself, Connor. How are you?"

He hurried up to her, his eyes bright with excitement. "Grampa and I were feeding the horses, but I gotta go to school."

"Oh, bummer." She patted his back when he gave her waist a hug.

The yellow Lab nuzzled Connor's hand, and he scratched the dog's ears.

In her peripheral vision, she saw Brady step out of one of the stalls and move toward them. She tensed but kept her smile in place for Connor. "When I was your age, I always wanted to stay with the horses instead of going to school, too. Especially on a pretty day like today! In fact, I was just about to go for a ride."

Connor peered up at her and nodded, then whirled to face Brady, who was making his way up the alley. "Brady, can I pretty please stay home today?"

Brady grunted and sent her a hooded look. "Sorry, buddy. Not this time. Go grab your backpack."

"But I wanna ride with Piper!"

She squatted in front of Connor and tugged his earlobe. "How about a rain check? We could ride together tonight." When he continued to frown, she added, "School's important, and you don't want to miss the bus."

"You promise tonight?" the little boy asked with an adorable wrinkle of his nose.

"It's a date." She shook his hand and pushed back to her feet.

Brady reached them and nodded a greeting to her. "Mornin'."

"Hi." She felt her breath leave her as she drank in the sight of his tall, lean body and broad shoulders. His faded blue jeans had always had a way of fitting his hips and hugging his thighs that teased her imagination, and today he wore his flannel shirt like a jacket over a dark blue T-shirt. The long sleeves were folded up at the wrists, and he glanced at the silver-toned watch he wore.

"Five minutes, Connor. Scoot." Putting a firm hand on Connor's shoulder, he guided his nephew toward the door.

"Come on, Kip!" Connor called as he and Brady headed out with the yellow Lab at their heels.

As they disappeared out to the ranch yard, she heard the scuff of boots as Roy approached. She faced their foreman with a grin. "Good morning, Roy. That's quite the little helper you've got there."

"He's learning. Make a fine hand one day."

She tugged her grin to the side. "Or foreman?"

He removed his hat long enough to comb his fingers through his thinning brown hair before resettling it. "Hey, now. I ain't in the grave yet. I plan on workin' as long as this old body will let me rope and ride."

She placed a hand on his arm and a kiss on his cheek. "And I wouldn't have it any other way." She glanced toward the end of the row of stalls. "I was hoping to go out for a while on Hazel. Has she been fed?"

"Yup. Need a hand saddling her up?"

"Thanks, but I think I can remember how." She gave him a wink as she started for Hazel's stall. "So…can I ask you something?"

"Sure. What's on your mind, sugar?" He kept pace with her as she moved to the end of the stable and collected a blanket and saddle.

"I was just wondering what you thought about the idea the guys proposed last night about starting an adventure ranch. I mean, now that you've had more time to think about it…and the guys aren't here looking at us with those eager puppy eyes they had last night."

Roy laughed. "They were pretty pleased with themselves and keen on their idea, weren't they?"

"But will it work?"

Roy widened his stance and folded his arms across his chest. "Welp, hard to say."

She arched an eyebrow and shot him a hard look. "Come on, Roy. Don't equivocate with me. I want your honest opinion."

He pursed his mouth for a second, then said calmly, "Don't know that ten-dollar college word you just said, but you know I always shoot straight."

"I do. That's why I'm asking you. Besides the fact you probably know more about this ranch than anyone else, my father included, I know I can trust you to give me the truth. How bad are things for the ranch? Are we really hurting that bad, business-wise?"

"Your daddy's in a better position to talk money with you, but—" He nodded. "The herd's taken a hit. When we go to market in a few weeks, we're lookin' at probably a thirty to thirty-five percent cut from last year."

"Thirty-five percent?" Her chest squeezed. That sort of herd loss was bleak. "How? Why?" Her father had always been such a savvy businessman, and she knew her brothers had been good students of the ranching industry, learning everything their father and Roy had to impart. This downturn baffled her, and she was sick to her stomach knowing the worry her family had been dealing with, unbeknownst to her.

"Fewer calves survived this spring, then we lost several head to the poisoning."

She stiffened her back as a fresh wave of outrage washed through her. "Zane and Josh mentioned that yesterday. Someone tainted the pond in one of the grazing pastures? They said it was probably vandalism, but...my God! Who would do such a thing? And why?"

Roy lifted a shoulder and shook his head. "Couldn't say, darlin'. Some people are just bad at the core. Spiteful."

"So...you think it was done to strike out at the Double M or the family? Not just some random act of thoughtlessness or meanness?"

He shrugged again, his expression flat. Roy had always been calm and low-key. She'd always believed their foreman's even disposition and quiet nature worked in his favor as he dealt with the animals and the occasional hot-tempered hand, but at the moment, Piper wished she could get a better read on his feelings. "But *why*? Has something happened while I was gone that no one told me about? What would make someone hate our family enough to hurt us like this?"

"*Hate*'s a strong word," Roy said, rubbing a hand on his chin.

"Roy, stop playing diplomat. Tell me what's happening."

"Don't know why."

She chewed her bottom lip. "So what do you really think of the guys' plan?"

He chuckled and shook his head. "Oh, no. I'm not going to tell you what to do."

"I didn't ask what I should do. Just—"

"Same as. All I'll say is, I've never been a risk-taker. Starting a new business when the ranch is already hurtin', that's a risk. But I'm not your brothers. Maybe they can make it work."

Piper huffed her frustration with his evasive answer and growled playfully. "You're no help."

Roy gave her a half smile, then ducking his head and pursing his mouth, he hummed as if in thought. Finally, he added, "Well, Zane has the organizational skills, and Josh has got the people skills. Putting your money sense and brains in the mix would sure seem the right combination to make a go of it."

Her gut flip-flopped. "Then you think I should take them up on the offer? That I should move back here and help with this adventure ranch?"

"I think…" he stepped closer and put a hand on her upper arm "…that is a decision only you can make. But for what it's worth, I'd sure love to have you back here." He gave her a small grin and dropped his hand as he moved away. "And so would Brady."

Her heart clenched at the mention of Brady's name. She swallowed hard. "You think so? I mean, about Brady?" As soon as she'd asked, she wished she could take it back. Showing her interest, her concern to Roy was just shy of showing her true heart to Brady.

Roy shrugged and arched one eyebrow. "I figure so. He don't talk about it, but seeing as he's not dated anybody else since you left, I'd say he's still sweet on you."

Piper didn't know what to say to that. She stood frozen for several painful seconds and tried to catch her breath. She'd suspected as much about Brady, which was one of the reasons she worked so hard to avoid him. She didn't want to add to his hurt or feed false hope in him. But hearing Roy say Brady still harbored feelings for her twisted inside her like a double-sided blade.

Schooling her face, she fought to breathe normally

again and walked slowly backward from Roy. "Well…
I, um…" She cleared her throat and hitched her thumb
toward Hazel's stall. "I'm gonna take Hazel out now.
See you around."

"Enjoy your ride." Roy turned and shuffled down
the alley to another occupied stall, stroking the horse's
nose as he entered.

Piper's mind spun as she readied Hazel for her ride.
Brady hadn't even dated in the last seven years? She
knew Boyd Valley was small and isolated, but the
town had attractive, available women. A man as good-
looking and kind as Brady should have been a hot com-
modity. Heaven knew her brothers were never lacking
for female attention. Maybe she needed to say something to him to make her position clear. As if the silent
treatment and distance she'd put between them weren't
enough to say *It's over*.

Hazel snorted and tossed her head, jingling her har-
ness.

Piper patted Hazel's neck and chuckled. "You're
right. Maybe that's something I should leave alone."

Once Hazel was saddled—Piper had to admit she
was a tad rusty with the chore that had once been muscle memory—Piper rode out on the property in search
of a quiet spot where she could think and reflect on
the choice her brothers had given her. Picking the right
place for her meditation *was* automatic. The route to
the place she called her *thinking spot*—in the tradition
of her childhood favorite, Winnie the Pooh—was in-
grained in her marrow. She'd made some of the toughest decisions of her life under her favorite cottonwood
tree. From deciding which of the Jonas Brothers was
her favorite to which college scholarship to accept,
she'd planned the details of her life from the bench

under her cottonwood. As she rode out to the refuge, she recalled the last choice she'd made at her thinking spot—the decision to leave Brady and put their baby up for adoption.

After Connor's school bus rumbled away in a puff of diesel exhaust, Brady headed back to the stable, hoping to find Piper still there. Instead, he found Karl Townsen, one of the only two hands the ranch still employed, scrubbing out an extra feeding trough. Karl looked up and greeted him with a jerk of his chin. At one time, when the ranch had been at peak production, the Double M had boasted as many as ten hands living on-site. But recent dwindling profits and scaled-down operations had meant a reduction in ranch staff and closing the bunkhouse. Karl and Dave, the other hand, both lived in Boyd Valley and drove in from town to work every day.

A quick search of the stalls proved fruitless, and he strolled back toward the hand. "Hey, was Piper around when you got here?"

Karl turned off the hose. "Yeah. She was just heading out for a ride. Took Hazel."

Brady considered his options for a moment, then asked, "Did you see which direction she went?"

Karl gave him a knowing look and a sly grin. "Maybe. What's it worth to ya?"

Brady ignored the ribbing. "What about my dad? He say where he was going?"

"Back to your house to make some phone calls, I think. Something about a shipment from the vet supply that was late." Karl began looping the hose in a coil to put it away. "You got a message for him if I see him?"

Turning toward the rack of saddles, Brady waved a

dismissive hand. "Nah. If anyone needs me, I'll be out on the property checking fences."

Karl grinned. "She headed out on the south pasture."

Feeling sheepish that he was so obvious, Brady saddled up his horse, a roan gelding named Cactus— because he'd been a prickly, stubborn cuss of a horse to train—and rode south from the ranch yard in search of Piper. Finding her didn't take long. She'd ridden to one of her favorite places on the property, a spot on a ridge that had a scenic view of pastureland and Wilson Creek in one direction and a view of the complex of ranch buildings in the other direction. Her father had built a split-rail bench under a large cottonwood tree on the ridge that he and Piper had frequented for long talks and a little making out as teenagers.

Even from a distance, he knew the instant she recognized him because her body language changed. Her back straightened. Her shoulders drew square and her chin lifted defensively. Frustration vibrated from her in palpable waves. As he approached, she strode stiffly to the spot where she had hobbled Hazel and gathered the reins in her hand as if to leave.

"Piper, wait," he called before she could climb into her saddle.

"Go away, Brady. I came out here because I wanted to be alone."

He reined in Cactus, and as he rode up beside Hazel, he took hold of the mare's reins from the other side. "Yeah, and I came after you because I need to talk to you in private."

Piper groaned and refused to look at him. "Brady, I don't mean to be rude or anything. The last thing I want is hard feelings between us, but…I can't do this. I can't pretend that everything is fine and have friendly chats with you as if we don't have the kind of history we have." Finally, she glanced over Hazel's back to him, and the pain he saw in her eyes sucker punched him. "There's a reason I've made myself scarce when I've visited all these years."

"Fact remains, there's something we should discuss."

Shaking her head, she blew out a ragged sigh. "Brady, please. It just...hurts too much. Nothing's changed. I can't—" Releasing Hazel's lead, she turned and stalked back toward the well-weathered bench.

"I know it's hard. It's hard for me, too." He dismounted and looped his reins loosely around a low-hanging cottonwood branch. Then, approaching Piper like a fawn he didn't want to spook, he walked slowly toward the bench.

She snapped up a gaze that warned him away. Her expression said clearly that she'd bolt if he tried to snuggle up next to her on the two-person seat.

"Is this about my brothers' plan to start adventure tours and take guests at the ranch?"

"No." He shoved his hands in the back pockets of his jeans. A cool October breeze swept across the ridge, making the yellow leaves of the cottonwood dance and whisper.

"I'm still shocked that they asked me to come back here. To be part of it." She flexed the fingers of one hand with the palm of her other.

"You are? Really? You have to know how much your brothers miss you. You three are the McCall Triplets. Three parts of a whole."

Growing up as the foreman's son, Brady had envied the McCall offspring, less for their ownership and position at the ranch than for the bond of family, of the siblinghood that they shared. Since he'd been the same age as them, he'd spent his time catching fireflies with them at dusk, tagging along on fishing trips and rough-housing in the ranch yard as kids. But even as a small boy, he'd always known he wasn't part of the special camaraderie and cohesion that bound the triplets. While he'd coveted their relationship, he'd also accepted being outside their sibling triangle.

Now, Piper gave him a dubious look. "The trip-let thing became more of a twins thing in junior high school. You know that. Besides, this is business. This is different."

"It's a *family* business. So, no, it really isn't that different. And the *triplet thing* may have changed some in junior high, but you'd have to be blind not to see what you mean to your brothers."

She opened her mouth as if to say something, but closed it again with a soft click of her teeth.

"Piper, they want you to be part of this new venture because you're part of the family, but also because they know you're one of the best at what you do. Why would they hire someone else to do the books and run the fi-nances when you're over there in Boston, setting the accounting world on fire?"

She snorted a laugh and cocked her head. "Who says I'm setting anything on fire?"

He shrugged. "That's what Zane and Josh tell me. Said you've already been promoted twice in your com-pany in three years and that you won some local recog-nition as one of the Top Thirty Under Thirty in Boston. Is that right?"

Again her mouth opened and closed before she waved it off. "Well, yeah, but that's…"

"That's great, Piper." He pitched his voice low and moved closer to the bench. "I'm proud of you. Always knew you'd be a success at whatever you did with your life."

She lifted a startled gaze, moisture filling her eyes. "Brady, don't. I…"

"Anyway," he said in a more businesslike tone. He knew his shift in tone had her ready to bolt, so he cleared his throat and plowed forward. Their conversation wasn't going to get any easier by postponing it any longer, "none of that is what I want to discuss. We have other stuff to talk about."

She inhaled a deep breath, shoving to her feet again with her hands balled at her sides. "No, we don't. The past is the past. Please, just let it go! I'm sorry things didn't happen the way we'd planned, the way we'd hoped. But—"

His own frustration and hurt bubbled in his chest, and he took a long stride toward her, seizing her arm to bring her around to face him. "Stop shutting me out, damn it. This is important!"

Her wide, blinking eyes and taut shoulders said his sharpened tone had caught her off guard.

Taking a second to gather his composure—he certainly didn't need to start on the wrong foot for an emotionally fraught and delicate conversation like the one he needed to have with her—Brady released his grip on her and said a mental prayer for guidance. Patience. Strength.

"Do you smell that?" Piper asked, a question so out of left field considering his own line of thought that he could only frown at her for a moment. She craned her head to look past him and lifted her nose like a hunting dog sniffing the air. "Smoke."

He took a test whiff and caught the subtle, dark scent. "You're right."

He wasn't aware of any jobs being done today that required anything being burned, so the acrid smell sent a prickle of alarm down his spine. He'd come out to find Piper, determined that nothing would stop him from having the conversation they needed to have. But a fire could be devastating to the ranch. He pivoted slowly, searching the horizon for any sign of smoke, and Piper did the same.

Pointing toward the fields north of the ranch buildings, Piper said, "There. No column of smoke. Just a haze."

Brady narrowed his gaze against the bright October sun and saw the wispy gray that curled up and lined the sky with a thin ominous veil.

"Not good," he muttered, his brain changing gears and shifting into emergency mode.

"Master of the understatement strikes again," she said, already striding toward Hazel.

He jogged to Cactus, ripping the reins from the tree branch and swinging into his saddle before she'd gotten Hazel turned around. "Go back to the ranch. Have someone call it in. I'm headed to the site."

She gave Hazel a kick with her heels and snapped her reins, calling, "Right! I'll meet you out there."

Brady paused only a second to appreciate Piper's form, the way her slim legs gripped Hazel's flanks and her jeans hugged her bottom as she galloped down the hill. In the years she'd been gone, she hadn't forgotten how to ride, hadn't lost her easy rapport with Hazel. Frustration ate at Brady as he set out in the direction of the rising smoke. Why couldn't Piper see that the ranch was in her blood? That a part of her would always be tied to this land, the animals, her family legacy?

He shook his head as he pushed Cactus to move

faster, cutting at an angle across the meadow below the ridge where they'd been talking, and stopping only long enough to let himself into the north pasture and close the gate again. The nearer he got to the cloud of smoke, the surer he was that the fire was in the field where they were growing alfalfa to feed the stock through the winter. There'd been no lightning this morning to start a fire, the most common source of naturally occurring wildfire. Which pretty much left human carelessness. Or sabotage.

When he crested a small rise that afforded him his first good view of the burning field, the more likely scenario became clear. Vandalism. Brady's heart sank as he scanned the growing flames. The pattern of fire, burning and spreading out from multiple spots across the entire field, made it clear this was not a simple case of a recklessly tossed cigarette. The oily smell of petroleum told him an accelerant had been used, as well.

Grumbling a curse word under his breath, he guided Cactus down near the edge of the smoldering crop. His gut knotted as he thought of the valuable feed being charred, wasted by the creeping flames. He unsaddled Cactus and took the saddle blanket from the horse, a pitiful tool against the spreading fire, but all he had until the fire department arrived. He couldn't stand by and do nothing while the winter feed was destroyed.

He beat at a line of flame near the edge of the field, taking out his anger and disgust toward the person who'd started the fire. Who could have such a bitter gripe with the McCall family or the Double M Ranch that they'd strike out like this?

Over the crackle of flames and his own choked breathing, the thunder of hoofbeats signaled the arrival of the cavalry. He blinked against the sting of smoke, expecting to see Zane, Josh, Dave, Roy…hell, the whole staff and the McCall family riding to the scene. Instead, Piper was alone.

"Where's everyone else?" he shouted over the low roar of the fire.

"Roy's calling it in. He'll be here soon. I sent Dave to round up my brothers and father." She cast a horrified gaze across the acres of burning crop. "How did you put it? *Not good.*"

Her expression said he needn't tell her what losing the crop would mean to the ranch. The expense of buying feed to make up for the lost alfalfa would be a heavy blow to her family's already struggling cattle business.

He continued to beat at the fire with his saddle blanket, and she grabbed his arm. "Do you really think that's going to make a difference?"

"Maybe not—" he pulled his arm free and went back to work "—but it's better than standing here doing nothing. I hate feeling useless."

"Yeah. There's that." She took a step back from him, surveyed the scene again and set her shoulders. Spinning back to Hazel, she unsaddled the mare and was soon standing beside him, whacking at the flames in the same, likely fruitless attempt to save at least some of the crop. Each thrash of the blankets sent up a poof of ash. Within minutes they were both bathed in sweat, stained with soot and red-faced from the heat of the flames.

Zane and Josh arrived on ATVs just moments ahead of Roy and Dave on horseback. Piper's father drove in by truck, leading the fire department pumper and tanker and a sheriff deputy to the field. The parade of emergency vehicles, lights flashing, stopped in a line along the edge of the field, and men scrambled out to begin soaking the field from the pumper truck.

After dismounting, Roy stood like a grim sentinel, rigid and silent, watching the flurry of activity. His expression was drawn and hard when Brady finally dropped his charred blanket and strolled over to stand quietly beside his father.

Michael hurried up to them as the firemen got to work, and Piper's father was as agitated as Roy was inert. "How did this happen? Did anyone see anything?" Michael raked his hands through his graying hair, leaving it chaotically rumpled, and gaped at the fire in dismay. "This can't be happening. I can't believe our horrid luck."

Piper abandoned her efforts beating the embers, and dropping the blanket, she rushed to her father and took him into her embrace. "Oh, Dad! I'm so sorry."

Michael held Piper tightly and, with his face twisted with despair and outrage, groaned, "Who would do such a thing? Why?" He glanced to his foreman, clearly hoping his right-hand man had the answers he didn't. "Roy? Did you see what happened? Did anyone hear anything?"

Taking off his hat and dragging in a slow breath, Roy shook his head. "Sorry, no. But judging by the scope and amount of damage, I'd wager it was intentional. Done outta spite, just like the poison in the pond earlier this year."

Piper muttered an unladylike curse as she pulled free of her father. "I'm going to talk with the sheriff. Something has to be done to find the person who's doing this! I can't believe there isn't *something* they can do to find the culprit."

Brady fell in step behind her as she stalked toward

the sheriff's vehicle, her body as taut as barbed wire between fence posts. They were met halfway by the uniformed deputy, who had a clipboard out and was making notes about the scene.

"Who's the property owner?" the deputy asked.

"My father. That's him in the blue shirt." Piper directed the man's attention to Michael with a flick of her finger. "But I can speak for the family."

The deputy asked for a recap of who'd spotted the fire, who'd been first to arrive on the scene and what, if anything, they could tell him about the cause of the blaze.

Piper filled the man in, and Brady added his comments when appropriate. When they'd finished giving their statements to the sheriff, Piper and Brady rejoined their families with nothing to do but watch the fire eat the winter supply of food. The deputy interviewed Roy, Dave and her brothers, as well, while Piper's father, his expression bleak, paced the edge of the field. "It will cost a fortune to buy replacement feed," Michael McCall said to no one in particular that Brady could determine.

"This is a setback," Josh said, catching his father's arm, "but not an insurmountable one. We'll figure something out."

Brady admired Josh's optimism and his attempt to bolster his father's mood in the face of this latest disaster to hit the Double M. Brady was finding it harder to stay positive, knowing that if the Double M folded, he, Roy and Connor would have to find another place to live and work.

He gave Piper's brothers a side-glance and could almost hear the wheels turning in Zane's head— calculating costs, reconfiguring plans and adjusting his aspirations for the adventure ranch. Now, more than ever, the family needed a new revenue stream. But the cost of winter feed would put the brothers even further in the hole.

An idea prodded him and nudged his blood pressure up a few points. Did he dare suggest such a wild thought? Did he dare not?

He stepped closer to Piper and, gripping her elbow, he tugged her aside without considering why his instinct was to consult her first. "Can I ask you something?"

"Now?" She waved her hand toward the burning field.

"Am I interrupting something?"

She grunted as if planning a retort but only blew out a shallow breath. "I guess not. What is it?"

"When Scott died, he left me a decent amount of money from his assets. I used a good bit of it to pay off his bills and the funeral expenses for the two of them, but I banked some, too."

Her eyes narrowed suspiciously.

"What do you think Zane and Josh would say to me investing in a share of the adventure ranch, helping them get it up and running?"

"Being a partner?"

He nodded. "I know they probably intend it to be a family business, and there are those who say don't go into business with your friends, but...I know they're strapped for cash." He nodded toward the smoldering alfalfa. "This will set your family back even further. I just thought that if I invested—"

"What about Connor? Shouldn't Scott's life insurance be earmarked for his son's care?"

Brady nodded. "The life insurance is. And a small trust fund. This is separate."

She glanced to her brothers, whose heads were together, clearly discussing contingency plans and debating who could have sabotaged them...again. "I think that's for them to say. Why ask me?"

"Because I value your opinion and have for a long time."

Her eyes softened. "Oh. Well...I'm flattered, of course, but..." She shifted her weight from one foot to another.

"Besides, you know your brothers better than I do, and I want to be sure before I ask them that my offer, should I make it, won't be taken the wrong way."

Her throat worked as she swallowed hard and lifted a bold gaze to his. "To be honest, I have been debating a similar offer to them. I've stashed away a little nest egg and thought I'd offer it to them as seed money."

A cloud of smoke drifted to them and, coughing on the dense smog, he guided her even farther from the fire. "I think they'll be stoked to know you want even a little part of the venture. To keep it in the family."

Her head tilted in query. "Is this what you wanted to talk about earlier, before we saw the smoke?"

He pressed his mouth in a grim line. "No." Shooting a glance toward the crowd assembled to watch the firemen work, he added, "That business will keep for a while."

Her shoulders drooped as she faced the charred crop. "Yeah. We have bigger problems to think about at the moment."

He didn't bother to tell her there was nothing more important than the business he had to discuss with her. His business was so important that he wanted to wait until he had her undivided attention. Instead, seeing her distress over the fire, he placed a hand on her shoulder and gave the knotted tendons a squeeze of support. Instead of relaxing, Piper tensed further and gave him a startled, even dismayed look. He shook his head as he sighed his frustration. "Jeez, Piper, you don't have to look at me like I'm something you have to scrape off your shoe."

Her eyes widened. "I'm not!"

"You did." He shoved both hands in his back pockets. "And you tensed up when all I was trying to do was show you some support."

"I—I'm sorry. I'm just…stressed." She glanced away, turning her attention to the firemen dousing the field. "I didn't mean to seem—"

"Bull."

She whipped her head around, blinking at him and frowning. "Pardon?"

"You've been tensing and shrinking away from me as if I had leprosy ever since you arrived." He shot her a wry grin. "Do you really find me that repulsive now?"

For several seconds she held his gaze, which he considered a victory in itself, before dropping her gaze to her boots and muttering softly, "Quite the opposite."

He held his tongue, waiting to see if she'd elaborate. But the moment was lost when her brothers strode up to them, both stiff-backed and tight-jawed.

"Dad says you two are the ones who first spotted the fire," Zane started. "Did you…?"

"Are you sure you didn't see anything that would tell us who did this, how it happened?" Josh picked up when his brother gritted his teeth in frustration.

"No." Brady shook his head to echo his answer. "Sorry."

"We were up on the ridge at the bench Dad built, talking," Piper said. "We smelled the smoke before we saw it rising from the field. We got here as fast as we could, but it was already too widespread to do anything effective to stop it."

"Thank God you saw it when you did. If it had spread to the pastures..." Zane sighed heavily and kicked at the dirt in disgust.

"I don't think the crop's going to be a total loss," Brady said, trying to offer some encouragement to his friends. "You all have survived worse than this. I know it sucks, but the McCalls I know can bounce back. I mean, your plan for the adventure ranch is proof of your resilience."

Zane and Josh looked at each other in that way they did that said they were sharing a private thought before Zane said, "This fire may be a sign that our plan is a pipe dream. Rather than funnel more money into new operations, we might be taking new loans to keep the ranch afloat."

Piper grabbed Zane's arm and rubbed his back. "Don't say that! Your plan is a good one. Don't abandon it now, or the punk who did this wins!" She waved a hand toward the fire.

Brady scrubbed a hand on his chin and angled his body to face the brothers. "This may not be the right time to mention it, but—"

"I have money saved up," Piper cut in, "money I want you to use to start the adventure ranch. It's not a lot, but it's a start."

Zane and Josh shifted their attention to Piper, their faces reflecting their surprise and intrigue with her proposal. Brady bit the inside of his cheek, trying to squash his irritation with her stepping on his figurative toes. Her offer didn't mean he couldn't add his to the mix. In fact, a four-way partnership could be even more enticing to the brothers. More resources meant more opportunity for success.

"If you're going to do this adventure ranch thing, why not let me help fund it? I want to be a partner with you."

Josh brightened. "Does this mean you're accepting the job as our financial officer?"

"I—"

Zane gripped Piper by the arms, smiling broadly. "Say *yes*. You know you want to."

She raised both hands and laughed awkwardly. "Whoa, whoa, whoa! I'm talking about helping underwrite the start-up expenses. I haven't decided anything about the job yet."

Her brothers' expressions dimmed, and Zane's shoulders drooped as he lowered his hands to his sides. "Come on, Piper…"

"My money may not prevent you from having to get a loan, but if I can help keep you two from going too far into debt, then the money is yours."

Josh pulled a lopsided, half-hearted grin. "Thanks. That's nice of you."

Brady squared his feet and rubbed his damp palms on his jeans. "I want to invest in the adventure ranch, too. I was just telling Piper, I have money from Scott—"

"Brady, no," Zane said, and Josh shook his head. "We can't ask you to do that."

The immediate refusal stung, reviving past days of living in the shadow of the ranch owner's children. "You didn't ask. I'm offering freely. Because I believe the idea is a good one."

Piper didn't say anything, but she gave him a poignant look before turning away.

"I have an interest in seeing the Double M succeed. And I believe the adventure ranch could be just the way to turn things around," Brady argued, as much to Piper as her brothers.

"But that money—" Josh began.

"Is mine to invest where I think best. Connor has been provided for. Have no fear there."

His assurance that none of Connor's trust fund was at stake seemed to reassure Zane and Josh.

"And while it's not a fortune," Brady continued, seeing the tide turn in his favor, "the idea is that if we combine our assets, all of us partners in the venture, it's more likely that the adventure ranch will work. You don't have to take on mountains of debt."

"Make you a partner, huh?" Zane mused, his brow furrowed in thought. He twisted his mouth and canted his head slightly as he considered the suggestion.

"I'm willing to put more than just my money into the adventure ranch. I'll put in my time and energy, sweat equity, as well. No salary needed. If I'm a partner, I'd expect to receive a commensurate percentage of the profit."

Josh scratched his chin and stared out at the burning alfalfa. "It's an interesting idea. I'd just assumed Zane and I were taking this on by ourselves."

"But it makes a hell of a lot of sense to turn this into a partnership," Zane added, looking from his brother to Piper. "If you're sure you want to give up your nest egg—"

"I wouldn't have offered if I wasn't sure."

Zane stuck his hand out to Piper. "Then you have a deal. We'd love to have you as a partner."

Piper's face lit with relief and joy as she shook first Zane's, then Josh's hands. Tugging her closer, Josh embraced his sister and gave her a peck on the top of her head. "Thanks, Pipsqueak. You don't know what it means for us to have your support."

Brady took a step back from the siblings as they cemented and celebrated another bond that bound them, leaving him on the outside looking in. Disappointment gnawed at his gut as he eased back another step, ready to head back to the stable.

Then Zane turned to him and said, "Hey, cowboy, you're not withdrawing your offer already, are you? Come here!" He stuck his hand out. "Put it there, partner!"

Brady blinked. "You're sure?"

"Positive."

Brady accepted Zane's handshake, and immediately Zane used the grip to reel him closer.

"Hey, bring it in." Zane slapped him on the back with a one-armed hug. "Josh, get her in here." And the next thing Brady knew, the brothers had sandwiched him and Piper against each other as they embraced, clapped shoulders, ruffled hair and laughed in celebration of the new partnership.

Their celebration was interrupted by an angry-sounding shout from Michael. All four of them turned in time to see Roy forcefully restraining Michael, who shouted at the lead sheriff deputy and aimed an accusing finger at the officer. The senior McCall was red in the face, fighting Roy's hold, while the deputy stood in a defensive position, one hand on his utility belt, clearly preparing to subdue Michael by force.

Chapter 5

"What the hell..." Zane grumbled as he sprinted back toward their father.

Piper's gut twisted, and she followed Josh and Brady as they, too, rushed to intercede in the confrontation.

Zane bodily blocked his father from approaching the deputy, while Josh and Brady aided Roy in dragging Michael away.

"You better get off my land!" Michael hollered at the deputy. "I'll report you! I'm no cheat!"

"Cool down, Dad. This isn't helping," Josh said over their father's shouts. "Please, don't make things worse."

Piper wedged her way into the fray and got in her father's field of vision. She caught his face between her hands, forcing him to look at her. "Stop, Dad. Look at me. What happened? What's wrong?"

"That...that *punk* all but accused me of setting the fire as part of an insurance scam." Her father's nostrils flared as he glared over her shoulder and sucked in ragged breaths. "Said he knew the ranch was struggling and that we'd filed a complaint about the poison in our pond earlier this year."

"Both of which are true," she pointed out.

Her father's gaze darted back to her. "It's the way he said it. Like I was staging all these disasters so I could collect on the insurance and bail the ranch out." He gritted his teeth, and a muscle in his tight jaw twitched angrily.

Piper swallowed hard. She'd only seen her father this upset a handful of times in her life. Once when Josh was fifteen and had cut school to go to a strip bar in Denver on a dare. Another time, when the family was out to dinner and they'd witnessed a man slapping a woman in the parking lot. Their dad had set the man straight about how to treat a lady, then spent the rest of the dinner lecturing Zane and Josh about showing women respect. Once when he'd argued about something with their mother, the topic of which Piper wasn't privy to. And most recently, when the Broncos had blown a huge lead in a game he'd bet money on.

"Dad, cool it. He's just doing his job," Josh said.

"By implying I'm a thief and a fraud?" Michael pointed at the officer again. "Innocent until proven guilty! I didn't do this!"

"Dad, think about your blood pressure. Settle down, okay?" Josh pleaded.

Piper blinked. *His blood pressure*?

Roy put a hand on her father's shoulder, and in his characteristic calm and even tone, he said, "Michael, nobody that knows you would ever suspect you of fraud. Don't let your stress and disappointment over the fire distort your perspective."

Michael glanced to Roy, then back at the deputy and exhaled harshly. "He needs to spend less time worrying about my insurance and more time looking for the bastard who did this."

Roy nodded sympathetically. "You're right. Now, what do you say I drive you back to the house? Okay?"

Her father squeezed his eyes shut and pinched the bridge of his nose for several seconds before raising a weary gaze to his foreman and nodding. "Yeah. Okay."

Roy cast a backward glance to the deputy. "Okay?"

The officer nodded once, granting his permission for the men to leave the scene.

Piper moved closer to Zane. "What's up with Dad's blood pressure?"

Zane looked at her as if she were stupid for a moment, then his expression cleared, and he blinked. "You don't know? His doctor put him on medicine for high blood pressure earlier this year. The stress with ranch finances hasn't done him any favors, but hypertension also runs in his side of the family."

"I remember. It contributed to Grandpa's death." Piper wrapped her arms around herself, feeling a sudden chill, despite the nearby flames. She angled her head and narrowed her gaze on her brother. "Why didn't anyone tell me?"

Zane shrugged. "I don't know. When's the last time you inquired about Mom or Dad's health?"

His tone was tinged with accusation, and Piper felt the barb to her core.

"I ask. They always say they're fine."

And she was all too happy to believe the generic reassurances that all was well with her family and at the ranch in her weekend phone calls, as if time had frozen when she left town. In her freeze-frame view of her home, no harm came to her family or their business. No one grew older or dealt with financial worries, vandals or health scares.

Her brother grunted and rolled his eyes in a manner that spoke for his disappointment in her passive acceptance of their parents' palliation.

As Zane walked away, Brady stepped up beside her. "I'm sure he didn't mean to sound so rough. Everyone's on edge because of the fi—"

"I deserve it. I haven't kept up with any—" Her voice cracked, and she paused to gather herself, to clear the phlegm the smoke caused from her throat. Brady slid an arm around her shoulders, and the dam of emotions she'd tried to hold in check broke.

Tears poured from her eyes, and she sobbed so hard she couldn't catch her breath. "I'm a t-terrible daughter!"

"No." Brady pulled her closer, holding her and rubbing her back. Her head told her to pull away, but the solace he offered and the comfort of his embrace were just the balm her aching heart needed. Just as they'd always been.

Brady had always known just what she needed and been right there to provide it. Be it a scraped knee in the ranch yard, a helping hand with her chores or a shoulder to cry on following preteen disappointments, Brady had been her champion.

"I sh-should have known about my dad's b-blood pressure. And the ranch's t-troubles. I should have asked more questions, not been satisfied with platitudes that made me feel safe." She buried her face in his shoulder, and he squeezed her tighter.

"They were trying to protect you. They didn't want to burden y—"

She raised her chin and shook her head. "No. That's no excuse. I'm not some helpless female that needs shielding from b-bad news." She paused to gulp a breath. The smoke and her tears made her nose run, and Brady produced a folded bandana from his back pocket. "I should have asked. I should have been more involved with the b-business." She blew her nose and wiped her face on the bandana, then leaned into his chest again.

"We all have our secrets, it seems," he said in a low tone. When she tensed, guilt stringing her tight, he stroked her hair and kneaded the tendons at the back of her neck.

"What does that mean?" she asked.

"Shh. Forget it. It's not important right now." His fingers worked magic on her muscles, and she found it easy to cant against him, allowing him to ease her worry. But as his massage, his embrace, soothed her distress, his touch wound her up in other ways.

Sparks of desire lit her nerves as he trailed a hand along her spine and dug his fingertips into her shoulder muscles. His breath fanned her temple as he held her close, and the well-worn flannel of his shirt gently caressed her cheek.

Home. Even more than being back in her old bedroom, back around her family's dinner table or following familiar ranching routines, being held by Brady felt like home.

She stood there, in the shelter of his arms, for several minutes, savoring the security and comfort, until Zane called to Brady, "Can you take care of getting Roy's horse back to the stable?"

He nodded and took a step back from her. "Okay?"

She sniffled and wiped her face one more time before nodding. "Yeah. Thanks." She started to hand the bandana back to him but paused. "I'll just…wash this and get it back to you later."

He grinned and winked as he headed to the area where the horses milled about, grazing.

Piper tucked the bandana in her back pocket and helped Josh load the charred saddle blankets and saddles on the back of the ATVs. Josh gave her a boost up onto Hazel, and she rode bareback to the stable.

Once Hazel had been settled back in her stall, she went in search of her father. She wanted to know more about his health issues and assure herself that he'd recovered from his outburst. Her first stop was her parents' bedroom, but no one was in there except Zeke, who'd curled in a ball to sleep on her mother's pillow.

Shaking her head at the liberties the cat got away with, she went next to her father's office. Instead of her father, she found Karl Townsen rifling through her father's desk. She furrowed her brow.

"Can I help you with something, Karl?" She pitched her tone in a manner that let him know his intrusion was improper and highly suspect. Why was he here instead of helping with the fire?

The hand jerked his head up and squared his shoulders. "No. Just…looking for a pen to leave your father a note."

"Could I give him a message for you?" She folded her arms over her chest and walked into the office.

He shrugged stiffly. "I just need ask him about taking next weekend off. Family business in Boulder."

Piper drew close enough to her father's desk to see the drawer Karl had been searching. There was an ample number of pens in plain view—as well as a flat money box where her father kept petty cash.

She pulled one of the pens out along with a small notepad and handed them to Karl. "How many years have you worked for the family?"

The hand pursed his lips as he thought. "About eight."

She nodded. "Oh, that's right. You came on my senior year of high school. That's a pretty long time. A lot of history between you and my family."

He rolled his shoulders and cocked his head to the side. "Yeah. And?"

Motioning to the pad, she added, "Oh, nothing. Just reminiscing. Go on and write your note. I'll see him in a few minutes and give it to him."

He balked, his face growing flushed. "Um, never mind. I'll just ask him when I see him later."

Piper arched an eyebrow. "Mmm-hmm. Karl, if I opened the petty cash box, would everything be there that should be?"

The hand stiffened, and his mouth grew taut. "Are you accusing me of stealing?"

She shrugged. "You have to admit it looks suspicious."

His expression became hostile. "I ain't stealing, just gettin' what I'm owed."

Piper blinked. "What you're owed?"

"Your daddy has always said he'll reimburse us for ranch expenses. I needed payback for some stuff I bought, so…" He shrugged as if his explanation excused his actions.

Piper cleared her throat. "So then you lied about leaving a note for my dad?"

Karl only glared at her.

"Did my father give you permission, today, to go in the cash box without him for your reimbursement?"

He narrowed his eyes but still said nothing.

"Do you have a receipt showing how much you spent when and on what?"

His glare darkened. "I don't like being accused of theft."

She squared her shoulders, unintimidated by the hand's glower. "Karl, taking money from my father without his knowledge or any kind of receipt qualifies as theft in my book." She drew a deep breath. "You're fired."

Karl bristled. "You ain't the boss."

"But I'm part of the owner's family, and that's close enough. Get your things and leave the premises."

"Forget *fired.* I quit!" He stomped toward the door where he paused long enough to send her a sneer. "Besides, this place is on its way out. I'm better off getting a new job before you all go belly-up."

Piper opened and shut her mouth in shock.

The thud of the ranch hand's angry steps echoed down the hall.

She dropped in her father's chair and stared at the cashbox.

"Crap," she grumbled on a sigh. What had she done? Maybe Karl had been pilfering from the petty cash, but confronting employees was her father's job. She should have brought the incident to her father's attention and left the rest to him. On a day when things had already taken a bad turn for the ranch, she'd managed to make things worse.

Wasting no time following the decision to make the adventure ranch a four-way partnership, the four new partners spent several hours, led by Zane, going over details of their new business arrangement. Zane had called the bank and made an appointment for the next morning to sign the paperwork to make the deal official. In addition, he'd negotiated terms for a business loan and made sure they could close that deal, as well.

Now, Piper gazed around the lobby of the bank where dusty fake plants and thin-cushioned couches attempted to make customers feel at home. Beside her, Brady bounced his heel, jiggling his leg in agitation.

"You can change your mind, you know," she said in a hushed tone. "If this makes you nervous—"

"No," he cut her off, shaking his head. "I'm still in. It's just waiting rooms make me nuts. Waiting rooms are where you wait for bad stuff. The doctor to tell you your mom's got cancer. The school principal to tell you you're getting detention. The ER to tell you your brother didn't survive his car wreck. The police station to tell you your dad will have to spend the night in the drunk tank."

She put a hand on his bobbing knee and squeezed. "I'm sorry."

He flipped one hand in dismissal.

"How about the airport waiting to go on vacation? That's good," she suggested.

He gave her a side-glance. "Never flown before. Only vacation my family ever took outside the state, we drove."

She frowned. She'd known that about him in high school, if she'd thought harder about it before she'd spoken. "Well, how about waiting at the airport for me to arrive this week?"

His knee stilled, and when he met her gaze she sent him a sassy grin, he returned a warm smile that made her toes curl and heat gather low in her belly. "Yeah," he whispered. "That was good."

"Hey, did you know Karl quit?" Josh said, looking up from his phone to Brady with a puzzled look.

Acid curled in Piper's gut, and she bit her bottom lip.

"What?" Brady said, his chin jerking up.

"Dad told me this morning. He didn't give any reason, but he was going to talk to him, try to change his mind. You know how short-tempered Karl is."

Piper scratched her temple and said meekly, "It's my fault."

Three pairs of eyes swung toward her.

"I caught him in Dad's office yesterday after the fire. He was going through Dad's top drawer where the petty cash is kept, and…" She blew out a breath, buzzing her lips. "I assumed the worst. I guess I was on edge because of the fire and…I basically accused him of stealing from Dad. I fired him on the spot."

"Piper!" Josh groaned.

"He blew up and said he quit, so either way…he's gone." She ducked her head, guilt gnawing her. "I told Dad, and he promised to smooth things over with Karl. But…well, I did what I thought was right."

"Did he say why he was in Dad's office?" Zane asked, his eyes narrowed. "He has no business being there."

She explained Karl's story about needing reimbursement, but before either brother could comment, a woman called to them from the door of one of the offices. "Zane McCall? Mr. Carver will see you now."

The foursome rose and followed the woman into the small but well-appointed office where Gill Carver, a former classmate of theirs, sat behind a desk most people would see as too large for the room. But Gill wasn't most people. He'd always been a pretentious troublemaker who seemed happiest when he was tormenting others. Gill had become especially hateful toward them after his father's ranch had gone bankrupt when they were in high school, and the Double M, among other nearby ranches, had acquired some of the Carvers' equipment and land at the bankruptcy auction. Piper had no doubt that family humiliation had been part of what had motivated Gill to get his degree in finance and get a job in banking.

Piper was galled by the notion that Gill would be managing the business loan, but Zane had researched the competitors and determined First Bank of Boyd Valley, small as it was, had the best interest rates and repayment terms. She might not like the idea of doing business with Gill Carver, but Piper trusted Zane's business sense.

Gill stood as they entered his cramped office, and when he recognized them, his smile took on a sardonic edge. "Well, well. Look at that. The three McCall Musketeers and their faithful sidekick together again."

Piper sensed more than saw Brady tense at being cast as sidekick. She knew he'd always felt he lived in the shadow of her and her brothers. As the employee's son. The odd kid out. The tagalong to their blood-bonded threesome. That Gill would make a point of highlighting that discrepancy after all these years spoke volumes to her. Gill was still a vindictive, petty jerk. She sent Zane a side look that said *Do we really have to do business with this cretin?*

Zane's returned expression asked her to overlook the slight and trust her brothers' decision.

"How can I help you today?" Gill waved a hand toward the two chairs across the massive desk from him.

Zane, who was closest to the chairs, sidled toward

the far chair, and Josh motioned for Piper to take the other.

"First we need a notary to witness the signing of partnership papers. Then we want to open a new business account."

Gill arched a manscaped eyebrow. "Partnership? You're finally making this little club of yours official, huh?"

Piper bit the inside of her cheek. Gill's smile was just shy of a sneer, and his contempt for her and her brothers was palpable.

"Zane?" she whispered under her breath.

"That's right. We're starting a business together." Her brother nodded to the unctuous banker and placed a hand on her wrist, giving it a quick reassuring squeeze. "When we finish the paperwork, making the business arrangements and opening the account, we'd like to talk about a short-term loan for the rest of the start-up capital."

"Another loan?" Gill gave a mocking frown. "Doesn't our bank already own several loans on your ranch? The mortgage on your house, a business loan for your father," he said, ticking them off on his fingers, "and, oh, yes, a second business loan to cover recent herd losses."

"If you check your records, as you clearly do, since you're so familiar with our family's debts," Josh said, his voice tight, "you'll see those loans are in our parents' names. Our new business is separate from the ranch holdings and balance sheets."

"That's smart, considering how far in the red your father has gotten himself." Gill's smarmy smile brightened, and he turned his attention to Brady. "Summers, are you sure going into business with the McCalls is in your best financial interests?"

Piper cast a side-glance to Brady, who stood in front of the closed office door with his arms crossed over his chest. His nostrils flared slightly in distaste, but the lethal stare he had fixed on Gill didn't falter.

"Positive."

Gill cocked his head to the side in a quick dismissive gesture. "Okay. I know you were never good at math in high school, but I thought I should give you the chance to back out before you cast your lot with a sinking ship."

Piper could hear Brady's teeth grinding, and she reached up to give his arm a squeeze—of support? To calm him? She wasn't sure, except that she did it automatically, instinctively.

"Can we get on with it?" Zane asked.

"Certainly. I assume you brought the papers you need notarized?"

Zane jerked a nod, opened the folder he had brought and slid them across the desk to Gill. Gill gathered the papers and, without looking at them, lifted his phone receiver to page his secretary. "Fran, I need you to witness a notarization." When he hung up the phone, he rocked his chair back and propped his feet on his desk as he scanned the pages and commented.

Piper rolled her eyes. She couldn't imagine one of the senior executives in her office or one of the bankers her office worked with being as gauche as to prop his feet on his desk during a meeting with a client. Muddy shoes at that, she noted, spotting the dirt in the treads and crusted on the edge of Gill's soles. Or was it mud? She looked closer and recognized the texture and color of the substance. Cow patty. Gill had stepped in a cow patty.

She curled her lips in to smother the grin that blossomed, and she quietly enjoyed the satisfaction the notion gave her. She hoped he tracked the mess into his car, his house—

"Equal partnership...investment of funds...rights of partners in business decisions...yada yada. What sort of business did you say this was?" Gill asked, peering over the top of the page to Zane.

"I didn't say."

Gill waved a hand, inviting one of them to answer. She noticed the flash of a gold wedding ring on his left hand and wondered briefly who Gill had married. A local girl?

Brady remained stoic, his jaw tight. Josh gave his twin a consultative glance before saying, "An adventure ranch."

Gill lowered his eyebrows and tipped his head in query. "Excuse me?"

"You heard me. We want to open the ranch to visitors and take them out on excursions that will include various high-adrenaline activities."

The banker seemed to contemplate Josh's answer for a moment before he asked, "Such as?"

"What difference does it make what activities they offer?" Brady asked, his tone not hiding his resentment.

"You all did want a loan to help finance this *adventure ranch*, am I right?"

Piper cringed at the mocking tone Gill used. She sat straighter in her seat, on the verge of a tart reply, when a soft knock preceded Fran's entrance. Brady had to scoot sideways to allow the door to open and the secretary to squeeze into the increasingly crowded office.

They busied themselves with the business of signing the partnership papers, opening the business account for *McCall Adventures* and drawing up the papers for the loan. Piper and Zane carefully studied the documents laying out the terms of the loan before nodding their acceptance to Josh and Brady. Zane, as the CEO of the new business, signed the documents for the loan.

When her brother pushed the completed documents back across the desk to Gill, Piper couldn't help but feel a trill of excitement. She knew how important this venture was to her brothers, the passion they had for high-risk outdoor sports and how much they wanted to be able to bring in enough revenue to keep the ranch afloat. Maybe even to return the ranch to its former glory. Knowing she had a tiny part of the new business, thanks to her investment, was deeply satisfying.

In fact, she found herself longing for more. She couldn't deny how much she wanted to take the job her brothers had offered. She wanted to be a part of the day-to-day operation. She wanted to see firsthand the growth of the adventure ranch. Like a newborn calf, the business would have a period of getting its legs under it, but as the company strengthened, found the right balance, she knew it would be up and thriving in no time. And she wanted to be a part of it, damn it!

"So," Gill said, leaning back in his chair and capping his obviously pricy fountain pen in a manner that drew attention to his toy. "Should I be expecting to hear from your father soon?"

"Why would you?" Piper asked and immediately regretted falling for Gill's bait.

The banker shifted his face into a false expression of concern. "I heard about the fire at your place. Burned up your whole winter feed supply, they say."

"They," Josh said, pausing to let his emphasis on the pronoun sink in, "are wrong. And you should know better than to give credence to gossip."

"You didn't have a fire?" Gill asked, feigning surprise.

Piper scoffed internally. He was so transparent.

"We salvaged some of the crop," Zane said, tucking his copies of all the paperwork into his folder and rising from his chair.

"Oh." Gill nodded and rose from his seat as well, tugging on his suit coat to arrange it and smoothing his tie. "I'd feared the additional loss might make meeting his loan payments a hardship this winter. If your family needs to rework the terms of your loan or discuss any problems with making payments—"

Brady snorted derisively, and Josh interrupted, "We won't. Our father is nothing if not diligent about repayment of debts. You have nothing to fear."

Josh gave their high school rival a tight look and snatched the office door open. Brady exited behind Josh, casting a disgusted glare at Gill. Zane, ever the gentleman, shook Gill's hand, and Piper summoned the composure to do the same. For better or worse, McCall Adventures now carried a debt that Gill oversaw. A modicum of professional courtesy was called for.

They joined Brady and Josh in the bank lobby, where Josh paced restlessly and Brady looked ready to bite the head off the next person who spoke to him.

"I feel like I need a shower," Josh grumbled as she and Zane approached.

"I feel like I need to go to confession and repent." Brady narrowed his gaze on Zane. "You know we just signed a deal with the devil, right?"

Zane frowned and headed out the bank's twin glass doors. "He's an ass, yes, but we are doing business with the bank. And First Bank of Boyd Valley has the best terms for business loans."

"Maybe so," Piper countered as they walked to Zane's truck, "but you know Gill would like nothing more than to see us fail. He's held a grudge against us since the first day of kindergarten."

"I never understood why he dissed you all so bad from the get-go. Did you do something to him?" Brady asked, opening the truck door for Piper.

"Not that I recall," Josh said. "But you remember how bitter he became in high school after his family's ranch went out of business? I understand his father's become a real sourpuss of a man, too."

"But I think it became more personal for Gill when you beat him out as the pitcher for the baseball team," Piper added and slid onto the seat.

From behind the steering wheel, Zane lifted his eyebrows and nodded acknowledgment.

Brady scooted across the seat and smooshed Piper up against her brother.

Josh flashed a smug grin from the open passenger door. "Yeah, then I started dating Belinda Malloy. That ate him up."

Piper frowned at her brother as the four of them squeezed on the bench seat together. "It's not funny. What if he uses his past grievances to make trouble with our loan?"

"Then we'll make trouble for him with the bank," Zane replied as he started the truck. "He has laws and regulations to abide by."

"By the way, I saw his wedding ring. Who did he

marry?" Piper angled her shoulders as she tried to get more comfortable.

"Her name's Annabelle. Someone he met in college. You wouldn't know her," Josh replied.

"Zane, next time we all go somewhere together, we're taking two vehicles or we're taking a car with four seats!" she said.

"Did Boston make you soft, Pipsqueak?" Zane replied.

"You could always sit on Brady's lap," Josh teased. "I know how much you used to like that."

She leaned forward enough to shoot a glare at Josh.

Brady turned his head toward her with half a smile and patted the top of his thighs in invitation.

"I'm fine," she said, hunching her shoulders forward to fit in the narrow space between Zane and Brady.

"Maybe I'm way off base here, but did it bother anyone else that Gill already knew about the fire in hayfield?" Brady asked.

"And he had cow patty stuck on his shoe," Piper added.

"He did?" Zane cut a glance at her.

She nodded. "Coincidence…or could Gill be the one who's been sabotaging the ranch all these months? You know, helping Dad fail to meet the terms of his loans?"

"But he wouldn't profit from that personally. The bank holds Dad's loans," Zane said, but he was clearly concerned about the possibility. "Besides, this is a ranching town. There are cow patties everywhere, even tracked into town on ranch trucks."

Piper lifted a palm. "Maybe so. But if Dad defaults on his payments, the bank could seize the ranch and sell it at auction for a whole lot less than it is worth. Gill could be looking to take possession of it. And even if not, you know he'd love to see our family flounder. He's petty that way."

Her brothers remained quiet for several moments before Josh smacked his fist on the armrest. "Damn it, she's right, Zane. Gill would love to screw us over."

"Everybody chill." Zane waved a hand at them. "I honestly don't think Gill is stupid enough to risk his career or *jail time* to try to bring down the ranch."

"But—" Piper started.

Zane cut her off by putting a hand on her knee and adding, "*But*... I'll mention it to Dad and run it by the sheriff to see if it bears investigating." He cast a side-eye to Piper, who gave him an unconvinced pout, and he added, "Don't worry, Pipsqueak. It'll be a cold day in hell before I let Gill Carver destroy our family."

Chapter 6

When they got back to the Double M, Brady caught Piper's arm before she'd made it two steps toward the house. "Hey, thanks to the fire and hammering out details of the adventure ranch partnership with your brothers, we never finished the discussion we started a couple days ago."

She pried her arm free of his grasp. "Yes, we did."

He pulled his mouth into a sarcastic grin. "Beg to differ. Pick the time and place, but we *do* need to talk. The sooner the better."

Piper's shoulders slumped. She'd thought she'd dodged the bullet of whatever history-reviving, pain-inducing conversation Brady wanted to have.

"Hey, Piper!"

She turned at the sound of the young voice to find Connor running across the yard with a fistful of wildflowers, the stalks crushed in his hand. His yellow Lab was at his heels. "These are for you."

She gave the boy a bright smile, charmed by the color in his cheeks and mussed hair that suggested he'd been playing hard in addition to picking her flowers. "Those are beautiful, Connor. Thank you!"

He slanted a bashful grin at her. "Grampa says girls love flowers. I got those from behind our house."

"I do love flowers. Your Grampa is right." She angled her head. "Why aren't you at school today?"

He shrugged. "Uncle Brady said I didn't hav'ta go."

She gave Brady a side look, to which he said, "Teacher in-service day. Kids get a long weekend." Then to Connor, "Have you eaten lunch?"

"No. Grampa's cooking hot dogs, though."

"Why don't you run and wash up, then. I'll be in soon."

Connor scratched his dog on the head. "Okay. Come on, Kip!" He gave a weak whistle as he spun back toward his house, and Kip loped after him.

"He's cute. Was the dog a present to help with his grief?"

"Nope. Kip's older than Connor. They've grown up together." He shoved his hands in his pockets and faced her. "Now about that talk…"

She grunted and raised her hands. "Fine. So talk."

He pulled a frown, casting his gaze around the ranch yard that was buzzing with activity. "Not here." He glanced toward the hillside where her favorite cottonwood and the bench her father built stood sentinel over the ranch. "Come on." He gripped her hand and tugged her along, headed to her *thinking spot*.

When they neared his house, he paused and said,

"Wait here. I have to get something, but I'll only be thirty seconds."

He disappeared inside for a moment, and the short wait only served to ratchet up her disquiet. What could he possibly be getting from inside? How did that something relate to their conversation?

Returning outside, he reached for her as they started the trek to the top of the hill. She sidled away. She didn't need him touching her, holding her hand or otherwise guiding her. She was still jittery and tingling from the ride home from the bank with her body smashed against his and the scent of his soap in her nose.

As they neared the top of the hill, anxiety overtook her like a summer storm sweeping down from the ridge of the Rockies.

Piper moved stiffly to the bench and took a seat, the whirl of tiny wings in her belly growing more frantic. She kept her gaze on the ground, knowing eye contact with Brady would only unnerve her more. His piercing green eyes had a way of seeing right to her soul, and she needed, now more than ever, to protect herself from his incisive gaze. She intentionally focused on trivial things—the collection of yellow leaves that had fallen from the cottonwood's branches, the slow progress of a beetle along one of those leaves and the incongruous presence of a gum wrapper among the leaves. Hating to see even that tiny scrap dirtying the scenic spot, she bent to pick up the bit of litter and stuck it in her pocket.

Brady took off his hat and fidgeted with the brim, flicking it with his thumb as he paced restlessly in front of the bench.

Piper didn't like his nervousness. His edginess boded ill for this conversation.

"Go ahead," she said, flipping up her hand in invitation, then tucking her hand under her leg when she saw it quiver. "You have my attention. What did you want to tell me?"

"Right," he said, drawing a deep breath. "When Scott and Pam died, Dad was too big of a mess to handle the arrangements or deal with the business of closing their house and accounts. It fell to me."

A sympathetic pang twisted in her chest, imagining how difficult that must have been for him. "I'm so sorry, Brady."

She waited patiently for him to continue, selfishly relieved that the topic wasn't their relationship but rather the loss of his brother.

"When I was at their bank, closing their accounts and emptying their safe deposit box, I found a letter addressed to me." He reached in his jacket pocket and withdrew a folded envelope. "This is what I stopped to get at the house." Again he fell silent, his eyes lifting to the rustling leaves, then shifting to stare down at the letter in his hand. She was disconcerted to notice the paper and his hands trembling.

Once upon a time, they'd shared everything. They confided in each other, dreamed with each other, supported each other. If she was completely honest with herself, she'd have to admit that she'd missed having Brady to talk to during difficult times, having his perspective for tough decisions in recent years.

As a teenager, pouring her heart out to him had been cathartic. Maybe he'd missed having her as a sounding board, as well. Maybe this conversation was simply an opportunity to spill his grief, share his burdens with someone he trusted. Clearly, Roy had been in no shape after Scott's death to help Brady. And while Brady and her brothers were good friends, she couldn't see Zane or Josh having a soul-deep, emotionally raw conversation with Brady.

She shifted her position on the bench and studied his furrowed brow. Despite all they'd once had, Piper was uncomfortable with the intimate direction the discussion was headed. If they were to break the bonds between them, if she wanted to keep her heart safe, an emotional conversation about his brother wasn't going to help.

"Brady," she said after he remained silent for several pregnant seconds, "I'm sure losing Scott was hard, and I *am* sorry you had to go through all that, but I don't think—"

"Yeah, it was hard. It still is. So…just bear with me. Okay?" The impatient edge in his voice surprised her. Brady was typically so calm, so easygoing.

She sat straighter and pulled her shoulders back. "All right."

His green eyes no longer avoided hers. He pinned her with his stare and flapped the envelope as he spoke. "I debated whether to show this to you or not. I admit that a part of me wanted to keep it from you. To punish you."

Her brow creased, and a shot of adrenaline coursed through her. *Punish her?*

"I know it was spiteful, but…you hurt me when you left. And finding this—" he waved the envelope, and his jaw clenched, making the muscles in his cheeks jump "—only poured acid on those wounds."

Piper narrowed her eyes, her gut writhing like a worm on a hook. What could possibly be in that letter that would cause him such grief? She knew she'd wronged Brady in terrible ways, and she lived with those sins every day. But no one knew about those transgressions except her. Guilt gnawed at her, filled her entire being with a bile that no amount of purging could ever fully cleanse.

"But..." Brady sighed and swiped a hand down his face before meeting her gaze again. "I loved you once. And for what it's worth, I still care about you. Still have a soft spot in my heart for you, despite my anger and hurt."

She held her breath, afraid of where this conversation was going. When he paused, his gaze drilled hers with an intensity that shot frissons of icy dread through her.

"The lies and secrets have gone on long enough," he said, slapping the envelope against his palm before extending it toward her. "So they end today. It's time we both laid all our cards on the table."

She stared at the letter with the handwritten *Brady* on the front as if it were a demon with sharp teeth waiting to rip her to shreds. When she didn't take it from him for several seconds, his scowl deepened, and he seized her wrist and jammed the envelope into her hand.

"Read it," he commanded, and his tone brooked no resistance.

Hands shaking so hard the paper rattled, Piper lifted the unsealed flap and slid the folded pages out. She took a shallow breath into her leaden lungs and began reading the handwritten note.

Dear Brady,
Today was Connor's second birthday, and after a day filled with celebration for the wonderful child who has completed our family, I feel I must

put these thoughts on paper. Please forgive Pam and me for any hard feelings or resentments this confession and my instructions cause. Our intentions are pure and loving.

As you know, we've named you in our will as Connor's legal guardian should—heaven forbid—anything happen to both myself and Pam. Pam's sister may fight you on this. She was upset when we told her our decision, but our choice is clear and resolute. And after watching you play with Connor at his party today, I felt it only right to leave this letter for you, so you will know the reason for our decision. We are completely at peace with the decision, because we know you to be a loving, hardworking, loyal and patient man. You have a good heart and are well-grounded. You can do this. I have every faith in you. But the choice boiled down to one simple fact—Connor is your son with Piper McCall.

Chapter 7

Piper's heart slammed violently against her ribs, like unrestrained cargo flung through the windshield in a car crash. She blinked, struggling for a breath, and read the last line again. Surely she'd misread it.

Connor is your son with Piper McCall.

Gasping for air, she shot a shocked glance at Brady. His face was rigid, accusing, mercilessly unflinching. She opened her mouth to say something—to defend herself, to ask one of the million questions ping-ponging in her brain, to deny that it could be true. But her throat locked and choked any sound from leaving her.

Hesitantly, she lowered her gaze to the paper again and continued reading. Tears stung her eyes as she perused the rest of the letter, soaking in every word, digesting them and reconciling Scott's assertions with what she'd believed for seven years.

Our plan began to form the night you came to our house so upset that Piper was leaving. You told us then you thought she was pregnant but had refused to marry you. You were devastated, and we were grieved for you, but also for ourselves. So many years of trying to have a child had been fruitless, and there we were, faced with the possibility of a blood relative going to another family. We were determined not to let your child be raised by someone else, when we wanted him so desperately.

We went to our lawyer the next morning to seek his advice, and by the end of the week, we had a plan in place. We hired a private investigator to find Piper in Boston and keep tabs on her, to alert us if and when she went to an adoption agency.

Again she jerked her head up to pin an incredulous look on Brady. "They were *spying* on me?"

He said nothing, his level gaze hard and unsympathetic. After a moment of exchanging silent glares, she continued reading, righteous indignation now part of the emotional soup that roiled inside her.

When we found her and the adoption agency she intended to use, we made sure that we got your son. We made sure no other potential parents saw Piper's file. Yes, we are guilty of underhanded, probably illegal, things. We cheated, we circumvented rules, and we pulled so many strings I'm not sure why the adoption didn't unravel. But we didn't care. We still don't. Because we got Connor. He is ours. And if you are now reading this, then it means we are gone…and now he's yours to raise. Forgive us for keeping the truth from you, and don't hold it against us. We love Connor with our whole hearts and know you do, too. He belongs with you.

I've enclosed information about our life insurance and Connor's college funds. There should be enough to cover his care for several years.

Brady, Piper doesn't know we adopted Connor. It is now your decision whether to tell her or not. I know you still love her. Maybe, just maybe, you two can find a way to be together and share the love of this precious boy you created. Thank you, Brady, for being the best brother a guy could ask for. For giving us Connor and for raising him now. I love you, little brother. You are up to the task of being Connor's father. Don't doubt that for a minute. Just love him and protect him, and the rest will fall into place. Just stay in the saddle, Scott

A teardrop plopped onto the letter, blurring the ink, and Piper swiped at her face with the back of her hand. She sat motionless and numb to the core, while she re-read the entire letter. Somehow, this had to be a mistake. The family that had adopted her baby lived in Massachusetts. She forced her paralyzed brain to recall the details of the adoption that for years she had worked to block out. The adoptive parents, whose names she'd never known, were from… Worcester, Massachusetts. Or were they? She worked to form enough spit to swallow. The law office handling the adoption for the parents was located in Worcester. She couldn't really say where the parents were from.

Her head spun, and beneath her, the bench seemed to tilt and the ground to sway. She had to brace a hand on the seat to keep herself upright. "I...I don't understand."

"What's unclear?" he asked, his tone bitter. "Maybe the part where you lied to me about what happened to our baby?"

She felt a viselike grip squeeze her chest, and she struggled for a breath. Air sawed from her throat in shallow gasps that only added to her dizziness. "Brady, I didn't—"

"Did you not think I had a right to know your decision about our baby? God knows I gave you plenty of opportunity to tell the truth, but you ignored my calls for weeks! Then when you did answer a text, you lied and said the baby was dead."

"That's not true! I never said the baby died!" She swallowed, and guilt washed through her as she confessed. "I...I just...let you think that when you assumed..."

He pulled his cell phone from his back pocket and scrolled through screens before reading, "You don't have to worry about the baby anymore. There's no longer anything to decide or discuss. Please stop calling. We both have to move on with our lives now."

She gaped at him, her heart thundering. "You saved the text?"

"I saved the text." He huffed a sigh, laden with anger and frustration. "And do you blame me for thinking that meant you lost the baby? Whether you call it an outright lie or not, you deceived me. You didn't give me a say in what happened to our baby. Then you brushed me aside like last week's news."

She squeezed her eyes shut, digging deep for the strength to face the giant she'd tried so many years to hide from. Over the years, she'd practiced what she might say to Brady if he ever found out, if she ever had the courage to tell him about the baby herself. But though she'd mentally rehearsed her responses a thousand times, words failed her now. Guilt and shame overwhelmed her, colored with anger for his brother's deception.

Connor is your son...

Then the truth of those words finally penetrated the blanket of her compunction, confusion and shock. Connor. Is. Your. Son.

She whipped her head up to stare wide-eyed at Brady. "Connor is our son? Connor is our son!"

He scoffed and twisted his mouth in a humorless moue. "That's kinda the point of this conversation."

Like a primed well, new emotions surged up and overflowed, adding to the flood that muddied her thoughts and swamped her senses. She raised a hand to her mouth, laughing and crying at the same time. Joy filled her soul, so pure and true she ached with it. The sweet baby that she'd felt compelled to give up, the tiny boy she'd given away so that he could have a better life than she could provide was back in her life. Safe, loved and...*living with his father.*

Her brain yo-yoed back to the fact that Brady had discovered her secret, her deceit, her crime against him.

She lifted her eyes once more to meet Brady's and met the accusation, fury and pain in his face. The see-saw of emotions left her winded, speechless. Her celebration over finding her child now became a sharp slice of regret that made her double over at the waist as guilt wrenched her gut in knots. "Oh, Brady, I'm so sorry."

His mouth tightened, and he shook his head in disgust. "Sorry? You think *sorry* makes up for denying me the right to be a father to my own son?"

"I know you're mad."

"Ya think?"

"Brady, I was a kid. I was scared, and—"

"I was scared, too. But I knew we could handle it together. That's why I offered to marry you."

She frowned. "You only proposed because of the baby."

"Hell, yeah! I'd have done the right thing if you'd given me a chance! You know that."

She exhaled a deep breath and said softly. "That's why I turned you down."

Brady cocked his head, his expression contorting in confusion. "Come again?"

"I said, that's why I turned you down. I didn't want a husband who only married me because we were reckless enough to forget birth control."

He gaped at her, his mouth working, but only strangled sounds came from his throat.

"We were too young to be thinking about marriage, Brady! We both had plans for college. You had dreams of veterinary school, and I couldn't take that from you."

He moved closer to her, sticking his face in hers. "What I had was the kind of mediocre grades that colleges find easy to turn down and a dazzling future as a ranch hand, shoveling horse crap for the rest of my life. Vet school was unrealistic. You were the real dream." He took a slow breath, and his eyes and voice softened even though his jaw remained taut with tension. "You were the only good thing in my life, Piper. And you left me. You left me, and then you lied to me."

A searing ache stabbed her chest, and moisture stung in her eyes again. She surged off the bench, knocking his shoulder aside, and marched away from him. She needed space to catch her breath, distance to collect her thoughts. After a moment, she pressed a hand to her swirling stomach and pivoted to face him. "Brady...a baby is the wrong reason to get married."

He threw his hands up. "Seriously? Sounds like a pretty *good* reason to me."

"Not if that's the only reason!" She raked her hair back from her face and sniffled as her tears made her nose run. "What about compatibility? What about *love*? Marriage is hard work under the best circumstances, and if you enter into it for the wrong reasons, you're setting yourself up for failure."

His eyebrows dipped. "Are you saying you didn't love me? Because I loved you with all my heart. I wanted to spend my life with you, Piper."

The fist of pain squeezing her chest clamped tighter, suffocating her. Her legs grew wobbly, and she wrapped her arms around her middle as she struggled to keep her knees locked and steady. "Brady, please. Rehashing the past doesn't help anything. It only hurts. What we have to deal with is *now*. What happens *now*?"

"No, don't change the subject." He strode over to her, taking her by the elbows and drilling a piercing green stare straight to her soul. "Answer me. I deserve to know. Did you love me?"

Brady felt the shudder that raced through Piper. Her cheeks drained of color, and if he hadn't been supporting her arms, he felt sure she'd have collapsed. And just how was he supposed to interpret that reaction?

She moistened her trembling lips, and he tracked the path of her tongue, fighting the desire to kiss her dewy, sweet mouth. If she'd had any doubts how he'd felt about her then, how he *still* felt about her, even after years of trying to cure himself of his addiction to her, he could end her speculation with one blow-your-boots-off, memory-making kiss. But he roped his desire and restrained it as he waited for her answer.

"I did love you. Of course I loved you, Brady."

He choked out a wry laugh. "*Of course? Of course* implies it should be obvious. But what was obvious to me was your disregard for my feelings when you said *See ya, pal* and up and left for Boston. You refused to answer my calls and then told me to move on with my life." After a short pause he added, "Without giving me a say in what happened to our child!"

Piper stiffened then, drawing herself up to her full height, even as tears streaked her cheeks. "I did what I thought was best at the time! Yes, I was wrong in so many ways. I know that in hindsight. But I never wanted to hurt you. It was because we'd dreamed together about our futures that I knew marriage at eighteen and starting a family so soon was *not* what you wanted. I wanted you to go to college, to become a veterinarian. You had dreams for yourself, and I would not be responsible for killing those dreams. I didn't want you to resent me or our baby, and I didn't want to give up the opportunity *I had* to go to Boston College on scholarship."

"Oh, now we get to the truth."

She aimed a finger at him. "Don't twist this around and make it what it isn't. Was it selfish of me to not tell you about putting the baby up for adoption? Yes. I've admitted that. Do I regret hurting you? Definitely. But my giving the baby up for—"

"Connor. That baby has a name. *Connor.*"

She shook her head slowly. "Actually, in my heart, I

named him after you. I always thought of him as *Brady Jeremiah Jr.*" She twitched a sad smile. "*BJ* for short."

Her revelation punched him in the gut, and he staggered back a step, dropping his hands from her arms. He sucked in a ragged breath.

"And, most importantly, I gave our baby up for adoption because I wanted what was best for *him*. I believed he'd have a better life with adoptive parents. I'd squandered my chance to be with you, and I didn't want to blow my best chance to give BJ…to give *Connor* a good life." She puffed out a shallow breath. "I made a really bad decision by letting you believe he'd died, but I swear I had good motives, ill-conceived though they were. I know you must hate me for what I did. I can't blame you for hating me."

He scoffed. "Hate you? I only wish I could have hated you."

She pulled a sad, wounded half grin. "Ouch."

"It would have been so much easier to get over you. I was furious with you, hurt by you, but…" He huffed his disappointment and stared at the ground near his feet. "I never quit caring. Even though you've made it clear in the years since that you've moved on, I've had a hard time accepting it. I still think about having all that we once talked about, the life we dreamed about sharing together."

"Brady…" she rasped.

"Learning the truth about Connor was bittersweet. I'd lost my brother, but…" he glanced up to meet her watery gaze, and the misery in her eyes slashed through him "…I got a little piece of you back, a little bit of the future we'd planned."

A tiny mewl of distress sounded in her throat, and a visible tremor shook her. The instinct to protect and possess her stirred deep inside him. He eased closer to her, his gaze roving over her face, reading every tic and shadow to gauge her heart. When one of the tears that had puddled in her gray eyes rolled down her cheek, the anger that had coalesced over the years into a hard ball in his soul cracked. The bitterness drained away, and he was left with a hollow space that clamored to be filled. With Piper. With new hope.

"My God, Piper, I've missed you," he whispered, reaching for her. Thumbing away the moisture on her cheek, he stroked her soft skin and cradled her face in his palm.

She sucked in a hiss of breath as if his touch burned. Brady's gut clenched, fully expecting her to pull away, to make excuses, to distance herself again. Instead, she angled her chin into his touch, releasing the breath she held with a sigh as soft as the autumn breeze. "I've missed you, too."

If he hadn't been standing inches away from her, his every fiber tuned into the minutest hints of her mood, he would have missed her whispered confession. But he did hear her, and the barely audible words were all the invitation he needed.

Sliding his hand to the nape of her neck, Brady coaxed her closer. His other arm circled her waist, anchoring her against him, and he dipped his head to take what he'd been waiting for. He poured seven years of suppressed desire, fruitless longing and painful patience into his kiss. He didn't bother with a polite kiss that eased into the embrace or with subtle nibbles along her cheek that teased her passion. No, he wanted her to know how serious he was about his feelings for her, the time they'd wasted, the need that clawed at him. He angled his mouth on hers, an urgent kiss that demanded a response from her. A deep kiss that claimed her as his.

After the initial surprise bowed her back, and she gasped at the crush of his lips against hers, her posture eased. She melted against him, bunching his shirt in her fingers as she clung to him.

As he grew more confident that she wouldn't bolt, that she was as swept up in the passion of the moment as he, and that maybe, just maybe, she still had feelings for him, one thought filtered through his brain—*At last.*

Ken watched the meeting between Piper and the cowboy with his jaw tight and his fingers gripping the high-powered binoculars so hard his knuckles were white. He was galled to know he'd been ignorant of a relationship that was obviously so key to her past.

The bark of the tree he'd climbed to have a better vantage point scraped his back, and the stench of cow pies and rancid mud permeated the air. How did Piper stand the filth and stink? She was better than this dirty ranch and the sweaty cowboys that worked it. No wonder she only returned for a few days each year.

Knowing how rarely she visited her family, how little she saw of this particular cowboy, should have eased his mind. But the discussion Piper was having with the ranch hand clearly had her upset. For her to be so moved by what he was saying, whatever was in the paper he'd shown her, meant she was emotionally invested. Their body language screamed of a deeply personal exchange. Which meant the cowboy was important to her.

Ken lowered the binoculars and stewed. He needed to find a way to break the bond she had with this Stetson-wearing John Wayne wannabe. The most obvious solution was to deal with him the way he'd dealt with Ron Sandburg. Eliminating the competition was the surest way to clear the path to his future with Piper. But knocking off the cowboy would be tricky.

He pulled out his pack of cinnamon gum and unwrapped a stick. Shoving the gum in his mouth, he let the wrapper flutter to the ground like one of the dead leaves dropping from the branches around him.

How would he get to the cowboy? The ranch was crawling with people from first light until well after dark. He'd stand out as an interloper here in Hickville, unlike the high-rise where Ron Sandburg had lived.

Expelling a frustrated sigh, Ken raised the binoculars again to monitor the exchange between Piper and—

Ken flinched at the sight that greeted him with such violence that he nearly fell from his perch. The cowboy had Piper in a lip-lock, his hands groping her like a randy octopus. And she did nothing, *nothing*, to fight him off. Ken saw red. Rage boiled in him, and his pulse pounded in his ears.

Piper belonged to him. Something had to be done about the cowboy. Nobody took what belonged to Ken without consequences. Yes, the cowboy would pay for his trespass, and Piper...well, he'd have to teach her a lesson, too.

Piper lost herself in Brady's kiss for long moments of bliss before sanity reared its head. She drew back from him with a sigh of dismay, averting her head from his kisses.

Brady stilled and released her slowly, obviously reading the returned distance in her expression. "What?"

"We can't do this." She pulled away from his embrace and stalked back toward the bench, raking fingers through her hair.

"Can't what? Kiss?"

"No. I mean, yes. I… We can't let sex muddle our heads while we figure things out."

"Figure things out…" Brady parroted, his voice confused.

She faced him, tipping her head in query. "Isn't that why you showed me the letter? So we can decide how to move forward? What we're going to do about Connor?"

Brady gave a harsh laugh and rubbed the scruff on his chin. Piper's own chin stung a bit from the abrasion of his stubble against her skin when they'd kissed. Her fingers twitched, wanting to touch the places where she still felt his mark on her, but she stifled the impulse.

"So…you want a part in deciding Connor's future?" The irony in his tone chafed, but she saw where he was going.

"Are you really going to punish me for what I did when I was eighteen?" She didn't bother to hide her hurt. The grip of emotions on her voice forced her to stand in strained silence with him for several moments, while she regained her composure and wiped the trickle of tears from her face.

His lack of denial spoke for itself. Her hands fisted. "Brady, I said I was sorry. I made a bad decision at a time when I was young and scared and confused and feeling that I'd failed my family and—"

She paused from her defense of her actions, even though she knew her decision had been indefensible, as a new realization hit her. "Wait…you got that letter from Scott's lockbox at the bank when they died… in *January*?"

He shrugged. With an exasperated sigh, he walked back to the bench. "Yeah."

"So you've known Connor was our son for, what, nine...ten months, and you're only telling me now?"

He looked at her as if she'd slapped him, then laughed bitterly. "Says the woman who hadn't let me know for seven *years* about our baby. You're something else, Piper. Throwing that in my face, when I still wouldn't know the truth about our son if not for my brother *dying*! Could you be *more* of a hypocrite?"

She raised a hand as she sprang up from the bench. "Fine. Fine. You win that point."

He grumbled a curse word. "It's not about winning points. Connor is what is important."

She bobbed a nod. "Agreed. Absolutely. But seeing as I'm just learning all this... I'm still processing..."

"By all means, process." He waved a hand of invitation. "This is important, and I have all the time you need to discuss it."

She took a moment to catch her breath and let her reeling mind find traction. "I...don't even know where to start. Connor is...our son."

She thought of the giggling boy who'd regaled her with kid jokes, loved his dog and brought her wildflowers. The boy with a curious mind, with Brady's eyes and a bright, heart-stopping smile. Her son. *Their* son.

Her pulse thundered as she grappled with the magnitude of the revelation. She stared out across the waving grass of the hillside, watched the tumble of leaves tossed by the breeze and soaked in the golden rays of midday sun as they filtered through the branches of the cottonwood tree. The simple autumn beauty, the peaceful setting should have calmed her. But learning the truth about Connor on top of the realities of the family's finances and the offer from her brothers to be a part of something big, something that could help save the family's ranch…

Her mind reeled in so many directions, she didn't know where to begin sorting it all out. She lifted her eyes to Brady, remembering how rock-solid he'd been in the past, how much she'd counted on his confidence and pragmatism when teen angst and life issues had rattled her in high school.

"What do I do?" she asked him, because turning to him for advice felt as natural as breathing. She sat back down on the bench next to Brady and pressed her fingers to her mouth. "What am I supposed to do with this? If you don't want my input on Connor's future, then why did your tell me about him?"

Brady angled an *are-you-kidding* look at her. His cool reception of her entreaty stung. The rancor in his expression spoke for how their relationship had changed. And she had only herself to blame.

"Because you deserved to know. You didn't give me that option, but I can't keep a truth as important as our son from you."

With a slow breath and hard swallow to force down the bile and regret that burned her throat, she determinedly trained her thoughts on the issues at hand.

"Does Connor know the truth?" she asked, then as more and more questions popped into her brain she lobbed them without waiting for him to respond to any of them. "Does your father know the truth? My family? Is that why they asked me to move back here? How do you think Connor will react? Maybe it's better we don't tell him. What's his state of mind since Scott and Pam's deaths? Are we supposed to share custody now, or are you—"

"Whoa! Jeez, slow down!" He shifted to face her, raising a hand in a *Stop!* gesture before pinching the bridge of his nose. "We don't have anything to decide about custody."

She jerked her head back in surprise and scrunched her face. "Excuse me?"

His eyebrows lifted, and he turned up his palm as he said flatly, "Scott and Pam legally adopted Connor. In their will, they legally gave full custody to *me*."

She blinked and made a choking sound in her throat. "I—"

"You signed away any claim to him when you put him up for adoption. Remember?"

She shot up from the bench, her hands fisting. "Are you kidding me? That was... But everything's changed! You can't mean—"

He shook his head and rose to his feet as well, squaring off with her. "I do mean it. Nothing has changed. Did you really think those adoption papers meant you gave up custody only until you changed your mind or your circumstances made it more convenient to be a parent?"

She clamped her lips in a tight scowl. "Of course not. But who could have foreseen—"

"No."

"Brady!"

"I don't want to fight you on this, Piper." He aimed a finger at her, his expression flinty. "But I will if you push me."

She took a calming breath and continued in a quieter tone. "I don't want to fight you, either. I...haven't even had time to think about custody. I've only known about this for five minutes, but..." She blew out a puff of breath as she narrowed a frustrated glare on him.

"I hate that you're being a mule about it from the get-go." She combed her fingers through her wind-ruffled hair, pulling strands from her mouth and eyes. "Yes, I signed papers when I was barely eighteen, not ever imagining the twists my life would take."

He jerked a nod as if to say, *Case closed.*

"But if I move back here to take on the job my brothers offered—" she persisted, and his eyes grew wary "—I'll see Connor every day. Don't you think I'll want a relationship with him?"

"You can have a relationship with him." His timbre warmed now, softening the hard edge he'd used earlier. "I encourage you to have one. Connor is a great kid, and I have no intention of standing in the way of you getting to know him." He stopped there, holding her gaze with his own, but her guilty conscience heard the unspoken *Like you did to me.*

She pressed a hand to her belly where the assault of winged creatures continued.

"But…" he added, his eyes narrowing slightly to emphasize his determination "…I won't let you break his heart. He's already lost one mother. He needs someone he can depend on. Your track record says that person is not you. And I won't let you take him from me. You'll never move him to Boston or force him to choose between the two of us. He's had enough disruption and upheaval in his life."

Even though an hour earlier, Piper could never have imagined taking Connor back with her to Boston, the rebellious streak in her chafed at being told so pointedly *You'll never...* The stubborn sister who'd been told by her brothers *you can't* simply because she was a girl bristled at the absolute. For years, she'd lived to defy expectations. She'd moved to Boston in part to escape the limitations and assumptions placed on her simply because she was the sister in the McCall triplets.

"I see," she said, straightening her spine and squaring her shoulders. "You've decided, and that's it? End of discussion?"

"In this matter, yes." His jawline was rigid, and his mouth set. The hard determination in his eyes, usually so kind and full of warmth, sent a chill to her core. As she studied his unflinching expression, she cataloged the other differences in his face. The loss of boyish softness to his facial lines. The tiny lines bracketing his eyes that spoke of stress and too much sun. He was the same man she'd fallen in love with, and yet…different.

"What happened to your plans, Brady? You say vet school was unrealistic, but I thought you were accepted to Colorado State. Why didn't you go?"

He twitched his brow, clearly startled by her change of subject. "As I recall, I said I wanted to go to college *with you*. Part of me wanted to get a college degree, yeah. Being a vet seemed a good fit for a kid who grew up on a ranch. But the goal was always to be with you. You were at the center of everything I wanted for my life. And then…there was my dad. I had a drunk father to take care of."

She closed her eyes and shook her head as a fresh wave of heartache washed through her. "Oh, Brady."

"You asked. Just being honest."

When she opened her eyes, she met the fire in his green gaze. Her body reacted the way it had so many times throughout the years. The reaction was instantaneous and powerful. A surge of heat in her blood, a flood of affection from her heart and a dizzying sense of destiny from her soul.

Though so many things swirled in a maelstrom of

indecision and heartache for her, one thing was clear. Her life was now bound even tighter to Brady's thanks to the sweet little boy they had made together.

Whatever they were discussing, Piper had high stakes in it, and the greater her connections with this dusty track of land and the equally dusty people, the stronger the pull away from Boston. Ken had overheard her tell Sara in marketing that she missed her family and the mountains of Colorado, but that she had no plans to return. Yet the rumor he'd caught wind of over his eggs and sausage at the tiny diner in town contradicted Piper's plan. Some schmuck in a pin-striped suit was grumbling about Piper and her brothers forming a partnership and starting a new business. A new business would make her ties to this cow town all the stronger.

His usual sources of information, Piper's emails and Facebook messages, had all but dried up, since she could communicate in person with her family about these plans. Ken shifted uncomfortably on the tree branch he'd claimed as his daytime monitoring station. Camouflaged with fall foliage, the branch afforded a secure perch across a pasture from the hill with the bench but also a straight line of sight to the main house. At night, he enjoyed the cover of darkness and the more comfortable bench where Piper and the cowboy had their private confabs. But the high-powered lens of his camera alone didn't give him nearly enough information. What was the highly wrought discussion she was having with the cowboy about? How could he get closer, learn more?

Ken gritted his teeth and slapped the rough bark of

his perch. He had to find a way to get onto the property and plant a listening device.

Piper was only scheduled to stay a few more days before returning to Boston, but he had a horrible suspicion that her return was in jeopardy. He had to do something to convince her this ranch was no longer the place for her. But what?

Chapter 8

For the next twenty-four hours, her discussion with Brady replayed in Piper's head a hundred times. Each time, she formed more questions, heard nuances that broke her heart one minute, then filled her with hope the next. Confusion and hurt reigned supreme. What in the world was she supposed to do?

I won't let you break his heart. He's already lost one mother. He needs someone he can depend on. Your track record says that person is not you.

The day of her parents' anniversary party arrived, and she went through the motions of preparation, helping tidy the living room, orienting the caterer in the kitchen and taking a long soak in a hot bath, trying to calm her whirling mind. Late in the afternoon, Piper pulled her dress for the party out of the closet and laid it across the end of the bed. For a moment, she stared at the dress, a fitted dove-gray number with cap sleeves and an empire waist, wondering what Brady would think of it, then returned to the closet. Brady's opinion shouldn't matter. She wasn't dressing to please him. The dress had been selected by her girlfriends in Boston from three she'd bought. Her friends said the fitted design showed off her figure best and the color made her eyes pop. All good qualities in a dress, but who was she trying to impress? Had she, even back in Boston, secretly been hoping to catch Brady's eye? The notion unsettled her.

She retrieved her shoes, medium-heeled, faux-eel pumps with sparkly embellishments on the vamp, and when she turned back to the bed, shoes in hand, she pulled up short.

Zeke had climbed on the dress and was settling in for a nap.

"Oh, no, you don't!" She waved a hand at the fuzzy feline, thankful for the dry cleaner's plastic bag that protected it from Zeke's plethora of long fur. "Get off, Zeke. Go!"

The Maine coon only looked at her with what she could only describe as a smug grin. Pure Cheshire cat.

"Now!" She dropped the shoes and hustled over to lift the cat—carefully, so that his claws didn't snag the dress through the plastic. Clearly thinking her intention was to cuddle, Zeke reached for her shoulder with his front paws and began purring loudly.

And just like that, she melted. Pulling him close to her chest, his large body draped over her shoulder like a baby, she snuggled Zeke and reveled in his soft fur. One simply didn't grow up on a ranch and not form a deep love for animals. Standing in her childhood bedroom, holding the feline like a baby, Piper flashed again to her conversation earlier with Brady.

Connor was her son. Had life unfolded a little differently, she might have cuddled Connor as she did Zeke right now and sung him to sleep. Now, like a lullaby, the low rumble of the cat's purr soothed her. She buried her nose in the fluff of belly fur and choked back tears of regret. She found herself swaying as she held Zeke, as if she were comforting a baby.

Second-guessing her decision to give Connor up for adoption served no purpose but to torture her. What mattered now was deciding how to move forward, how to heal the wounds she'd caused Brady and find a way to maintain an amicable relationship with him. For Connor's sake.

Amicable. She scoffed a laugh under her breath. "That kiss we shared today was a little more than *amicable*," she told the cat. "More like *amorous*."

Zeke nuzzled her hand, demanding that she pat his head. With a snort of amusement, she scratched his cheek and grinned as he rotated his head so that his chin and other cheek got similar attention.

"Piper?" her mother called from the hall.

"In here." She set Zeke on the floor with a final pat on his rump. "All right, beastie. Let me dress."

Her mother stuck her head in the door. "Who were you talking to?"

"Zeke. He's doing his best to impede my progress." She dusted cat hair from her bathrobe and cast a sideglance to her mother.

Her mother squatted, talking baby talk to Zeke as she stroked his back. "Who's a good boy? Yes, you are."

"Did you need me?"

Her mother rose and flicked fur from her fingers. "I will later. My gown will be a bugger to zip."

"I'd be glad to, but can't Dad—"

"Nope. Like on our wedding day, I don't want him to see my dress until I join the party." Her mother flashed a coy grin. "A little mystery helps keep the romance alive, you know." Melissa stepped farther into the room and set a jewelry box on the dresser. "Thought I'd offer to help you with your hair. Have you considered wearing it up?"

Piper eyed the black velvet box but didn't mention it. "I thought down would be easier. Maybe hot rollers for some curl, but…" She shrugged.

Zeke had moved to her wastebasket and stuck his head over the rim, examining the contents.

"Oh, but darling, this dress…" Her mother lifted the dress from the bed and pulled the dry-cleaner plastic off it with a sigh of awe. "This dress demands you show off your lovely shoulders and neck."

"I have *lovely shoulders and neck*?"

"You have *lovely* everything, Piper. And you don't dress up nearly enough and show yourself off."

"Product of my environment. Jeans always suited me better." She sent her mother a wrinkled-nose look. "And since when do I need to show myself off? You make me sound like the prize steer at auction."

Her mother chuckled. "Far from it. You're my beautiful daughter, and for a change, I get to see you all spiffed-up and looking like the princess you are in my mind." She wagged a finger, but her smile softened the scolding effect. "It's my party. I've hired a photographer to take pictures and if I ask you to pull out all the stops getting dolled up, are you really going to say *no*?"

"Well, no." A thunk drew her attention back to the cat who'd now tipped over the trash can and was dragging out the plastic safety overwrap Piper had removed from a bottle of aspirin.

"Oh, honey, get that from him. He'll swallow bits of it and get sick."

Grunting, Piper swooped down to snatch the wrapper from Zeke, who meowed pitifully when his prize was taken away. "Your cat is weird, Mom."

"Hmm. Indeed. Now, about your hair…" She draped the dress over the end of the bed again and lifted the jewelry box. "Wearing it up will also better show off these." Melissa cracked open the box and showed her the strand of pea-size silver-toned pearls.

Piper gasped. "Mom, those are gorgeous. Are they for me?"

"Someday. They were my grandmother's, and you'll get them when I die."

"Ugh! Don't say things like that. You're not allowed to die, Mom."

Her mother pulled a lopsided grin and smacked a kiss on Piper's cheek. "But for tonight, I think they are the perfect complement to your dress…" her grin brightened "…and your lovely neck."

Piper took the proffered box and brushed her fingertips over the smooth pearls. "They are gorgeous."

"So…" Her mother stepped behind her and twisted up a handful of Piper's hair. "Will you let me put your hair up? Being surrounded by so many macho men all the time leaves me no outlet for doing the girly things I love."

"What?" Piper asked in mock surprise. "Zane and Josh won't go on spa days with you?"

Her mother's face split with a wide grin. "Oh! A spa day. That sounds wonderful! Will you have time to go into Denver for facials and pedicures before you leave? My treat!"

Piper choked on a laugh. "I didn't mean… Mom,

when did I ever do girly stuff growing up? You know I don't—"

Her mother's crestfallen expression broke her heart, and she swallowed the rest of her dismissal. Instead, she wrapped her mother in a hug and squeezed her tight. "Okay. For you, I will let someone buff my calluses and paint my toenails." She levered back from her mom. "And I'm leaving my hairstyle up to you tonight. Just don't go crazy with the hairspray. Okay?"

The delight that filled her mother's face was reward enough. "Oh, thank you, sweetheart! Wait right here. I'm going to get my curlers and bobby pins."

As her mother hurried out, Piper spotted Zeke back at the wastebasket, his raised paw trying to tip the can over. "No!" She shooed the cat away, chuckling. "You are certainly stubborn like a McCall, furball." She picked up Zeke and deposited him gently in the hall. "Go on. No men allowed while I dress."

She returned to the bedroom, giving the strand of pearls another admiring glance before snapping the box closed and sliding it onto her crowded dresser top. In the process, she managed to knock off a music box Brady had given her for Christmas the last year they were dating. The lid flipped open when the music box landed sideways on the floor, and the tinkling notes of John Denver's "Annie's Song" played into the quiet room.

Piper froze, the notes like poignant daggers to her heart. The music box had been his mother's. Brady had called the tune *their song* because the words expressed how he felt about Piper. She had been unfamiliar with the song, and Brady had had to pull out Roy's dusty cassette tapes and play the oldie for her.

"John Denver was my mom's favorite. Dad hasn't

listened to any of these since she died," he'd explained. "But I remember her singing this one, and now it makes me think of you."

Now, standing in her bedroom, hearing the music that had moved her so deeply took her back to the first time she'd heard the romantic words and sweet melody. To the swell of love she'd felt toward Brady for his sentimental gift. Their future together had seemed so certain, so bright, so full of love and cherished moments to come.

Her knees buckled, and she sank to the floor as the sting of moisture rushed to her eyes. Crawling toward the fallen music box on trembling arms, she allowed the torrent of tears to flow and chest-racking sobs to break. The last few days had tested her ability to bottle up the memories and keep up the pretense that she didn't miss Brady with every breath. The strain her family was under thanks to the financial worries, the threat of some unknown vandal whose attacks had escalated...

It was all too much. She sat on the floor, ugly crying, and reached for the music box. Torn between closing the lid to shut off the heartbreaking tune or letting it play to educe the bittersweet ache that had simmered in her soul for years, she stared without seeing at the dried flowers preserved in the box's glass walls and lid.

"Okay, I think I've got everything I'll need," her mother said breezily as she returned. "I can—" Her gasp cut her off. "Piper? What in the world...?" She deposited the armload of hair products and beauty tools on Piper's bed and crouched beside her. "What's wrong?"

Turning to her mother, she held out the music box with a trembling hand. "B-Brady gave me this."

"I know." Her mother lowered her bottom to the

floor and scooted closer to Piper. "I remember." She tucked Piper's hair behind her ear and knuckled a tear from her daughter's cheek. "Why the tears?"

Piper waved the music box. "It fell and s-started playing. I j-just…"

Her mother took the music box from Piper and, flipping the lid closed to silence the tinkling notes, set the box aside. "Talk to me, baby. What's going on?"

Piper draped her arms around her mother's neck and buried her face on her shoulder. "It hurts, Mom. It still hurts so much."

"Of course it hurts. You still love him."

Heart pounding, Piper jerked her head up and gaped at her mother.

"I don't—"

Her mother caught Piper's chin with her fingers and narrowed a warning look on her. "Don't you dare try to lie to me by denying it. I've seen the way you still look at him."

Piper's heart seized with panic. What had her mother seen? Was she really that transparent? What else might she have given away in her expressions or body language without knowing?

Her mother drew her eyebrows together. "And don't think I don't know that he's the reason you come home so rarely."

"I— Mom, it's…complicated."

"Psh," her mother dismissed, pulling Piper close again and rubbing her back as she held her. "Life is only as complicated as you choose to make it. With most things, you can narrow your choices down to basic priorities. What matters the most to you? Love? Family? Money? Happiness?"

Piper groaned. "That's a great slogan for a T-shirt,

Mom, but kinda oversimplifying the reality. There are things you don't know about why Brady and I split up. Things I've never told anyone."

"Anything you want to share now? Clearly, keeping it bottled up hasn't been working too well for you."

Piper tensed. She needed to tell her mother the truth about Connor. She was bound to find out sooner or later, and the shock and hurt her parents would feel wouldn't be eased by waiting. But now wasn't the time. She didn't want to spoil her mother's evening, a celebration her parents had every right to savor.

"I...will. But n-not now." She swallowed hard, feeling as if she had a fish bone stuck in her throat.

"All right," her mother said and sighed. "I won't push. But remember this—life is too short and full of the unexpected to waste even a minute harboring regrets. Forgive yourself for mistakes, let go of past hurts, and...don't ignore the opportunities right under your nose to be truly happy."

Piper sniffed and gave her mother an ironic laugh. "Subtle, Mom."

"So sue me for wanting my daughter to be happy. And I have never seen you as happy as you were when you were with Brady." She leaned back and thumbed another tear off Piper's cheek, then holding her damp digit up for Piper to see. "Or as miserable since you went your separate ways."

Grunting her frustration, Piper tried to pull away. "Not helping, Mom."

Melissa angled her head and twisted her mouth in a moue of disagreement. "Oh, I get it. You want me to pat you on the back and help you justify walking away from the man you love." She placed her hand under her chin, patting her cheek with her index finger as if thinking hard. "Okay. Let's see... Well, he's certainly not good-looking or kindhearted. And he's definitely lazy—"

Piper clenched her teeth, frustrated with her mother's persistence. And the heartrending truth she illuminated with her sarcasm.

"And he's humorless and dishonest and probably not very—"

"Mom!" She shot her mother an angry glare that instantly dissolved into a new round of heaving sobs.

"I'm sorry, Piper, but I can't pretend that Brady is somehow a mistake for you. I want you to be happy, of course, but I—"

"I kissed him."

Her mother fell silent and blinked her surprise. "Well... I don't see why that's a problem. If you still love him—"

"I don't!" Piper shook her head, then amended, "I can't. I mean... I don't want to care so much about him, because it hurts, but... Oh, jeez, Mom, it's so complicated."

"So you've said." Her mother squeezed Piper's hand. "You've always needed order and logic. It's your left-brain way of processing information. But love isn't about logic, darling."

"The question of loving Brady isn't the problem, Mom. I—" Piper met the loving smile her mother gave her, and before she could stop them, words started tumbling from her tongue. The secrets that she'd kept busted free like a wild stallion kicking down a stable door. "I got pregnant, Mom. In high school, before I left for college, and I had the baby in Boston. That's why I didn't come home for so long during my freshman year. I couldn't. I didn't want you to know how terribly I'd let you down."

Her mother's eyes widened, and her face paled. "Piper?"

"Wait, there's more." She tried to swallow, but her mouth was arid as she forged on. "I gave the baby away, Mom. I didn't tell Brady what I'd done and—the baby was his—"

Her mother pulled a face that said the last had been understood.

"And, well, I couldn't face him all these years because of what I'd done. I felt so guilty, and then..." She paused only long enough to draw another breath. "Connor... Connor is my son. Mine and Brady's. I didn't know. Scott and Pam didn't tell Brady. He didn't know until they died and he found a letter Scott had written him and—" She felt a knot back up the air in her lungs. "Oh, God, Mom, I have a son. We have a son. Brady and I. Connor is... I don't know what to do!"

Her mother looked poleaxed for a moment, but she took a few breaths and looked Piper straight in the eye. "You will love your son. That's what you will do."

Piper exhaled harshly. "I know. But...how? And what does it mean for me and Brady? Do I try to get shared custody? Do I pretend I don't know and let Brady raise him by himself? That seems to be what Scott and Pam intended. What do I tell Connor? What do—"

Her mother pulled her into a tight hug and shushed her. "Whoa, baby. Slow down." She gave a stiff laugh. "I just learned that I have a grandson, and I need a moment to savor that before we solve world hunger and plan your entire future."

"I'm sorry. I didn't mean to spoil today for you, what with your party tonight and—"

"Spoil it?" Her mother pushed her to arm's length, laughing even as her eyes grew teary. "You gave me the best gift today I could ever have hoped for! I'm a grandmother to a precious little boy. However this plays out between you and Brady, that fact remains, and I cherish it."

"You're not mad at me?" Piper bit her bottom lip and winced. Why was it that no matter how old she got, she still wanted, needed, her parents' approval?

Her mother's expression sobered, and she was clearly choosing her words carefully. "No. Not mad. I'm…hurt that you didn't trust us, trust enough in our love for you and our ability to help and support you through anything to tell us sooner."

She lowered her gaze as her mother continued, "I'm disappointed in the choices you made throughout, but…"

When Piper's shoulders drooped, her mother put a hand under her chin and nudged Piper's face back up. "Look at me, honey, and listen. Hear me. You were young. You were scared. You had limited life experience to deal with the very adult situation you got yourself in. We all make mistakes, and we all have to live with the consequences of our choices. Maturity means doing better when you learn better. Don't beat yourself up over Brady or Connor or how it all played out. What matters now is now."

Piper rolled her eyes. "And we are back to the original question. What do I do now?"

Her mother was silent for a moment, her expression reflecting her deep thought and concern for Piper. "Trust your instincts. Deep down, you know what is best for you. Trust your heart. Don't let fear stand in the way of your honest feelings and your chance to be happy. And trust your family this time. Know that we are with you and will support you and love you through whatever happens."

Melissa leaned forward to press a kiss to Piper's forehead. "Now, we both need to pull ourselves together and get ready for the party. Huh?"

Piper nodded. The party. She needed to collect herself and finish dressing for the party. Where she'd see Brady again. A little shiver rolled through her.

You better get used to seeing Brady from now on, a voice in her head warned. *You share a child, so you share a future, whether it is spent together or not.*

Brady ran a finger under the collar of his shirt, wishing he could loosen his tie. He'd never been cut out to wear a monkey suit like some white-collar stiff. Seeing the McCall brothers approaching, drinks in hand, he quit fidgeting and nodded a greeting.

"Right there with ya, bro." Zane slapped him on the back and handed him a cold bottle of beer. "We appreciate the sacrifice for our parents' sake."

"More specifically, our mom's sake. Dad's humoring her with this dress-up business." Josh took a pull of his beer and surveyed the room that was filling with friends and family. "If Dad had his way, this shindig would be barbecue with a bonfire, and the closest thing to an hors d'oeuvre would be those little pig-in-a-blanket things made from cocktail weenies."

"Oh, those are great!" Zane said and patted his stomach. "Man, I could go for some of those about now."

Brady grinned and nodded. "I'm with you there."

Josh raised his beer. "To cocktail weenies."

The three laughed and clinked bottles. As Brady took a large swig of his brew, Piper entered the living room from the front hall. Brady sucked in a sharp breath at the sight of her, managing to inhale beer into his lungs. Covering his mouth to avoid spraying his mouthful, he choked the beer down, then resigned himself to a paroxysm of clumsy coughing.

Josh laughed and pounded his back. "Whoa. You all right? Remember how I told you not to drink and breathe at the same time? This is why."

Brady flashed a half smile as the brothers guffawed, and he continued coughing.

"Funny," he rasped, keeping his eyes on Piper as she drifted from one fawning guest to another. Clearly, he wasn't the only one enraptured by the formfitting dress and high heels that made her legs look especially long and shapely. Most every man in the room turned to stare as Piper made her way across the floor toward him.

"Day-um," Zane drawled, but Brady only half listened as Piper's brothers bantered.

"What?"

"I think I know why our friend here forgot how to drink. Look what just walked in."

After a pause in the brothers' exchange, Josh echoed his brother. "*Day-um* is right. Who knew she cleaned up so well?"

Brady wiped his hands, damp from the beer bottle's condensation, and cleared his throat one last time following his coughing fit. Piper's eyes held his, her expression anxious as she strolled nearer.

"When did she become a girl?" Zane asked.

"I don't know, but I don't like it. We may have to

punch some faces before tonight's over. Do you see how Hannigan's looking at her?"

Zane growled his disapproval, a low rumbling that echoed how Brady felt about the male attention Piper was receiving. Then Zane nudged his brother with his elbow and jerked his head, signaling they should leave. "Careful, Summers," he said. "Remember, that's our sister."

As the two edged away, Josh's expression read *Yeah. What he said.*

Piper frowned and slowed her steps when she saw her brothers depart. Too late to politely change course, she approached Brady and asked, "Was it something I said?"

"Not exactly. More like what you wore."

Wariness filled her eyes, and she cast a quick glance down, smoothing her hands over her dress as if searching for a flaw she'd overlooked. "What's wrong with how I'm dressed?"

He gave her a slow smile, his heart swelling as he studied her up close. She smelled as heavenly as she looked, and the sheer glimmer of lip gloss made her mouth look as ripe and sweet as raspberries. To keep himself from grabbing her and hauling her in for a kiss, he squeezed his beer bottle until he thought the glass might break.

"Nothing's wrong with it," he murmured, his tone thick with a desire he couldn't hide. "You look…" He fumbled for the right word to express his awe. *Beautiful. Sexy as hell. Like heartbreak.* "Breathtaking." She smiled her appreciation, a pink tint creeping to her cheeks, and he added, "Quite literally. I tried to inhale my drink when you walked in." He leaned closer and

Index

added, "That only works if you're a fish, by the way, so…I don't advise trying it."

She chuckled, and the moment of levity helped ease the nervous tension.

"So…where did they go?" she asked craning her neck to search for her brothers.

"Somewhere not here."

She lifted one eyebrow. "Obviously. Why? Are they really avoiding me because of my dress?"

"Not exactly. More like giving us privacy."

His answer seemed to unsettle her. "At your request?"

"No, but…I'm not gonna argue."

"Oh." She fiddled with her pearl necklace, her posture stiff, and her gaze drifted around the room. "Good turnout."

He hummed his agreement. "Can I get you something to drink?"

With an awkward smile, she shook her head and fell silent again.

"Are we going to talk about it?" he said after a moment.

"Not here. And not now," she said without looking at him.

"Okay. Trite banter it is." He raised his bottle toward her. "You really do look great tonight."

She flashed a wry grin. "What? This old thing?"

"Yes, *that old thing*. You have turned quite a few heads."

She said something under her breath that sounded like *Only one head I care about.*

"Pardon?"

She forced a smile and shook her head. "I said *thank you*. You look really nice, too."

He wanted to scream his frustration with the stiff, too-polite, completely pointless conversation. Maybe she was right. Any discussion about their unresolved differences of opinion regarding Connor should wait for a less public forum. And any reference to the kisses they'd shared would only make him want a repeat performance. Also out of line in the midst of her parents' friends. But, damn…with her hair swept up in a loose bun, wispy ringlets on her nape, she looked like something out of a fairy tale. His mouth watered, wanting to taste the delicate skin behind her ears and nibble his way along her slim throat.

Piper's gaze moved over the gathering before returning to him. "Is your dad here? I haven't seen him."

"He's supposed to be. He was still getting dressed when I left. Told me not to wait on him." Brady sipped his beer and tried to quell the lust curling through him.

"And Connor?"

"Not coming. When I told him it was an adult party, he opted for video games and a sleepover at his friend's house."

"Oh."

He heard the disappointment in her tone. He took it as a good sign that she wanted to spend time with their son.

The clink of a utensil against a glass rose above the conversations in the room and slowly quieted people, and Zane stepped toward the center of the room, calling, "Can I have everyone's attention, please?"

All of the guests turned to better see Zane, and a hush fell over the room. "Thank you all for coming tonight to help us celebrate thirty years of marriage for our parents, Michael and Melissa McCall."

A round of applause and a few whistles lifted from

the assembly, before Zane raised his bottle of beer. "I'd like to be the first to offer a toast to the happy couple. Mom and Dad, I couldn't be happier for you…"

Piper leaned toward Brady whispering, "Help me! I'm supposed to give a toast after Zane's, but I'm afraid of either sounding too mushy or trite and insincere."

"What do you want me to do?"

"Give me something to say. You know words have never been my thing." She wiped her hands on her dress, then flexed her fingers.

"Um…wish them *happy anniversary*, and…" Brady fumbled. "I don't know…"

"So here's to the best parents a guy could ever have," Zane said, raising his drink, and the rest of the party attendees joined him. "May you have many more years of happiness."

The crowd cheered and clinked glasses, and Brady cast a gaze around for one of the caterers' trays. As a white-shirted teenager carrying a tray of drinks squeezed between the couch and a cluster of ranch hands, Brady swooped in to snag a flute of champagne. He scuttled back and held it out to Piper as Zane called, "And now my sister, Piper, would like to say a few words. Piper?"

Her eyes were wide and anxious as Brady shoved the drink into her hand and murmured in her ear. "Favorite memory, they're role models, something about the future…"

She bobbed a nod, swallowed hard, and he took a step back, giving her the limelight.

"Uh…" She paused to clear her throat. "I just want to add my congratulations and, um…" She glanced to Brady as if seeking support, and he gave her a subtle thumbs-up. "Growing up, all of my fondest memories include times when we were all together as a family, and Mom and Dad were laughing together or encouraging us."

Piper drew a slow breath and continued, "I know they didn't always agree on everything, but they found a way to work together, to compromise…and they always had my back. I forgot that for a few years, during a difficult time in my life, but I had a very clear reminder today that, even though I've grown up and moved away, nothing can ever change that truth." She glanced at her mother, and Melissa blew her a kiss. "Just this afternoon, Mom was ready with her love and advice when I needed her."

Brady raised an eyebrow, wondering what had transpired this afternoon. Had Piper told her mother about Connor?

"My parents have…" When she returned her gaze to his, Piper stumbled a bit over her words. "Uh…they m-modeled the kind of solid, loving marriage that someday I hope to have."

Brady couldn't help but wonder if her image of her future marriage included him.

"They've set a pretty high bar for happiness," Piper said and smiled to the gathered guests.

"Piper, I'm s'rry. I know'm late, darlin'," a voice called from behind Brady, and he cringed. Not only did Brady know the voice, he knew the slurring speech that indicated how much Roy had been drinking. Brady tensed as he turned. The rest of the crowd sent curious looks Roy's way.

"But you're wrong. S'all wrong." Roy staggered in from the kitchen, clearly having entered through the mudroom door instead of the front hall like the other guests. "It'za lie." He waved a finger like an old schoolmarm scolding a class. He wore a dress coat and tie, but his collar was unbuttoned, and his tie was askew. His shirt was tucked in but haphazardly, and his hair had been combed but looked as though Roy had been raking his fingers through it ever since.

Brady issued a curse under his breath and pushed through the crowd, making his way toward his inebriated father. Heat flashed through Brady. Embarrassment. Anger. Frustration.

"No marriage'z all happy'n roses. They got s'crets. I got secrets. My wife…she had se—" he hiccupped "—secr'ts."

A low buzz of conversation filled the room.

"Dad, stop," he said quietly as he approached Roy.

Piper divided a concerned glance between her parents and Roy. She seemed uncertain whether to continue her toast or wait for the interruption to play out.

Roy aimed his finger at the senior McCalls, shouting, "Tell 'em the truth, M'lissa. Michael. Not always so happy."

Brady grabbed his father's arm but, with a surprising strength and determination, Roy shook him off and stumbled farther into the crowded room.

"Roy, what are you doing?" Melissa asked sternly, her complexion pale.

"I know the truth," Roy shouted back as guests shifted uncomfortably with the growing tension. "But I c'n keep y'r secr'ts. I c'n keep secr—" His loud belch interrupted his rant.

Gritting his teeth in fury, Brady seized his father's arm again. "Let's go, Dad. You're making a scene."

Waving his hand toward the McCalls, his father chortled. "I'm not makin' a scene! I'm just cel'bratin' thirty years for…" He waved his finger as if he was struggling to remember the McCalls' names. "Michael and M'lissa."

Josh appeared from the cluster of party guests and took Roy's other arm. "Let's get him to your house and sober him up, huh?"

A fresh wave of shame washed over Brady, and he kept his eyes down as he jerked a nod and helped wrestle his father toward the back door.

"Ask 'em!" Roy yelled as he was dragged from the party. "Ask 'em how happy they was fift'n years 'go! Not s'happy then!"

The click of high heels followed Brady and Josh as they hustled Roy through the kitchen, drawing the attention of the catering staff. With a backward glance, he confirmed that Piper had followed them. "Sorry about the interruption, Piper. Go back to the party. We've got this."

"Let go of me," Roy snarled.

"What is he talking about?" Piper asked, still trailing them as they pushed Roy out the door and into the chilly night air.

"I don't know." Brady hitched his head toward the kitchen. "Seriously, Piper. Go back in. Finish your toast."

Roy pointed at Piper. "You broke my boy's heart. Still after…all these years."

"Dad," Brady growled, giving Roy's arm a tug, "Shut up. Don't say another word."

His father turned a glare to him. "You know she hurt you. Connor is proof o' that!"

Piper gasped, stopping in her tracks and cutting a worried look to Josh.

Josh slowed to a stop. He frowned and angled a curious look toward his sister. "Okay, this is getting weirder by the minute. What does any of this have to do with Connor?"

"Forget it," Brady said at the same time Roy slurred, "He's their kid."

Brady might have been able to bluff his way through the moment, but Josh faced his sister, searching her face. "Piper?"

Her guilty expression and the ragged breath she drew as she averted her eyes were all the answer Josh needed.

"Who told you that?" Brady asked his father, an aching pit growing in his stomach.

"Found Scott's letter in y'r room."

Brady huffed an angry sigh. "You had no right to read—" He cut himself off. He'd save his recriminations for later.

Josh shifted his hard stare, narrowing his eyes. "Brady, Piper, I think you have some explaining to do."

Piper rushed over and put a hand on Josh's arm. "I'll tell you everything. Later. Just…let me tell Dad first. And…not tonight. I—"

Josh gaped at his sister, hurt and betrayal accompanying his shock. "Just Dad? Does Mom know?"

"Too many secrets," Roy muttered, wobbling as he tried to pull free of Brady's grasp. Then, with a half snort, half snore, Roy's head lolled to the side, and his legs no longer supported him.

Brady and Josh shifted their hold on him just in time to keep him from collapsing.

"Look," Brady said, his gut pooling with acid. "Let's get him inside and squared away. We can talk about everything else…" he met Piper's resigned gaze "…later."

The back screen door slammed, and Zane jogged across the yard toward them. "Can I help?"

Brady heaved a weary sigh, and as the third McCall sibling trotted up to them, witnessing his humiliation, he muttered, "Look, you guys, I'm sorry about all that in there. I know it's no big surprise that my dad's a drunk, but I hate that he spoiled your parents' celebration."

Zane waved him off. "Nothing's spoiled. Dad made a joke and a few statements about there being nothing hidden between them other than his real weight and Mom's occasional splurge shoe purchases, and the party got back on track. Don't lose sleep over it." He rubbed the back of his neck and grunted. "What a night…" Zane paused, squinting in the direction of Piper's favorite cottonwood and bench on the hill.

She cast a glance the same direction. "What?"

"I thought I saw…something." He shrugged while Josh and Brady each turned to peer toward the hill. "Never mind." Zane stooped to grab Roy's feet. "Piper, get the door?"

She nodded and hurried to the front door of the house.

Once Roy was deposited on his bed and Brady had pulled his dad's boots off and covered him with a blanket, he joined the McCall siblings in the living room.

"I think I'll stay here. Make sure he doesn't try to make an encore performance if he wakes up." Frowning, he scrubbed a hand over his jaw. "Not sure how welcome I'd be after this anyway."

"Of course you're welcome!" Josh protested.

Piper put a hand on his wrist. "You're not to blame for anything your dad says or does. Don't beat yourself up over this."

He shrugged. "I know. Usually I can stay on top

of things with him, keep him out of trouble, but tonight... I just..."

When he didn't finish his sentence, Zane asked, "Do
you have any idea what he was talking about? What secrets do my parents have? What secret is he keeping?"

"Zane!" Piper drilled him with a warning glare.

Brady shook his head. "I honestly don't know. It
could have been just drunk rambling or delusions on
his part. Please apologize to your mom and dad for
me." He paused and shook his head. "No, I need to do
it. In person. First thing tomorrow."

"Your dad is the one who needs to apologize." Piper
squeezed his wrist, and he covered her hand with his.

"Do you think..." Brady drew his eyebrows together,
his gut tightening when he considered the fallout of
his father's drunken display. "Will this cost my dad
his job? I wouldn't blame your folks if they did let
him go, but..."

"I can't imagine they'd let this get in the way of so
many years of loyalty and hard work. Your dad is a
great foreman," Zane said. "We need his help and guidance more than ever, considering the events of late."

Brady chewed the inside of his cheek, not bothering to tell the siblings how much of his father's slack
he'd picked up. Especially since Roy's drinking had
increased following Scott's death.

Josh cleared his throat and shuffled his feet. "Um,
about that other thing he mentioned, about—"

Piper shook her head, her eyes imploring. "Josh,
don't. I told you I need to talk to Mom and Dad about
it first."

"What thing?" Zane asked, his brow beetled in confusion.

Piper drew a finger across her throat, signaling Josh to stop talking.

"Josh already knows," Brady said softly. "What does it hurt to tell Zane now?"

"What does Josh know?" Zane pressed, obviously growing agitated.

Piper sighed, her face dark with consternation, and Josh divided a look between Brady and Piper, obviously waiting for permission to divulge what he knew.

Zane spread his hands, looking from face to face. "Someone want to fill me in?"

"Connor is mine and Piper's." Brady gave Piper an apologetic look and shrugged. "I don't see the point of waiting when Josh already found out." He returned his attention to her brothers. "I only learned the truth after Scott died. He left me a letter. Piper just found out the whole story this week."

Zane gaped at Brady, while Josh shoved his hands in his pockets and clenched his back teeth.

"Please," Piper whispered, her voice thin and strained. "Don't say anything. I told Mom this afternoon, kind of without planning to, but I need a chance to talk to Dad, to explain."

Zane shoved a hand through his hair and blew out a puff of air. "Wow. I don't even know what to do with that." He shared a shocked glance with Josh, then added, "What are you going to do?"

"You are going to do right by her, aren't you? You'll marry Piper?" Josh said, his questions sounding more like commands as his eyes narrowed.

"Hey!" Piper stepped over to Josh and poked him in the chest. "I'm a big girl now, Doofus. I think I can decide what's right for me without your help!"

Josh leveled a challenging glare on her. "Fine. And what about what's best for Connor?"

She gasped, and tears blossomed in her eyes. "Don't be a jerk, Josh. I only learned the truth yesterday. I'm still trying to wrap my head around it all myself."

"Connor's best interests are our top priority," Brady said evenly. "But they're also for Piper and me to decide."

Zane squared his shoulders. "You're right. This is just…a shock to us."

"Tell me about it," Piper muttered. In a nervous gesture, she raised a hand to her hair to rake her fingers through the chocolate-brown waves, then stopped with a grimace when she encountered the upswept arrangement and hair pins.

"I take it you haven't decided a way forward, then?" Josh folded his arms over his chest and gave his sister a concerned look.

She shook her head. "No. Everything's muddled together—the fire in the field, the news about Connor, your proposal about the new business… I have so much to consider. I don't know where to start, and… I'm scheduled to go back to Boston day after tomorrow."

"I know where to start," Brady said.

The three McCalls turned their eyes to him.

"You can't rush important decisions like the ones you're making. And I know you. You'll want things settled before you go."

She gave him a resigned nod.

"Then you can't leave yet." He placed a hand on her shoulder and squeezed. "You should extend your stay. Indefinitely."

Chapter 9

Piper lingered in Brady's living room after the twins returned to the party. She stood by the back wall and looked at the family pictures hung there. Framed photos of Roy and Brady's mother at their wedding. Brady and Scott as young boys. Scott helping Brady learn to ride his first horse. Canned studio shots of the four of them that had been taken when Brady was about six, Scott closer to thirteen. A rare trip to Florida when Brady was seven. Little did he know that was the last family trip they'd make. His mother had died the next winter.

Her death had wrecked Roy. That was when his drinking started in earnest. At least, that was when young Brady had noticed his father's problem.

Now, he moved up beside Piper and stared at the photos with her. "You should go back to the party."

"Soon."

"You have to finish that eloquent toast to your parents."

She elbowed him in the gut. "Ha ha."

After a few strained moments, she cut a side-glance to him. "Look, Brady..." she pivoted to face him "...obviously we have a lot to figure out. I can extend my stay a couple days, but not indefinitely. Maybe we should have dinner together tomorrow. Talk things out?"

He shrugged one shoulder, trying to appear casual, even though his pulse was thrumming like an engine in overdrive. "Of course. I'll send Dad and Connor out for pizza, and we can eat at my place."

"No, don't impose on them."

He curled his lips in a grin. "Trust me. Pizza is no imposition for Connor."

"But Roy—"

"He owes me. Especially after tonight. Don't worry about him."

She fumbled with her pearls. "Actually, I was thinking you and I could go out. Maybe to Zoe's?"

His mind flashed back to numerous dates at Zoe's Bar and Grill, and he experienced a sharp twang in the center of his chest. He rubbed absently at the spot and sighed. If he wanted to avoid places that held sweet memories with Piper, he'd have to move to a new town. He couldn't think of a single place in Boyd Valley where they hadn't made memories. "If that's what you want, sure. So long as we talk."

"Talk," she repeated emphatically. "Not yell or accuse."

He lifted a hand of acquiescence. "Of course."

She shifted her weight from one foot to another, and a shadow skittered across her face. "Because I truly want to do what's right. For everyone, but…especially for Connor."

"Agreed. Same here." He tugged up a corner of his mouth, and she drew and released a slow breath that seemed to calm her.

She looked so damn beautiful standing there. The soft glow of the living room lamp made her dark hair shine with chestnut highlights, and her plum lip gloss tempted him to take a bite. He moved closer to her, staring deeply into her quicksilver eyes. "Piper, forgive me."

Her brow dipped. "For what?"

"This." He cupped the back of her head and caught her lips in a fierce kiss. Her startled gasp faded into a pleasured sigh, firing his desire. Slanting his mouth across hers, he drew her closer. His hands settled at the small of her back, and she canted her hips forward.

That alone encouraged him to be bolder. He held her tighter, kissed her more deeply and dared to hope that they'd turned a corner in their relationship.

Piper feathered a soft stroke along his cheek, then speared her fingers into his hair. When her lips parted and the tip of her tongue darted out to tease his, he groaned and met her invitation.

He moved his kisses to her throat, and Piper tipped her head back, offering better access. He nibbled his way along the curve of her chin to the hollow of her collarbone where he encountered the sleek strand of silver pearls. As pretty as she looked tonight, what he really wanted was to see her dressed only in the shimmering necklace and her high heels. The image he conjured in his mind sent a flash of heat through him. He wanted her so much, he ached from it. Seven years.

He'd waited and prayed to have her back in his arms for seven long years.

"Piper," he murmured against her skin as he moved his lips to where her snug dress caused the top of her breast to swell above her dress.

"Shh," she whispered, the sound muffled as she pressed kisses to the crown of his head.

"I've missed this. Missed you so much," he said, ignoring her shush. He slid his fingers up her spine to the pull of her zipper. He dragged it down an inch, then another, pausing to give her time to protest. She didn't.

Turning her with a slow dance step, their bodies swaying together, he walked her backward toward the couch. Then hesitated. How many make-out sessions had they shared on that very couch as kids? He couldn't count them all, but he could do better than a worn-out couch for her now. He didn't want to make out with her. He wanted to make love to her.

He tugged the zipper an inch lower, enough that one of the cap sleeves of her dress slid off her shoulder. The front of her gown puckered out, and he slid a hand up her ribs to cup her breast. He lifted the ivory swell and sucked in a sharp breath as he brought the full of it into view. Her nipple was darker than he remembered, a dusky pink, and it beaded when he flicked it gently with his thumb.

She caught his head between her hands and, murmuring a husky "Please," pulled him down to her breast.

Covering her with his mouth, he suckled and lashed the taut nipple with his tongue. The sexy hitch in her breathing brought back memories of their bodies wrapped around each other, of cries of ecstasy in an empty hayloft, of sensation so sweet and pure his younger self had wept for joy. He skimmed his hand up her thigh, under her dress. He squeezed her bottom and felt the tremor that shook her.

When he shifted his other hand down her back and prepared to lift her, to carry her to his room and relive all those special, sensual moments, her arms looped around his neck in silent agreement. He glanced up at her, smiling as he hoisted her up. Her legs wrapped around his hips, and he kissed her mouth again. Hard.

He turned to take her down the hall, and—

Stopped.

"Brady?" his father said, squinting at him from the hallway. "Where's Conn'r?"

Piper gasped and dropped her feet to the floor, struggling to right her dress and smooth out the evidence of their foreplay.

"He's at Joey's, spending the night," Brady growled, knowing that the moment with Piper was lost. Already she was pulling away, straightening her clothes and backing toward the door. He wanted to throttle his father for interrupting. Not because he wanted the sex so badly his body hurt, but because he'd felt inches away from really breaking through the wall Piper had erected between them. If he could rekindle the intimacy between them, he could remind her how well they meshed, how perfectly they fit emotionally as well as physically. "I told you that earlier. Go back to bed. You're drunk, and you've done enough damage tonight."

Roy's gaze moved to Piper, and Brady tensed. If the old man said one thing about…

"Piper. Is the party ov'r? Your parents'?"

"Uh…no." She drew a deep breath and flashed a nervous grin. "And I really should get back to it." She hurried toward the front door and gave him a backward glance. "Tomorrow night then? We talk?"

He nodded. "Tomorrow night."

Chapter 10

"I shouldn't be out late," Brady told his father as he pulled on his coat to leave for dinner.

"Don't cut the evening short on my account. I can handle the boy just fine."

"Make sure Connor brushes his teeth before bed. Lights out at nine thirty if I'm not back yet." Brady started for the door, then paused. "Bye, Connor. Listen to Grampa and behave yourself."

"Okay! Bye!" he shouted back.

Brady put on his nicer cowboy hat, meaning the one not covered in dust and all forms of ranching detritus, and headed to his truck. Piper was waiting for him near the front door of the McCalls' house.

She swung up onto the passenger seat and brought the waft of female scents—fruity shampoo and sweet lotions—with her. Her skin glowed with a natural rosy hue no makeup could recreate, and her hair shone with golden highlights from the setting sun. She'd donned a short dress with knee-high boots and a snug cardigan that left no secrets about her womanly curves. Tiny gold hoop earrings winked in the glow of the amber sunset, and his heart bucked when he recognized them as ones he'd given her when they were dating.

Brady had been starved for dinner when he left his house, but one whiff, one glimpse of Piper had him hungering for something altogether different. Something only Piper could sate.

"Hi," she said with a smile as she settled in and fastened her seat belt. "I'm famished. Where are we going? Zoe's?"

He didn't answer right away, and she waved a hand in front of him. "Yoo-hoo. Brady?"

"Um…not Zoe's. Too public. I made reservations at Cam's Lakeside Bistro." He tugged up a corner of his mouth. "You look beautiful, by the way."

Her face brightened, but she ducked her head. "Thank you. Just…remember, this isn't a date. It's business."

Her chiding served as cold water to his nostalgia, and he put the truck in gear to head out. He squelched the growing heat in his blood, knowing he needed to keep the business of Connor's welfare at the fore tonight, unmuddled by his desire for the boy's mother. "Right. Of course. Sorry I complimented you."

"I didn't mean…" She grunted. "Can we start over? I want an amicable dinner. I want to be on good terms for our discussion, but I didn't want you to think…" She sighed and turned to face the window. "And isn't Cam's just as public as Zoe's?"

"Maybe so. But there should be fewer Boyd Valley

people. I prefer not to be the source of gossip or risk someone we know overhearing our conversation."

"Yeah. I get that. It's just… Cam's is—"

"Where we had our first real date. I know. But short of driving into Denver, we don't have many options around here."

She continued to stare out the window.

"Is it a problem for you…going to Cam's Bistro?"

She drew a deep breath and faced him with a warm smile. "No. In fact, I'm looking forward to their trout almondine."

As if by silent agreement, they didn't broach the topic of Connor on the twenty-minute drive to the restaurant. Instead, they managed an easy banter about what high school friends were doing now, humorous misunderstandings she'd had with coworkers because of their Boston accents and plans Piper had heard her brothers making in regard to setting up their grandfather's land for the adventure trips.

"They're going up to the property later this week to clear an area to be the main campsite. They've been in touch with a company out of Jackson Hole to come and rig the lines for the zip-lining, and Josh thinks they can set permanent anchors for the rock climbing without outside help."

"Did they get any word back from the insurance company about rates to cover the liability costs yet?" he asked, taking the turn down the narrow street that led to the lake where he and the McCall triplets had gone to swim, sail and water ski every summer since they'd been old enough to want those warm-weather entertainments.

"I think Zane has figures from a few companies, but

he's still shopping around for the best rates. It's pricier than they thought."

"Gotta be covered, though."

Piper nodded her agreement, and her gaze swept the lake and surrounding buildings. "This place never changes. It's so peaceful and pretty."

The wooden building next to the bait shop and ski boat rental was a refurbished cabin that housed the small bistro, with a large deck overlooking the mountain lake. Brady agreed that the setting was magnificent, and the bistro owner had enhanced the restaurant ambience with the perfect touches of landscaping and lights.

"I hope Cam's children don't sell out or close the bistro when he retires. Zoe's is good, but no one beats Cam's fresh fish or barbecue pork." Brady parked on the gravel lot near the front door and escorted Piper inside with a proprietary hand at the small of her back. To her credit, she didn't shrink away from his touch, and when a chill breeze buffeted them as they neared the door, she even tucked herself closer to him, giving a squeak of displeasure at the biting wind. Though recent days had been pleasantly warm, tonight the temperature had dipped dramatically ahead of a cold front that held the potential for freezing rain and sleet in the next couple of days. He almost questioned Piper on why she hadn't worn a coat but decided he rather liked the idea of her cuddling close for warmth, and he didn't want to start the dinner with anything she could take as criticism.

They were shown to a table on the deck, tucked in a corner out of the breeze and near a large stone fire pit, where a cozy blaze crackled. Tiny white lights were strung in the trees, and tiki torches burned at the perim-

eter of the porch. The indoor dining room had a view
of the lake and surrounding mountains through plate-
glass windows on two sides of the room.

When their server arrived at their table to take drink
orders, Brady's hope of avoiding anyone who knew
them burst like a bubble on a pin.

"Oh, my gosh! Brady and Piper together again," the
familiar woman gushed.

Brady racked his brain for her name, but he'd not
been as popular in high school as Piper had, and he
couldn't be sure he'd ever known her name to begin
with. "Well, well. I'd heard you two broke up. It is so
great to see you together again!"

Piper gave their waitress a strained smile. "Hi, Jodi."

Jodi, then. But…he was still at a loss for her last
name.

"This isn't what it looks like." Piper rushed to explain. "We're just talking business."

Jodi looked disappointed, but then brightened again,
saying, "Business? Oh, that's right. The new adventure tours company. You two are partners with your
brothers. And I heard you may even be moving back
to take an active role in the company?"

"Wow." Piper chuckled wryly. "The grapevine has
been working overtime. Where'd you hear all that?"

Jodi shrugged. "Here and there. Gill Carver comes
in once a week for the prime rib special, and he told
me some of it."

"Gill told you?" Brady growled.

"Yeah. He's at the bar now, watching the hockey
game on the TV with Steve, our bartender."

A coil of disgust twisted in Brady's gut. He craned
his head to see through the plate glass to the bar, but

Piper kicked his leg under the table and sent him a look that said *Forget Gill*.

She was right, of course. He wouldn't let Gill spoil their evening.

"You remember Steve Ponticelli, right?" Jodi wrinkled her nose as she tipped her head to study Brady. "Cam's grandson? He was in the class behind us."

Brady bobbed his head vaguely.

After Jodi took their drink orders, Piper leaned across their table. "We can go somewhere else if Gill's being here bothers you."

Brady gritted his teeth. "Hell, no. I'm not gonna let that jerk run me off. He'd better keep his distance, though."

Piper looked unconvinced but didn't push the issue. "The fire's nice. I'd forgotten how nippy it gets this time of year around here."

"We're not really going to talk about the weather, are we? Have we fallen that far?"

She winced. "Sorry. A weak attempt to stall."

"You're dreading the conversation?"

"In a way. No. Well, I guess it's just…so explosive. Potentially. I don't know where to start." She bit her bottom lip, then shook her head. "No, I do know. Tell me about Connor. Tell me what he likes, what his first words were, how old he was when he walked and all the stuff I've missed."

"All of it?" He chuckled and reached for Piper's hand, curling her cold fingers into his warmer ones. "That's a pretty long conversation. And tonight we have to cover our plan going forward."

She dropped her gaze to their joined hands but didn't pull away. "So hit the highlights."

"I could let you see his baby book. Pam kept a detailed scrapbook of his early years. I only saw him occasionally back then. Holidays, the sporadic dinner invite. Back then he was just my nephew, and while I loved him, I didn't have a deep interest in the minutiae of his day-to-day life."

She twisted her lips in a moue of disappointment. "So we both missed the milestones of his babyhood."

He only grunted in reply. He wouldn't make the obvious statements about why that was true. They'd covered that before, and tonight was about reconciliation and moving forward.

"Brady," she said softly, squeezing his hand tighter. Her sad, guilty expression told him where she was going before she spoke.

"No need, Piper. Not tonight."

"But… I feel like I have to preface this whole discussion with…something." She stared at their joined hands, worrying her bottom lip with her teeth for a moment, and he kept quiet. Waiting. He stroked her thumb with his in silent support.

"Please, please, know that everything I did back then, I did because I honestly thought it was the best for everyone involved. I didn't want you trapped in a marriage you thought you had to be in because of the baby. I didn't want our baby to miss his best chance to be raised by two loving parents, instead of one struggling single mom. I didn't want to disappoint my parents. I didn't want to quit college." She jiggled his hand, as if making sure she had his attention, and she met his gaze straight on. Her eyes were damp. "But most of all, you have to know I didn't *want* to give up Connor. I almost changed my mind…when I held him and saw you in him…" She inhaled deeply before continuing. "But the adoptive parents' lawyer arrived to pick the baby up—" she shook her head and raised her eyebrows "—little did I know he was going to his uncle and aunt—and I let him go. I cried...big ugly crying with a snotty face and hiccups and the works, when they took him away. I *did not* make the choice to give our son away lightly." She paused a beat for a breath. "And I am so grateful, despite all the lies and deception and secrets—"

He stiffened as defensiveness clawed his spine.

"—on both sides, that I have a second chance to be part of Connor's life."

He quashed the edgy resentment that had nipped at him, focusing on the moment and the possibilities that lay ahead if he played his cards right. He was here with Piper. They had a child together and a second chance—a viable, promising second chance—for a future together. Though Piper had made a life for herself in Boston, she now had two very strong reasons to move home. The new adventure business and Connor. Her confession regarding her struggle with giving Connor up fueled his hopes that she'd choose to return.

"To second chances." He raised her hand to his lips and kissed her palm. The sough of her breath catching sent an answering tickle to his belly. The stirring of a dormant desire that Piper alone could conjure. A yearning that was more than physical, more than simple attraction. His soul was involved. Everything he'd ever wanted from life, his dreams of family and fulfillment. Piper. She'd always been the one. And now he stood on the edge of that future, looking forward with more hope than he'd had since he was eighteen.

"Oops. Sorry to interrupt," Jodi said with a wink to Brady as she set his beer and Piper's wine on the table.

He'd been so focused on Piper, he hadn't seen their

server approach. Piper gently withdrew her hand from his and sat back in her chair.

"I think I know the answer to this question, but... have you had a chance to look at the menu?" Jodi gave them an impish grin.

"Don't need to look," Piper said, lifting her chin and smiling politely. "The trout almondine."

"Make it two. And bring us the artichoke dip to start."

Once the waitress nodded and left them in peace, Piper dove right in. "I guess the big question in front of us is how to divide custody. I want visiting privileges, of course."

"Visiting?" Brady furrowed his brow. "That sounds kind of...distant." A chill snuck into his heart, and he narrowed his eyes on Piper. "Unless I've misread things. What sort of arrangements are you thinking of?"

"A lot depends on whether I move back here to be part of my brothers' new company."

"*Our* new company," he amended. "You have an equal stake in it, just like I do." He folded his arms over his chest and regarded her with a quizzical stare. "Do you mean you still haven't decided whether to move back home and take the job they offered?"

"Um...not really." She fiddled with her fork and flashed a sheepish grin. "And my home has been in Boston for the last few years."

He shook his head. "No. Your home is here, and it will always be. Boyd Valley is where your family is. The Double M. Your heritage and legacy." He wanted to add *Where I am. Your soul mate.* But he swallowed the words. He may have believed they belonged together, but Piper clearly still hadn't reached the same conclusion. That stung. A lot.

"Whether or not I move back here doesn't change the question of how we divide custody of our son."

His hackles rose a bit. "*Divide* custody?" He gave a short, harsh laugh. "That sounds rather…well, divisive. I thought the idea was to work together. I'm not interested in a plan that would mean Connor got shuttled back and forth. He needs roots. Permanence. He needs us to be a team."

"Um…right. Semantics."

"Is it?" Brady's heart beat faster, a growing concern for the direction this conservation would go.

"It would be helpful if I made a decision about where I was going to live, if I want to move back here and…" She waved her hand, letting him fill in the rest. Her eyes shifted away briefly, her gaze distant and thoughtful. "If I'm honest, there's never really been a question about accepting. Being part of something like this, helping rescue the ranch, playing a part in my brothers' business and being included is what I've always wanted."

"Then, you'll accept?" Brady's spirits, which had been growing heavier by the minute, now lifted. "Are you saying you're going to move back and be the CFO for McCall Adventures?"

Chapter 11

The ranch grounds were quiet. Ken scanned the yard carefully, watching for any activity. He'd seen a truck leave by the front drive just as he was settling into his lookout spot near the hill where Piper had been groping the cowboy. The image still filled him with rage. But the cowboy was gonna pay. Tonight.

Zipping up his black coat and raising the hood to cover his ears and light brown hair, he eased out from his hiding place behind a scrub brush. He moved quickly down the hill, stopping occasionally behind a tree or outbuilding to check for activity. At night, with the autumn chill bearing down from the mountains, the ranch stayed pretty quiet. Ranchers, he'd discovered, were of the early-to-bed, early-to-rise community. Which suited him fine. He hit his stride about 11:00 p.m.

With a last look for anyone leaving the stable or visible through a window, Ken made his final approach to the smaller house that sat at the edge of the ranch yard. The house he'd determined was the cowboy's.

He eased close to the outside wall that faced away from the main house, staying in the shadows. Ken silently cursed when he stepped on the small fallen limbs and dry leaves cluttering the yard, sending a cracking sound skittering through the still night. From behind the house he heard a clinking, like dog tags, followed by the unmistakable rumble of a dog's growl.

Freezing in his tracks, he waited to see if the dog appeared. He'd brought his handgun with the silencer in case of emergency, and he placed a hand on it now, ready should he need it. His goal was to move in fast, do his work and be gone just as quickly. He didn't want anything that could draw extra attention to him or his handiwork. Shooting the dog would be a last resort, since a bullet in the mutt's head was a loose end he didn't want to leave for the cops to find. He had to cover his tracks, stay under the radar.

When all was quiet again, he snuck closer to the house, the rattle of leaves under his feet unavoidable… damn it!

Again the dog tags jingled in the dark, and a light-colored dog, probably the yellow Lab he'd seen so many times in the ranch yard, appeared at the back corner of the house. The dog spotted him and launched into a full-out warning bark. Ken grumbled a foul word and pulled the gun and silencer from the holster at his thigh.

He aimed and—

"Kip!" Door hinges squeaked, and a back light flicked on. "Kip! What are you barking at, you dumb mutt?"

Ken shrank back against the side of the house, staying in the shadows, and held his breath.

The dog turned and gave a softer yip, her tail wagging.

"Either come in or be quiet!"

Ken lowered the gun and even that much movement attracted the dog's attention again. Another series of harsh barks followed.

Ken gritted his teeth. *If that damn dog blew his cover...*

"Kip! Shut it, dog. You're going to wake the whole ranch!" the man at the back door, out of Ken's line of vision, shouted. Then he whistled, calling, "Just come inside. C'mere. Kip, come!"

With a last *ruff* toward Ken, the dog trotted away. A door slammed. The back light went out.

Ken exhaled and flexed his hands to loosen the tension that had him strung tight as a noose. Then he set to work.

Piper met Brady's anxious stare, her pulse pounding in her ears. She blinked twice slowly, and a smile tugged the corner of her mouth. "I think...yes. I will accept the job." She heaved a deep sigh as if relieved to have made her decision. "I'll give my two-week notice when I go back to Boston."

Having made her decision, Piper felt as if the bull that had been standing on her chest had finally been corralled. She could breathe again, and the niggling disquiet that had plagued her since she'd first heard her brothers' proposal disappeared. Fear, she realized, had held her back. The fear of returning to a position in her family where she felt she was on the outside looking in. But her brothers wanted her skill set. Needed her.

Included her in something that was important and exciting for the family.

She'd also been afraid of being back in Brady's vicinity and how it would break her heart. But her worst fears, having her secret discovered, having to face the past and dissecting all the elements of their relationship…well, that had all happened already. Too late to close the barn door on that count.

Now, in addition to the new job and promising venture with Zane and Josh, she had a new perspective on her past, new insights…and a new reason to want to be in Boyd Valley. Connor.

"So," she said, exhaling and letting the tensions that had wound her in knots go in the breath, "that makes things simpler in terms of our decisions regarding Connor, huh?"

She gave Brady a broad smile, savoring the release of the needless worry she'd been carrying. She was coming back to Boyd Valley. Back to the Double M. Back to her family.

Brady was right. Maybe she did belong at the ranch. The choice to return certainly felt right. Predestined.

A weightless laugh bubbled up from her core, and she felt the smile she gave Brady shine through every pore, warm and invigorating. His answering grin stole her breath. Had she needed any confirmation she'd made the right decision, Brady's confident nod and glowing expression cinched the deal.

She couldn't wait to tell Zane and Josh she was on board. She started to dig for her phone to text them but balked. This was news she wanted to give them in person.

Their appetizer arrived, followed soon after by their dinner, and Piper tucked in, savoring every bite.

"If I'm going to be here, living just steps from you and Connor, then shared custody makes sense," she said.

He nodded, but his expression was guarded.

"What?"

He took a measured breath. "Shared custody requires a commitment from both of us."

She gave him a leery look. "Riiiight. What's your point?"

"The boy's been hurt enough, Piper. If I allow you to share custody of him, I need to know you're committed."

She sat straighter in her chair. "And you doubt my commitment because I put him up for adoption before?"

She saw his throat work as he swallowed and his eye dimmed with hurt. "No, I'm speaking from personal experience. I thought you were committed to me, once. And you left me."

His words hit her like a shard to her heart. "Brady—"

"Losing you was the hardest thing I ever had to face. So if you're not ready to see this through, not ready to give one hundred percent to Connor, then you should call it quits now, before he forms a bond with you."

Pain stabbed her and stole the breath from her lungs. "Brady, I—"

"But..." he squeezed her wrist "...I'm willing to give you a chance, give us a second chance for the sake of our son."

She blinked rapidly to fight back the sting of tears. "I will not let Connor down. I promise. I want to be a good mother to him."

Brady chewed the inside of his cheek for a moment before he said, "And another thing... I'm of the opinion that he's still too young to be told the truth about us being his parents. Scott and Pam were his parents, for all intents and purposes, until last January. Telling Connor he was adopted—" Brady screwed his mouth up in displeasure. "It feels too much like taking his parents away again."

"Oh." Piper took a sip of her wine and pondered his point. "I can see that. But…someday he deserves to know the truth."

Brady nodded. "Someday. It will be easier on him when the pain of losing Scott and Pam isn't still so raw. When he knows both of us better, has a bond with us. Knows deep down that we love him as much as Scott and Pam did."

"Okay. Agreed. We'll wait and tell Connor we are his real parents…later. When we think he's old enough to understand." She cleared her throat and angled her head. "It's…weird, this discussion about waiting for him to know us better when I realize I don't really know him."

Setting his fork on his plate, Brady leaned back in his seat with a measured look in his eyes. Her heart wrenched with guilt, and she braced herself for the you're-the-only-one-to-blame-for-that remark.

Instead, Brady said quietly, "Let's see… He's a good kid. Smart. Inquisitive. He loves to ask questions about what we're doing around the ranch and why." He grunted a laugh and shook his head. "*Always* wants to know the why. I usually have to answer with, 'I don't know why. That's just the way it's done.' Or 'Because I'm the adult, and I said so.'"

She scrunched her nose and laughed. "Oh, no! You've become my mother!"

"Your mother? Ouch! Fathers can say trite parentisms, too, you know."

"Have you used *We'll see* yet?"

He screwed his face into a sheepish frown, and she laughed harder.

"Yeah, you're laughing now, but just wait. You'll say those things, too. I guarantee." Grinning, he shook his head at her as she continued chuckling at him. When she finally got herself under control, he continued, "As you may have noticed, he has a powerful sweet tooth. He loves all the typical little boy stuff. Dinosaurs, Legos, getting dirty."

"Well, there is plenty of opportunity to get dirty on a ranch." She sipped her wine, soaking up all the details she could about the little boy. Her little boy. Her breath snagged in her lungs every time she thought about it. Connor was her son with Brady. A permanent, wonderful link between them. A few weeks ago the notion would have terrified her. Now? Well, she had to admit it still caused a stir of angst in her gut, but it also filled her with a warmth unlike anything she'd ever experienced before.

Brady told her all he could remember of Connor's early years, admitting he hadn't paid as close attention as he might have had he known Connor was his son. "He started walking…hmm, I think it was around Easter, so he was maybe fourteen or fifteen months old?"

"Hmm. A late bloomer," she muttered more to herself than to Brady.

"Was he? When do kids usually walk?"

"Closer to twelve months, I think. Go on. Do you remember his first words?"

Brady shrugged. "Not specifically, but I do remember *no* was a favorite word of his early on." He sent her a wry grin. "He's always been quite stubborn."

"Really? *Where* could he have gotten that?" she said, chuckling.

Brady returned a comically puzzled expression and joined her laughter. A lightness and joy filled Piper, and she took a moment to cherish the moment. Teasing with Brady again, sharing a meal and constructive conversation boosted her optimism for the future. She was on a better path now than just two weeks earlier. All the changes and revelations in her life were a bit daunting, but exciting, as well. Invigorating. A dark veil of guilt and sadness had been peeled away from her life, and the fresh air that infused her made her giddy. And she had to admit that a great deal of her giddiness had to do with her revived relationship with Brady.

She lifted her wineglass and sipped, studying Brady over the rim. The past several years had only made him more handsome, honing boyish softness into rough-hewn angles. His shoulders had grown broader, and his stubble-dusted face more weathered by sun and wind. But his eyes were still the deep green of a Colorado lake and full of a warmth that melted her bones.

She'd told him this wasn't a date, and she'd meant it. But that didn't stop her heart from softening each time she met his eyes or keep her pulse from galloping when his hand touched hers.

From the speakers above their table, music played. Soft rock tunes from past decades. She seized an impulse and pushed her chair back from the table. "Do you want to dance?"

His expression reflected his surprise. "Um…you've seen me dance. At prom?" His gaze sparkled with humor. "Remember? I think you called my moves *random flailing*?"

"No flailing required." She pointed through the window to the dance floor where another couple slow-danced. "If you're worried about your moves, I'll lead."

His eyebrows lifted in challenge. "No need. I can manage a slow dance." He stood and held out his hand to her. "But if I step on your toes, remember that this was your idea."

She accepted his hand, and a thrill spun through her as his warm fingers wrapped around hers.

As he led her inside to the dance floor, a whisper in the recesses of her brain nagged at her, telling her not to let the intimacy of the evening confuse her. She couldn't recapture what was lost, and she'd only get hurt if she pretended everything between her and Brady was like it used to be.

Worse yet, she could hurt Brady again by giving him false hope about what she wanted going forward. Because while she'd made several important decisions in the past few days about being a mother to Connor and moving back to Boyd Valley to work with her brothers, she had no idea how to proceed on a personal level with Brady. She'd spent the last seven years trying to expel him from her heart. Reversing the progress she'd made, when their relationship going forward was still so full of unknowns, would be foolish.

Even as they stepped onto the dance floor and he nestled her against his chest with his hand splayed securely at the base of her spine, her brain shrieked its warnings. But Brady's body was familiar and enticing. Pressing close to him was a welcome homecoming. The October chill that had nipped at her while they ate vanished when he wrapped her in his arms. She swayed with him as Justin Timberlake and his *NSYNC bandmates crooned a ballad from her and

Brady's junior high school days. Brady hummed along, slightly off-key.

And the rest of the room faded away.

With her eyes closed, Piper could pretend she was thirteen again, falling in love for the first time. Or sixteen, holding on to her date for the Sadie Hawkins dance. Or seventeen, savoring the embrace of the boy who'd given her a turquoise promise ring after prom. The central figure of all of these memories was Brady. The only man she'd ever loved.

Her chest contracted when she thought of him in those terms. *Love.* They'd told each other *I love you* many times. The meaning and truth behind the declaration had changed over the years. No longer bright and shiny, *love* bore the patina of time and pain now. Maturity. Perspective. Wisdom. But the framework was still solid, the foundation strong. She and Brady could rebuild what they'd once had. If they dared.

A shiver chased through her, and she snuggled closer to him. *NSYNC yielded to Snow Patrol, asking her to forget the world. He stroked a hand along her hair and pressed a kiss to her temple. The gentle brush of his lips on her skin set her body thrumming. Her fingers reflexively curled into his back, and a raspy sound purred from her throat. It took a moment for Piper to notice they weren't dancing anymore.

Heart pounding, she tipped her chin up. Brady's lips were *right there*. So close. So tempting. She wasn't sure who moved first, but by her next breath, their mouths were sealed, slanted across each other in a blissful reunion of taste and sensation and pure emotion that reverberated to her core.

Brady framed her face with his hands, cradling her cheeks as he deepened the kiss. Piper canted toward him, shutting out the clamor of the voice in her head that said too much was still unsettled between them. She viciously stamped down the nagging sense that rushing into an affair with Brady would lead to another heartache.

Instead, she dragged her fingers through the hair at his nape and swept her tongue along the seam of his lips. When he moaned and met her tongue with his, a flash of heat rolled through her. His hands roamed down to cup her bottom and tug her hips closer, to stroke the length of her spine and leave a trail of tingles sparking her nerves. She'd missed this. Good God, how she'd missed this! Not just the sex, but the feeling— no, the certainty—that Brady cherished her. The connection they shared was so much more than physical, and yet the bond was most profound when they kissed. When they made love. When they shed pretenses, allowed themselves to be vulnerable and real, sharing raw emotion as well as unrestrained passion.

Seven years of pent-up need and hunger clawed at her now, and she poured that focused energy into her kiss. She wanted—

"Get a room," a dark voice snarled, splashing icy water on the fire inside her.

Brady jerked his head up, and she felt the tension that yanked his body tight. "Go to hell."

Piper turned her head to see Gill leaning against a chair at the edge of the dance floor, a drink in his hand and a sneer on his face. "Is that any way to talk to your loan holder, Summers?"

Piper squeezed Brady's arm, cautioning him, hoping to calm the fury she could see rising in his eyes.

"At the bank, you're my loan holder. Here, you're just an ass bothering me and my lady."

Gill twisted his mouth in a sarcastic grin. *"Your lady?* So you two are an item again? And here I thought Piper was just having a vacation fling with her favorite boy toy." He lifted his glass. "Congratulations, Summers. Maybe this time you won't screw it up."

Brady made a move toward Gill, but Piper blocked him, whispering, "He's not worth it."

She heard Gill scoff, and she pivoted on her toe to face him. "I find it interesting that you're so interested in the status of our relationship. Could it be that you're not getting what you need at home and have to live vicariously through us?"

Gill's expression dimmed. "Schoolyard insults, Piper? I gave you more credit."

"What do you want, Gill?" Brady asked in a low tone.

The banker shrugged one shoulder. "Just came over to say hello."

"And now you have." Brady squared his shoulders. "Now leave us alone."

"So you can continue the NC-17 floor show?" Gill gave Brady a thumbs-up. "Be my guest."

Piper's cheeks burned as she watched Gill stroll away. "He's right," she said softly. "Things were getting too heated for public."

"Are you ready to leave?" Brady asked, disappointment heavy in his voice. He motioned back to their table. "We could get dessert."

She patted his chest and shook her head. "No. But thanks. Let's go."

Brady said good-night to Piper at the main house door, his mood high, his body vibrating with desire… and a niggling sense that despite how well the evening seemed to have gone, so much was still unsettled. As he made his way back to his house and let himself in the mudroom door, he tried to pin down the odd sense of imbalance. Like a musical chord meant to inspire and swell one's emotions with one note flat, the evening was almost perfect. Except...

Brady brushed aside the niggling doubts as he entered the house quietly, not wanting to wake his family. Kip rose from her dog bed and, her tail wagging, trotted over to greet him. He rubbed her ears and gave her flank a pat. "Did you watch the house like a good girl?"

Kip answered with a thump of her tail on the cracked linoleum. Moving from the kitchen to the living room, he found his father in his recliner, asleep. Brady shook Roy's shoulder. "Dad, I'm home. Don't you want to go to bed?"

Roy blinked and sat forward in the chair. "Wha' time's it?" he asked, his voice a tad slurred.

Brady heaved a sigh. "Late. You've been drinking, haven't you?"

Roy pinched the bridge of his nose. "No."

"What if something had happened, and you'd had to drive Connor to the hospital, or...?" He blew out a harsh breath. "I'm so sick of this."

"I didn't drink!" Roy shoved to his feet, his tone defensive, yet he wobbled as he took his first step.

"Go to bed, old man. I've had enough of your lies, and I won't let you ruin what has been a pretty damn good night for me." Brady turned and strode briskly to his room. He could hear his dad bumping into things and stumbling about as he got ready for bed. Brady stripped down, yanked on a pair of sleep pants and an old T-shirt and crawled into bed. Only after he'd settled deep in his covers and reflected again on his dinner with Piper did the nagging disquiet crystalize.

Piper had decided to move back to the ranch, was eager to form a bond with Connor and share custody of their son. But she'd made no promises, no mention really of a future for them. Despite their kisses on the dance floor, she'd dodged giving him reason to hope for their relationship. And her lack of commitment glared at him like an angry bull.

A loud crash woke Brady some hours later, and he struggled to rouse himself. He blinked, trying to focus on the alarm clock beside his bed, but the numbers swam in a blurry glow. Rubbing his eyes, he sat up, his arms feeling especially weak, and his head pounding at the change of position. He grunted to himself. He hadn't had *that much* to drink at dinner, had he? Hearing another crash and the sound of retching down the hall, he gritted his teeth, knowing the source. Rising on unsteady legs, he staggered to the door and into the hall, his anger rising.

As he suspected, he found his father on the floor of the bathroom, gripping the toilet as he vomited. Around him were the items Roy had knocked to the linoleum from the counter around the sink. Toothbrush and cup, medicine bottles, razor, soap…

"Damn it, you were drinkin' t'night, you liar!" he growled, his words sounding somewhat slurred. What the hell?

Brady gripped the door frame and pinched the bridge of his nose. His head was throbbing, and he was having trouble focusing. Why was he feeling so weak?

His father raised his head to look at him. "Didn't. I swear. I…don't think…"

Turning back to the commode abruptly, his father retched again.

"Right. Look't you!" Brady shook his head in disgust and immediately regretted it.

Roy groaned in misery, clutching the toilet seat like a life preserver. So hard, in fact, that his fingernails were dark pink, almost red.

Brady swayed drunkenly, then stumbled to the sink to get the aspirin from the medicine cabinet. As he closed the mirrored cabinet over the sink, he noticed his slightly blurry reflection. His cheeks were unusually pink. Could he be coming down with something? Was that why his head hurt and he felt so unsteady? His stomach rolled with a touch of nausea, and he gripped the counter harder when his knees buckled. Brady gave his father a side-glance. Roy had slumped down on the floor with his head at an angle against the side of the bathtub. The idea that something was off tickled his brain, but he struggled to make sense of it. His head hurt so badly, and his stomach had started to churn…

He stared at his own face in the mirror for long seconds. Rosy cheeks, dull eyes…

He couldn't quite capture the thought that wafted around his head, but something felt off about the situation. He wasn't drunk. Red cheeks, red fingernails. Confused…

A pang of concern sent him staggering into Connor's room. If he and his father were sick, maybe…

"Conn'r?" He stood at the door of his son's room and peered through the dark at the body-shaped lump under the covers. Connor didn't stir. "Conn'r?" he said again, louder, not sure why he was waking the boy other than from his vague sense of alarm. When Connor slept on, still, silent…deathlike, Brady's unnamed worry spiked.

Chapter 12

"Connor!" he called louder, moving to the bed to shake the boy. He snapped on the bedside lamp and jostled Connor's shoulder. "Wak'up."

Connor gave a weak sigh and rolled his face toward Brady. His son's cheeks were flushed bright pink. Adrenaline flashed through Brady, fueling his limbs. Without examining why, Brady dragged Connor into his arms and staggered with his precious burden toward the bedroom door.

"Dad!" he called as he hurried, swerving as he made his way to the back door. The chilly October air slapped him in the face as he lurched into the dark night. He set Connor on the grassy lawn under the oak tree nearest the house and knelt beside his son. Though outside the circle of the halogen light halfway between their house and the McCalls', the security lamp provided enough illumination to see Connor's face and limp arms. Patting the boy's cheeks, he sucked in deep breaths of the crisp autumn air. "Conn'r. C'you hear me, buddy? Wake up!"

"No," Connor grumbled and rolled away from him, shivering.

Relief swamped Brady when he saw his son stir, and he struggled to focus his thoughts on the source of his sense of urgency. What was wrong? What next? Blanket. Connor was cold. He was cold. Roy? Was his father ill?

He glanced back at his house, then to the McCalls', trying to dispel the fogginess in his brain. A light was on in Piper's bedroom. He shoved unsteadily to his feet and jogged with wavering steps to her window.

"Pip'r!" he called as he rapped his knuckles against the glass. "Pip'r, you awake?" A moment later the curtain was pushed back, and she cupped a hand to her eyes to block the room's light and gaze out at him.

"Brady?" she said through the glass, then unlocked and opened her window. "What in the world? Why...?"

"Cannu watch Conn'r?" he slurred. "He's o'er th—" When he turned to point back toward the oak tree, he lost his balance and fell against the house, shoulder first. He grabbed the window ledge to steady himself.

"Good grief! Are you drunk?" she hissed.

"No...som'thins wrong. Dad's still..."

Piper opened her window farther, and the weathered wood and metal protested with a creak and scrape. "What's wrong?" She cupped her hands around her eyes again to squint across the dark lawn. "Is that Connor under the tree?"

"Yeah. Need you..." He paused long enough to grab his aching head.

"Hang on." She ducked back inside briefly, then appeared again with her bathrobe on, a quilt in one hand

and her cell phone in the other. She climbed out the window and wrapped the quilt around him before shoving her shoulder under his arm. She started walking him back across the dimly lit ranch yard, using her cell phone as a flashlight. "Now tell me what's going on."

"Not sure. Can't think. Something…" He inhaled deeply and blinked, noticing his vision had cleared some. "Roy's sick. Me, too…maybe. Red…"

"What do you mean Roy's sick? How? Where is he?"

"Bathroom. Throwing up."

"He's drunk, you mean?"

Brady shook his head. "I don't know. Something's… wrong. I don't feel…right."

Piper stopped and looked at him with a narrowed gaze. "You do look sick. Your face is flushed." She glanced back toward the oak tree, her expression growing concerned. "Connor." She snapped her head back around to him. "Is Connor okay? Why is he outside?"

"Red…cheeks. Roy, too." Brady sucked in another deep breath of cold night air and tried again to collect his thoughts. To rein in the warning that circled the edges of his mind.

"Is Connor sick, too? Why is he out—"

Brady stopped short, tensing as his muddled thoughts sharpened at last. "C…O." He squeezed Piper's arm as the symptoms clicked into place. Carbonox—poisoning." He couldn't make his tongue say the words, but Piper's eyes widened and her back straightened. She understood.

"Carbon monoxide?" She whipped a glance toward the house. "And Roy's still inside?"

He bobbed a nod, then pushed away from her. "He needs air. Call f'r help." He trotted unsteadily back toward the house, and Piper followed.

"You can't go back in there! Brady, wait!"

"Go to Connor. Call help." A sense of urgency and deep breaths of clear night air gave Brady renewed strength and better clarity.

"Let me go in for Roy…" Piper argued, tugging on his arm "…or my brothers. You need to stay out here in the fresh air." With the thumb of the hand holding her phone, Piper started tapping in a call.

"You're not strong enough…to drag him." He wrenched free of her grasp, knocking the quilt off his shoulders, and headed toward his house. Time was wasting.

"Neither are you in the shape you're in. You can barely walk straight!" She snatched up the quilt he'd dropped and followed at his heels.

She was right about that. He wanted to run but only had the energy, the strength, to trot. She easily kept pace with him, her phone to her ear.

Brady heard a muted voice as someone answered her call, and she pressed the phone closer. "It's me. I need both of you at Brady's house. Now! Hurry!"

She disconnected without explanation, shoved the quilt into his arms and sprinted past him into his house. He paused briefly at the tree to check on Connor, who was groggy but awake and watching the proceedings with wide eyes. He covered his boy with the quilt, noticing for the first time the sweet smell of honeysuckle, Piper's scent, which clung to the bedding.

"What's wrong, B-Brady?" Connor asked, clutching the quilt around him, teeth chattering.

"Don't worry, buddy. Ev'thing's gonna be okay." He lifted Connor's chin and peered into his eyes. He could tell his slurred speech was concerning the boy so he spoke more slowly, working to control his tongue. "Are you okay?"

"My stomach hurts. And my head."

Brady gritted his back teeth, wishing he could magically take away any and all discomfort Connor had. He'd gladly bear ten times the amount of pain or illness if it would spare his son. Instead, all he could do was kiss his forehead and give him an encouraging smile. "Keep taking slow, deep breaths. You'll...feel bet'r soon. Stay here. Understand?"

Connor nodded, and Brady pushed to his feet to hurry inside. Despite all the grief he gave his father over his drinking, he didn't know what he'd do if anything happened to Roy. Losing Scott and Pam had been hard enough. With anxiety streaking through his core, Brady whispered a prayer that his father would be spared and charged back inside the oxygen-deprived air of their house.

Piper slowed her steps only long enough to dial 9-1-1 as she sprinted into the Summerses' house. She gave the operator the critical information as she searched for Brady's father. She found Roy on the floor of the back bathroom, and telling the emergency dispatcher she was putting the phone down to help Roy, she hastily worked to find the best way to move him. She tried dragging him by his feet first, but decided bumping his head along the floor couldn't be good for him. Shifting to hoist him by sliding her arms under his armpits, she lifted the foreman's torso with a grunt of exertion.

Even with adrenaline powering her muscles, she staggered under the man's weight. She growled her frustration, knowing that in days past, when she'd been doing ranch chores on a regular basis, she'd been in much better shape for this kind of task. Boston and her desk job had made her soft.

She heard footsteps and glanced behind her to see Brady lumbering down the hall. Her pulse spiked with concern for him. "Get out! You shouldn't be in here!"

"Not 'til Roy's out." He moved into position beside her, taking one of his father's arms.

"Brady, you can't—"

"Pull!"

"Mule!" Seeing that she wouldn't dissuade him, Piper funneled her energy into rescuing Roy. Side by side, her body grazing Brady's as they wrestled his father toward the back door, they worked in concert, scooting Roy a foot or two at a time.

Brady grumbled a curse as he wiped a fine sheen of sweat from his brow. "I should be able to throw him over my shoulder. This sucks!"

"It's not your fault. You're oxygen-deprived." She clenched her teeth as she mustered all her strength to pull Roy another two feet across the kitchen floor. "You shouldn't even be in here."

"Piper?" Josh called from outside.

"In here!" she shouted. "Hurry!"

Her brothers burst through the back door, and Zane frowned at the sight that greeted him. "What's wrong?"

"We think there's a carbon monoxide leak. Get him outside!" she said, standing aside so that Josh could take over.

"Where's Kip?" Brady asked.

"I'll get her," Zane said, heading down a hall in search of the dog.

Josh crouched and grabbed Roy under the arms. In a matter of seconds, he'd moved their foreman outside, and Zane came out on their heels carrying the dog to the tree where Connor waited.

Once Roy was laid out on the grass and Brady had collapsed beside his father, sucking in deep breaths of air, she moved to Connor's side and eyed her brothers.

Both were dressed in jeans, boots, even jackets. She wrinkled her nose at them. "Seriously! I call you with an emergency and you take the time to *dress*?"

Josh arched a black eyebrow, and even in the dim glow of the security light, she saw the spark of mischief in his eyes. "You'd rather I'd come out here in the buff?"

Cuddling Connor close, she sputtered. "Uh, wh—"

He grinned. "That's right. I sleep in the raw."

She pulled a frown and shook her head. "Jeez, Josh. TMI!"

"Trust me, Pipsqueak," Zane added, "The few seconds it took us to dress meant we were better prepared to help." He nodded to Connor. "Is he all right?"

"I think so. Have you called 9-1-1?" Brady asked, lifting a worried gaze from his father.

She remembered the phone she'd set on the bathroom floor. "I did. My phone's still inside. I put it down to get Roy out."

Zane stood from the crouch he'd assumed checking on Roy. "I'll get it."

"No, Zane." She waved him back to the tree. "It's not going anywhere. Don't go back in until the firemen say it's safe."

The distant whine of sirens drifted to them over the chirp of crickets and light stir of the leaves.

Brady braced on one arm as he leaned over his father, sucking in deep lungfuls of air. He gripped his father's arm and gave it a hard shake. "Dad, can you hear me?"

"Is Grampa gonna die?" Connor asked, a frightened quiver in his voice.

"No, sweetie," she said automatically, wanting to allay his fears. Then with a heavy sinking sensation in her chest, she realized she couldn't be sure of that outcome and amended, "Let's pray not."

"What about Kip?" the boy asked.

She glanced over to where Zane held the dog and saw Kip's tail move. "Zane's taking care of her, sweetie."

Piper hugged her son tighter and kissed his head. Sitting there, comforting Connor was the first truly motherly act she'd ever performed for her son, and she wanted to get it right. Tears pricked her eyes, not only in worry about Roy and knowing how tragic the whole situation could have been, but because she knew she'd missed so many mothering moments in Connor's life, moments Pam had filled with tenderness, instead of Piper. Clearly, Pam had done a terrific job raising Connor, but she was gone. Despite all the excellent male role models her boy had in his life now, no one could take the place of a mother.

But was she prepared for all it meant to be Connor's mother? Not just occasional guest appearances, but a full-time, ever-ready parent at her son's beck and call? An active caregiver, teacher and protector? Her head swam, and she knew it wasn't from any excess carbon monoxide she'd inhaled while saving Roy. The magnitude of taking responsibility for a child, her child, was overwhelming. She hadn't even worked up the courage yet to tell her father that Connor was her son. How did she find the wisdom and strength to be the parent she needed to be?

She squeezed her eyes shut as she clung to Connor, and she forcibly shoved those thoughts away. Now was not the time to weigh the life-changing choices she'd made tonight and the repercussions of her new reality. She needed to focus on now. On Connor. On the crisis at hand.

As the wail of sirens grew louder, she glanced over at Brady and Roy. Her brothers were huddled over the Summerses, murmuring in low tones. Roy's eyes were open, and with a sigh of relief, she jostled Connor. "Look, your grampa is awake. That's a real good sign."

Connor raised his head to cast a teary gaze to Roy. When her son tipped his head back to send her a watery smile, her heart rent wide, filling her with a bittersweet agony.

A fire engine led the emergency vehicles that bounced down the gravel drive from the main road, and Connor sat taller, craning his head to see, clearly intrigued by the arriving cavalry.

Josh jogged to meet the arriving help, directing them past the main house toward the Summerses'.

"Everything's gonna be all right now, buddy," Brady said over his shoulder. "You do what the ambulance workers tell you to do. Okay?"

Connor wiped his cheeks, and when an ambulance rolled to a stop in front of them, he peered up at Piper with a nervous look. "Will I have to ride in the ambulance to the hospital?" he asked, pronouncing the word *am-bull-ence*.

"Maybe." She flashed him a smile. "Would you like that? Wouldn't that be exciting?"

His furrowed brow and wrinkled nose answered for him. Then, obviously trying to appear brave, Connor shrugged. "I guess."

"What if I rode with you?" she asked. "Would that be okay?"

He glanced to Brady and said, "Will Grampa and Uncle Brady come, too?"

"Don't worry, Connor. I'll stay right beside you," Brady said, and she could feel the tension leave Connor's small body.

She knew Connor didn't know or trust her the way he did Brady. But the unintended snub still cut her. She could only hope that in the months to come he would learn to love her the way he did Brady.

A female EMT, her red hair pulled back in a ponytail at her nape, knelt in front of Connor and Piper and smiled. "Hi there, cutie. Are you my patient or is your mom?"

Piper's pulse tripped, and though she would have glossed over the EMT's technically correct assumption, Connor didn't.

"My mom's dead."

The woman looked concerned, glancing toward the house and then toward the spot where her partner was assessing Roy.

"I'm a friend," Piper offered as the only explanation to correct the wrong turn of the conversation. "And yes, Connor here is your patient. There was, as best we can tell, a carbon monoxide leak in their house."

"Oh," the EMT said, patting Connor on the knee. "I see. Can I take a look at you?"

He nodded shyly. "Will you help Kip, too?"

The woman's eyes lifted to Piper's.

"Their dog." Piper nodded toward Zane and Kip.

"We'll do everything we can for Kip. Okay, sport?" The EMT ruffled Connor's hair. "Why don't you and your friend come over to my big van where I'll have more light and you can wear a cool mask like a jet pilot?"

Piper accompanied Connor to the open end of the ambulance, noticing that a second ambulance had just arrived. The red-haired EMT pointed the newly arrived crew toward Brady.

Drawn by the hullabaloo in the ranch yard, her parents emerged from the main house in their bathrobes and cast anxious looks around the crowd.

While Piper held Connor's hand, the EMT secured an oxygen mask, then checked his temperature, blood-oxygen level and blood pressure. The EMT hid her concern well, but Piper saw the shadow cross her face when she read Connor's blood-oxygen level.

"Hey, sport, we're gonna go for a ride, okay? I want the doctors at the hospital to check you out."

The other EMTs rolled Roy to the end of the ambulance on a gurney, and Piper's father hurried over to check on his foreman.

The redheaded EMT glanced up at Piper. "You'll have to meet us there. No room for you with two patients."

"But I promised him—"

"Sorry. Rules are rules." The EMT climbed in the back of the ambulance and prepared to help her partner lift the gurney inside.

Connor's eyes grew large, and Piper felt a catch in her chest. She hated that she was being forced to break the very first promise she made the little boy. Leaning close to give Connor's forehead a kiss, she whispered, "Hey, Grampa's gonna ride with you, and Brady and I will meet you at the hospital. Lickety-split."

"Promise?" he asked.

"Cross my heart."

She struggled for a breath of the cold night air as the ambulance pulled away, red lights flashing. She'd just been reunited with her son. The thought that she could have lost him tonight sent a spike of icy fear to her bones.

Piper made her way to the second ambulance where Brady sat on a stretcher with the oxygen mask in his hand. A sheriff deputy was holding a mask over Kip's nose while Zane patted the dog and their mother hovered behind him, her face pale with worry.

Crouching next to her brother, Piper rubbed Kip's ear. "How is she?"

"I've called the vet. They'll keep her at the clinic on oxygen for a few days. He's on his way to pick her up."

After nodding to Zane and giving Kip's head a pat, she moved to Brady's side. "How do you feel? Why haven't they taken you to the hospital yet?"

"I told them I wasn't leaving until I talked to the fire department. And made sure Kip was okay."

She opened her mouth to protest, and he caught her fingers with his free hand and squeezed. "I'm feeling better by the minute. But then..." He frowned. "I wasn't exposed to the carbon monoxide as long as Connor and Dad."

Brady's gaze shifted to something behind her, and she turned to find one of the firefighters striding across the yard. As he approached, the fireman held out a wad of plastic sheeting in his hand. "Found your problem. It wasn't a leak. This was stuffed in the ventilation pipe, completely blocking the escape of the bad gases."

Michael frowned at the man and took the balled up plastic from him. "What do you mean, it was stuffed inside? How could that happen?"

The firefighter shrugged. "Only way I know is someone put it there. It didn't get there on its own."

A chill shimmied up Piper's spine. "You mean, someone intentionally blocked their ventilation?"

"Seems that way." The fireman turned as a sheriff's deputy stood and approached. He held the offending plastic out to the officer. "Here's the culprit. Found it in the main ventilation pipe."

The deputy's posture reflected his surprise, and his countenance darkened. He asked the fireman the same questions Piper just had and drew the same conclusion. The deputy divided a look among his audience. "You realize this means the nature of our investigation changes? We have to consider criminal intent."

She nodded, and a shiver shook her to her core. Piper cast a side-glance to Brady and her brothers. They all wore the same angry scowl.

"We'll need to question all of you privately." The deputy pulled a pen from his breast pocket. Glancing to the fireman, he added, "That's evidence. I need you to make a statement about where you found it and sign paperwork confirming the chain of custody."

Criminal intent. Piper's head spun as if she were the one who'd been deprived of oxygen. Someone had tried to kill Brady and his father? And her son. Or was the malice directed at one of them in particular and the other two were written off as collateral damage? Who could want to hurt the Summerses, and why? What the hell was going on at the ranch? Arson, poisonings, attempted murder…

Nausea churned in her gut, and she met Brady's stunned gaze with her own.

With a shrill whistle, the deputy summoned another

officer and shouted a request for an evidence bag to be brought over. "Well, what do you say? Ladies first?"

An ambulance had been called, and the blocked pipe discovered before it had finished the job. Damn it!

Ken lowered the night-vision binoculars and stomped over to kick the cottonwood tree under which he'd watched the emergency vehicles arrive. He'd been so sure he'd found the best way to eliminate the cowboy. A peaceful death in his sleep was even a merciful way to go. Ken clenched his back teeth. He should have just put a bullet in the guy and been done with it.

Except it would have been too easy for the cops to trace the shooting to him. He paced a tight circle while the emergency vehicles' lights blazed in the valley below. Enough of eliminating the competition and waiting for Piper to come to her senses concerning him. He obviously needed to take his efforts up a level. If he wanted to be with Piper, he'd have to take his case straight to her. Lay it all on the table and make it happen. She'd resist at first, he knew. He'd seen her independent streak. But he'd break her pride, humble her. She'd learn that he was her destiny and accept it. Or she would die.

Chapter 13

Two hours later at the hospital, Piper sat in the room on the pediatric floor where they were keeping Connor for observation and oxygen treatments, and she reviewed everything about the evening. From her dancing with Brady and their kisses, to his pain-borne terms for sharing custody. Then finding him at her window as she went to bed and discovering someone had purposely blocked their ventilation pipe. Like the evening's ups and downs, her emotions had roller-coasted from one extreme to another. She was physically and mentally exhausted. But she couldn't sleep.

She wouldn't sleep. Not while Connor was dealing with oxygen deprivation. His doctor said he was lucky. Brady had gotten their boy out before permanent brain damage could be done. Connor would be fine and was resting comfortably. But she was compelled to hold vigil beside his bed and monitor him, protect him. She held Connor's small hand and willed his body to feed on the oxygen and revive.

The room door opened, and Josh pushed Brady into the room in a wheelchair. Brady wore an oxygen cannula attached to a tank that he held in his lap with one hand, while he guided the IV stand with his hydration drip with his other hand.

"Hi. How's he doing?" Brady whispered.

"Pretty good, all things considered." Piper filled him in on everything the doctor had told her, and Brady visibly relaxed. "What about you and Roy?"

"I'm okay. Going home tomorrow...or rather as soon as they dismiss Connor. Roy is conscious and recovering, but his heart rate is off so they're going to keep him at least twenty-four hours."

"He was well enough to talk to the sheriff about the incident," Josh added.

Piper straightened in her seat. "Did he know anything?"

"Only that he'd heard Kip making a fuss about eight o'clock and brought her inside." Brady took a slow breath before continuing. "He thought it might be coyotes or some other nocturnal creature. Didn't see anything, though."

"What did my parents say? Did they see anything? Did anyone?"

"Nope." Josh angled the wheelchair in a corner and took the only other chair in the room. "Just like no one has any info on the poison in the pond or who started the hayfield fire or any of the other crap that's happening around the ranch." He scowled and gave her a level look. "The sheriff's department is still acting like it's an inside job."

"That's insane!" she said louder than she intended

and immediately winced and quieted. She glanced to the bed where Connor slept. He stirred slightly but didn't wake. In a whisper, she continued, "Pointing fingers at the family is just their way to excuse their lack of progress finding the vandal." She shuddered. "Except *vandal* isn't strong enough anymore." She gave Brady a pointed look. "Whoever it was tried to *kill* you, Connor and your Dad."

She could tell he wanted to deny her assertion, but instead, he slumped back in the wheelchair and frowned.

"That's the only reason someone might have for purposely blocking that pipe." Piper divided a look between Josh and Brady. "There has to be something that happened in the last few months that set this person off. Did one of you get in a car accident or pick a fight in town or stand a woman up or…something? Think!"

"Don't you think we've been racking our brains?" Josh replied, his dark eyebrows furrowed.

"Could Karl have done it? For spite?" she suggested. "I mean, I know I'm the one who angered him, but…"

Josh shook his head. "Dad talked to Karl about the incident in his office. Smoothed things out with him, he said."

Piper squared her shoulders, a bit startled by the announcement. "So Dad is bringing him back on?"

Josh shook his head. "No. Karl already took another job somewhere else. But Dad said they parted on good terms."

"Oh." She nodded stiffly. "Well…good."

"Hey, if we're going to have a big discussion about this, maybe we should go into the hall?" Brady suggested, nodding to Connor's bed. The boy had roused and was rubbing his eyes.

"Where am I?" Connor asked.

Piper turned to him and stroked his cheek. "Hey, sweetie. You're at the hospital. Don't you remember riding in the ambulance?"

Connor's eyes widened. "The hospital? Am I gonna die?"

Her heart flip-flopped. Of course. The boy's last experience with a hospital must have been when his parents died.

"No," she said and squeezed his hand. "You're going to be just fine. The doctors just want to keep an eye on you for a little while. How do you feel?"

"Sleepy. My head hurts." He raised a hand to the nasal cannula and tugged at the tubes. "What's this?"

She gently guided his hand away. "Don't pull on that. It's giving you special air to breathe to make you stronger."

His gaze moved past her to Josh and Brady. He crumpled his forehead seeing Brady in the wheelchair and hooked up to IVs. "Brady? Are you hurt?"

"No, buddy. Just need special air, like you." He patted the oxygen tank on his lap.

"Why do we need special air?" Connor asked, raising his arm and frowning at the IV tube taped to the back of his hand.

The three adults looked from one to the other, and finally Piper launched into a simplified explanation, leaving out the fact that the bag blocking the pipe had been malicious. Intentional. The thought sent a chill to her core, but also fired a resolve to find the perpetrator. Whoever had been vandalizing the ranch, trying to hurt the family's business, had escalated to attempts to harm people she loved. They had to be stopped at all costs.

* * *

The next morning, after returning to the ranch for a couple hours of sleep, Piper found her mother in the mudroom, just coming in from the stable after her morning ride. "Brady and Connor have been released from the hospital."

Her mother glanced up after pulling off her first riding boot and smiled. "Oh, that's good news!"

"Can I borrow your car to pick them up? The guys are busy…you know, covering for the shortage of hands at the moment, so I thought—"

"Of course." Her mother caught Piper's hands with her own. Melissa's hands were cold from being outdoors, but the gentle squeeze she gave Piper's fingers sent warmth deep to Piper's core. "You know where I keep the spare key, right?"

Piper nodded. "Thanks, Mom."

When Piper started to pull away, Melissa tightened her grip slightly, and her expression darkened. "Do you know how Roy is this morning?"

"Holding his own, Brady said. But the doctor wants to keep him a while longer for observation and one more treatment in the hyperbaric chamber. They expect him to be fine. No permanent damage."

"Mmm," her mother hummed in acknowledgment then gave Piper's hand a pat before releasing her. "Good to know."

Sidestepping Zeke, who wound around her legs and meowed for attention, Piper turned to leave, but after two steps, pivoted back to face her mother. "The other night at the party…" She hesitated, stooping to scratch Zeke's head and debating whether to press the topic. "Do you know what Roy was talking about?"

Her mother paused in the middle of tugging off her

second boot. Worry dimmed her mother's eyes, and Piper hurried to add, "I'm not saying I think you've kept big secrets from us or anything. I'm just—"

Her mother finished shucking her boot and raised a level look to Piper. "Roy's been with us a lot of years, Piper. I'm sure in all the time he's been here he's found more than one thing to be upset about. All I can say about the other night for sure is that he was drunk, and drunks don't always make sense." Her brow furrowed. "It's no secret he drinks too much, but your father and I decided years ago that as long as it doesn't interfere with his work around the ranch, we'll look the other way."

"Sweeping it under the rug doesn't help anything."

"True." Her mother shrugged out of her coat and hung it on a peg over the boot rack. She, too, gave the persistent cat a belly rub when Zeke flopped at her feet. "Roy has to want help before we can do anything for him."

"Maybe so. I just hate what his drinking is doing to Brady. And now Connor."

"Brady's a smart man." Melissa lifted Zeke, draping the large fuzzy cat over her shoulder like a baby and giving him a thorough head scratch. "He knows his dad needs help, and when Roy's ready to do the hard work to get sober, I know he'll see that his dad gets help."

Stewing over the rough road Brady had ahead of him, Piper slid her hands in her back pockets as she turned on her toe. Growing up, she'd taken for granted the unconditional love and support her parents gave her, and she missed her family while in Boston. She wanted Connor to grow up with the kind of love and support her own mother gave her.

She retrieved the extra set of keys to her mother's

Camry, and from the mudroom she heard her mother talking to her cat in a higher-pitched voice. "Who's a good kitty? You're just a big baby, aren't you? Good boy, Zeke."

Her mother's coddling of the cat made her smile. She would be a great grandmother to Connor. No doubt about that. Yet on the heels of that reassuring thought, Brady's remonstrations from the night before echoed in her head.

I won't let you break his heart, Piper. He's already lost one mother. He needs someone he can depend on, and your track record says that person is not you.

Brady's assertion twisted a knot in her chest. Would she ever live down the mistakes of her past? She had a second chance to have her son in her life. She *had* to prove to Brady that he could trust her to be a constant and trustworthy mother to Connor. But what did that mean for her relationship with Brady? Could she risk a second chance with her child's father, the only man she'd ever given her heart to? Would he dare to trust her with his heart again after the way she'd hurt him before?

She shook her head to clear the troubling thoughts. One thing at a time. Get the guys home from the hospital, get the adventure ranch up and running and begin building her relationship with Connor. Her future with Brady… Time would tell.

"Back in an hour or so," she called to her mother as she headed out to the driveway, weaving through the wiggling dogs that followed her to the car. She gave the dreary gray sky a considering glance, hoping the predicted rain-and-sleet mixture would hold off until she got Brady and Connor back home. The twisty moun-

tain roads were dangerous enough without adding in-
clement weather to the mix.

As she bumped down the gravel lane that led from
the ranch property out to the highway, Piper reflected
on the conversation with her mother. Brady had a lot
to handle between his father's drinking and raising
Connor.

Piper flicked on the windshield wipers as the sky
began to spit a light mist. She gripped the steering
wheel tighter and shoved thoughts of Connor and
Roy aside to concentrate on her driving. And how
she wanted to approach Brady and the issue of joint
custody. She didn't want to be a part-time mother to
Connor. That was exactly the kind of thing Brady was
adamant about avoiding. *All or nothing.*

She flicked a distracted glance to the car behind her.
The blue coupe had its bright lights on and was following too closely. With an irritated shake of her head, she
dismissed the coupe and returned her attention to the
oncoming traffic on the narrow mountain road and her
dilemma with Brady.

She wanted to commit her all. To Connor. To her
family. To…Brady?

Her heart gave a hard thump. She'd long ago given
up the idea of a future with Brady. How could she
be considering such a significant commitment again?
She bit her bottom lip. She'd given up Brady knowing
the gross injustice she'd done him. She'd felt sure he'd
never forgive her, and yet now that everything was on
the table between them…

The glare of light reflecting from her driver-side
mirror called her attention to the car behind her as it
made a move to pass her. She frowned, noting the dou-

ble yellow line indicating a no-passing zone. "What the hell are you doing, idiot?"

She backed off her speed, giving the dangerous driver better opportunity to get past her. If he insisted on illegally passing, she'd yield to him in order to minimize the risk.

But rather than pass her, the blue coupe pulled even with her in the oncoming traffic lane and stayed there. Piper's pulse spiked. And she thought Boston had crazy drivers! This guy took the ca—

The coupe swerved into her, scraping the side of her mother's Camry and nudging her off course, her right tires going onto the shoulder.

"Hey!" she shouted and battled down the urge to swipe him back. These were, after all, one-ton vehicles driving at highway speeds, not bumper cars at the carnival.

The coupe finally sped up and passed her—narrowly avoiding a head-on crash with a truck that blasted a long, loud honk as it passed.

Piper growled an ugly epithet under her breath. She braked again, wanting to give the other driver a wide berth. His erratic and dangerous driving had her full attention now. The car was a rental, she noted, seeing the bumper sticker advertising the rental company. She made a mental note that the coupe was a Ford Fusion with tinted windows. She read and repeated the license-plate number, fully intending to call the rental company—or the police—and report the driver.

Keeping her eyes locked on the road and car ahead and a firm grip on the steering wheel with one hand, Piper reached for her purse on the passenger seat. She felt for her phone, then remembering there'd be no service on this stretch of road, she abandoned her search.

She repeated the license plate number aloud to reinforce it in her brain.

The brake lights ahead of her flashed on, and she gasped, realizing how quickly she was coming up on the blue car's back bumper. She stomped on her brakes. The car skidded on the freshly wet road and crashed into the back of the coupe. As the Camry lurched to an abrupt halt, Piper bit her tongue and tasted blood. Her seat belt jerked taut across her chest, and her head whipped forward and then back. The airbag smacked her face and chest as it deployed.

Shock rendered her motionless for a few stumbling heartbeats. She released a shaky breath as she took a quick assessment. She shook with the aftereffects of adrenaline but counted herself lucky she hadn't been driving any faster, hadn't spun off the edge of the highway. Piper coughed on the powder released by the airbag.

Her mother's car had a considerable amount of damage thanks to the jerk in the blue Fusion. Even as she squeezed the steering wheel, seething at the driver's recklessness, which had caused the accident, the driver's door of the Ford opened, and a man in a heavy black coat with the hood up stepped out.

Piper gave an involuntary shiver as the man approached her, his shoulders hunched against the cold and drizzle. She was all too aware that she was alone, isolated on this stretch of the highway, and without access to cell phone service.

She locked the doors on her mother's car, then rolled her window down a mere inch to talk to the man who stalked to her driver-side door. A throb of irritation battled the swirl of apprehension for priority. She had no way of knowing what she'd encounter with the erratic driver. He could be high on meth, or vindictive or a scam artist looking to cash in on her insurance. Flexing her hands on the steering wheel, she exhaled a slow breath, trying to relax, even as her stomach bunched in dread.

A sixth sense told her something was off about the situation, but before she could fully work through her options, he was at her door. Only when the man got right up to her window was she able to see past the shielding hood of his coat and get a glimpse of his face. She sucked in a sharp breath of surprise. "Ken?"

The familiar face filled her with equal parts relief and confusion. She rolled her window down farther to talk to her coworker from the Boston accounting office. "What in the world? What are you doing in Colorado?"

"A guy can't go on vacation?" the husky accountant returned.

She chuffed a laugh. "What are the odds that we'd run into each other out here?" She waved a hand toward the crumpled fenders. "Literally."

He shrugged. "Yeah. What are the odds?"

His blithe attitude and the reminder of the way he'd been driving spiked her blood pressure. "What did you think you were doing, driving like that? Passing in a no-passing zone? You nearly hit that truck! And then slamming on your brakes in front of me?"

He straightened. "Are you saying this is my fault? You rear-ended me!"

"I—" She blinked her shock. He was *not* blaming *her* for this mess! "Seriously?"

"Oh, yeah. I'm serious." He narrowed a squinty-eyed stare on her.

Fed up, Piper opened her door and shoved up from the driver's seat. She pushed past him and stomped to the front bumper of her mother's Camry. "Look at this! You passed me, then stomped your brakes. On a wet road, how was I supposed—"

Ken seized her arm with a viselike grip, and Piper whipped her head to gape at him. "What are you—? Let go of me!"

"Not a chance." He yanked hard on her arm, and she stumbled into his chest. "I've worked too hard to get to this point." He grabbed her other arm now, and even through her coat his fingers dug into her arm in a painful grip.

"Ow! Stop it!" She struggled to free herself, a bud of panic growing in her chest. "What are you talking about? Worked too hard to get where?"

A car whizzed past them, the driver giving them a curious look as he drove by. Piper realized too late that she needed to signal a passing car. Her coworker was acting oddly, and the clutch of fear was strangling her breath.

"I've been trying to get your attention for months, but you've ignored me." Ken started toward his rental car, dragging her in his wake.

"Let go. Now!" She infused her tone with as much authority and determination as she could muster, but he seemed not to even hear her. Piper's survival instinct flared, hot sparks of panic flooding her veins. She tried to dig in her heels, to pull out of his grip, to strike him hard enough to win her release. "Stop it!"

She landed a flailing blow to his eye, and he paused long enough to narrow a glare on her. "You'll pay for that."

With a swift, twisting motion, he bent her arms behind her back and lowered his shoulder into her belly.

Air rushed from her lungs as he lifted her over his shoulder in a fireman's carry.

She screamed, squirmed and kicked—anything to win her release. A punch of adrenaline fueled her muscles and fired her pulse. But even that boost was no match for his strength. He dumped her facedown on the driver's seat of his rental car and planted his knee in her back, pinning her down. Piper struggled against his hold, trying to wrest even one hand free, but his large hands caught her wrists and held them securely behind her back.

"You belong with me, Piper. One way or another, you *will* be mine!" he said in a low growl. His grip shifted, and the screech of tape ripping from a roll sent a shiver through her. He clutched her hands together and wrapped the tape around her wrists, binding them tightly.

Bile surged into her throat. If she'd had any doubt before of his intent, she didn't now. She was his hostage. "Ken, don't do this. Please!"

"I've seen you with that sorry-assed cowboy. Kissing and groping each other like a couple wild animals. You're better than that, Piper. I'm better than that. We belong together."

She cast her glance around her limited view of the front seat, searching for a weapon. She saw nothing but clutter and trash. The floor was littered with fast food cups and cinnamon gum wrappers. *Gum wrappers.* Like the one she'd found under her cottonwood. She trembled to her core, realizing that he'd been on the ranch, watching her. *Stalking* her. The thought of him following her here to Colorado sickened her. Terrified her. But she refused to go quietly. She was no stranger to fighting and self-defense. She tried rearing her head back, hoping to smash his nose. To no avail.

"You're insane!" she shouted. "Get your hands off me! You'll never be half the man Brady is!"

"*Brady*, huh? That's the punk's name?" Ken leaned close to her ear and spittle sprayed her cheek as he snarled, "Brady's gonna die. No one touches my woman and lives to talk about it. Ask Ron Sandburg."

Piper froze. A chill crept through her as his meaning became clear. "Y-you killed Ron?"

"Ya huh," he replied, his Boston accent thick. "He got in our way. You and me…we have a destiny together." His breath was hot and smelled of cinnamon gum.

Her shock and fear rendered her weak for the precious seconds it took Ken to shove her deeper into the car. She collapsed, half on the floorboard and half on the passenger seat, the impact of the rough landing stealing her breath.

Her captor shouldered his way into the rental car and slammed the door. Digging under the driver's seat, he extracted a handgun and aimed it at her.

"The choice is yours, Piper. Will we be together in life…or in death?"

Chapter 14

"When is Piper gonna be here?" Connor asked, voicing the question that had been rolling through Brady's mind repeatedly in the last hour.

"Soon." Brady checked his watch for the third time in five minutes, his impatience and concern growing. Piper had said she was leaving right away to pick up him and Connor and drive them back to the ranch. Even allowing a generous extra half hour for delays, Piper was ninety minutes late.

Connor was growing increasingly restless and hungry, but Brady had been holding out for Piper to arrive before taking him to get some lunch. He'd have much preferred a meal at the diner in Boyd Valley—heck, even fast food—over the hospital fare they'd had the last twelve hours.

Brady resisted the urge to call Piper's cell phone again. He'd done that twenty minutes ago, and it had gone to voice mail, indicating she was driving and didn't want to be distracted. A good habit, he acknowledged, but one that didn't give him any answers about her ETA.

Instead, he called the phone in the main house, and Melissa answered on the third ring with a bright "Hello?"

"Hi, it's Brady. I was just wondering if you'd heard anything from Piper. She hasn't arrived yet, and I was trying to get an idea of how much longer it might be."

"Piper is on her way. She left, oh…" Melissa paused, presumably checking the clock "…about…hmm. Well, more than two hours ago. Almost three hours. Do you mean to say she's not there yet?"

"No, she's not. So…" he scrubbed a hand through his hair, an uneasiness nipping the back of his neck "…she hasn't called to say she was delayed or had a flat tire or anything?"

"Not that I know of. Let me ask the boys."

Brady heard a muted "Joshua! Zane!" and then a thump followed by silence as Piper's mother apparently went in search of her sons.

"I'm sooo hungry!" Connor complained. "When is lunch?"

Brady sighed in resignation. "When I get off the phone, we'll get something from the lunchroom downstairs."

Connor flopped on the foot of Roy's hospital bed and groaned. Roy lifted the plastic cover over his lunch and waved a hand at it. "You want my pork chop and yams? They're extra dried out and chewy, just the way you like 'em!"

Connor pulled a face. "Yams? Blech!"

"Sorry to keep you waiting, Brady. I can't find Zane, but Josh said he hasn't heard from Piper. He's willing to come get you if you want. And he can check the roads on the way to see if Piper is stranded with car trouble or something."

"Well—" Brady scratched the side of his nose, undecided "—I hate to have him drive all this way if Piper is coming already. But then again, if she's this late…"

"I'm sending him," Mrs. McCall said. "If for no other reason than I'm concerned about what is holding Piper up. Call if Josh doesn't get there in an hour. Okay?"

Another hour. More than enough time to get Connor something to eat in the cafeteria downstairs. "Right. Will do. Thanks, Mrs. Mac."

He should have felt relief that a backup driver was on the way, but Brady couldn't shake the prickling sense that something had gone very wrong. He'd had the same precognition the night Scott and Pam were killed.

"All right. Let's go get our grub on!" He pasted on a strained smile for Connor, not wanting to alarm his son, but he could see on Roy's face that his father saw through his charade. He herded Connor to the elevator, listening to his little boy chatter about what he wanted to order. But eating was the last thing on Brady's mind at the moment.

Piper was almost two hours late and not answering her phone. He couldn't help but fear that she was in trouble.

Piper was in trouble. Or at least she'd had some trouble and left the scene without letting the family know where she was going.

Josh had spotted his mother's Camry on the narrow shoulder of the mountain highway leading from Boyd Valley to the main road into Denver and had parked behind it to examine the evidence of Piper's mishap. The front bumper of their mother's car was smashed and the hood had buckled. Piper had hit…something. Another car? An elk? Other wildlife?

Josh turned a full circle scanning the road, the hillside beyond the guardrail, everywhere he could see from his vantage point. Whatever had done this damage to the Camry was gone. And so was his sister.

The mystery of where she might have gone—clearly, she'd ridden with someone to either call a tow truck or phone someone in the family—didn't bother Josh nearly as much as other details of the scene. First, she'd left her engine running. A completely inexcusable oversight he couldn't see Piper letting slip by. Also, her driver's door was open.

Josh swallowed the dark taste of anxiety that crept up the back of his throat. He wouldn't panic. There had to be a reasonable explanation for the apparent oversights. He crunched over the gravel on the side of the highway to cut the engine and lock up his mother's car until a tow could be arranged. Could she have felt sick or needed to go to the bathroom and hiked into the trees a little ways?

Josh scanned the highway and remote landscape of aspens, tall pines and dead grasses on the steep hillsides. "Piper! Hey, Pipsqueak, you out there?"

His shout startled a pair of birds from a nearby scrub brush, but no one answered.

Leaning into the Camry, he turned and removed the ignition key. As he backed out, he spotted Piper's purse on the floorboard, the contents spilled out. Her wallet, her lip balm, her brush. And her phone.

A chill raced through Josh. His sister simply wasn't foolish enough to leave her purse and her cell phone behind in any circumstance. A sinking reality swamped Josh, and his gut filled with acid. Something bad had happened to Piper. Something very bad.

Brady called Piper's phone. Again. And the call was answered.

"Hi, Br...y."

Despite the bad connection, he knew the voice belonged to Josh, but even with the sound dropping out, he recognized the timbre of dejection and anxiety.

Brady's stomach pitched. A sinking dread flowed through his veins like wet concrete. "If you're answering her phone, the news isn't good, is it?"

"No. I f...her car aband...left her purse and ph... behind."

Brady propped his elbow on his knee and braced his hand against his forehead. "Have you called the cops yet?"

"Not yet. Only...in cell range. I'm on...to get you. We...talk then."

Brady's throat tightened. He didn't know how he'd stand it if anything happened to Piper. "Okay. But I'm calling the cops and having them meet us here."

"...jurisdiction. I'll call Za...him alert the local auth..." Josh said.

"What should I do?" He couldn't be idle. If Piper was missing, he had to be doing *something*. Anything.

"Sit tight. I'll...there in...minutes."

"I can't do nothing!" he argued. "I can call Dave and Helen and get them to start looking. Asking around town. What about your parents? Do they know?" Silence answered him. "Josh?"

He muttered a curse under his breath as he disconnected and raised his gaze to his father. Roy, as expected, was watching him with a deep furrow lining his brow.

"What's happened?"

Connor, who'd finished his cafeteria hamburger and had his nose buried in a handheld video game, looked up, as well. Brady reached in his pocket for some money and held it out to his son. "Hey, buddy, why don't you take this to the nurses' desk and see if anyone there has change."

Connor got up from his chair slowly and took the bills. "Is something wrong?"

"Nothing for you to worry about." He tousled Connor's hair and gave him a nudge toward the door. "You can use the change to buy yourself some candy or a drink from the machine, okay?"

The boy brightened a bit with that news. "Okay."

Once Connor was out of earshot, he explained the situation to Roy as succinctly as he could.

After removing the oxygen cannula from his nose, Roy tossed the covers back and tried to get out of bed. "I'll dress and help you look."

Brady planted a hand on his father's chest. "No. I won't have you passing out or worse because you left the hospital too soon. Stay and recoup. Besides, I need to leave Connor here with you."

Roy clearly wasn't pleased with the idea of not being part of the search for Piper but, to his credit, he didn't argue. "Where could she be? Piper's not the sort to do something reckless like leaving her car and purse sitting unattended on the side of the road."

Brady took a deep breath, shaking his head in agreement. His hands fisted, and anxiety tied his gut in a knot. "She's not. That's why I suspect foul play."

Chapter 15

Twenty nerve-racking minutes later, Josh finally arrived at the hospital, and Brady had his jacket on in seconds. After exhorting Connor to behave and not give Roy or the nurses trouble, Brady matched Josh's long-legged stride as they rushed out of the hospital.

"I reached Zane on the way in. He's calling the sheriff and rounding up extra hands to search." Josh pushed the elevator button and only waited about three seconds before balking and heading for the stairs. "Dave and Dad were in the pasture working on a cow with a split hoof, but Dave's joined the search," he said over his shoulder as he pounded down the steps. "Mom is beside herself…"

"Understandable."

"…so Dad decided to stay with her. He can monitor the phone, draw up fliers, coordinate efforts with the police from there."

"And what has the sheriff's department said?"

"Not much yet. They've gone out to canvass the scene, and deputies were going to the ranch to get Piper's picture and other info to distribute to other agencies."

Given his recent oxygen depletion, Brady was breathing hard, and his temples pounded by the time they reached the bottom floor and the side exit of the hospital. So much for his doctor's orders to take it easy for the next few days.

Panting a little as he jogged beside Josh, Brady said, "I've been thinking…"

"Yeah?"

"Rather than randomly searching, as if she were a lost dog, we need…a plan. A strategy."

"Such as?" Josh asked, slowing to fish his keys from his jeans.

"Talk to people…in town. If we believe someone took her—"

"Looks that way," Josh said, his tone grave and his eyes flinty. He pressed the fob on his key, and his truck's taillights blinked as the doors unlocked.

Brady took a labored breath as he grabbed the door handle on the passenger side. "So we have to figure out who. Why."

"That's the crazy part!" Josh ranted as he slid behind the steering wheel. "She doesn't even live here anymore! Piper doesn't have any enemies."

"Of course that is *our* gut reaction. And that may be true. This could be a random act. But…"

Josh held Brady's gaze, his worry for his sister etched in the lines bracketing his eyes and the grim slash of his mouth. *"But?"*

"We have to move past that gut reaction and be logical. Think critically and analyze everything. We have to find the missing piece of this puzzle." He swallowed hard as bile began to fill his throat. "And quickly. Time is not our friend. Statistics say the longer it takes to find her, the less likely we'll find her alive."

Josh and Brady met Zane in the parking lot of Zoe's Bar and Grill. The restaurant was as good a place to start as any when you had exactly zero information or ideas.

They convened at the front bumper of Josh's truck, hoping the meeting would be brief and productive and they could get busy finding Piper.

"So I've been thinking since I talked with you guys," Zane said, his breath forming a white cloud as he talked. "We need to call some of Piper's friends and colleagues in Boston. We don't know of any rifts or enemies, but that doesn't mean she didn't tick someone off in Boston."

"We were thinking the same thing," Brady said.

"But before we go down that path—" Zane faced his brother with a narrow-eyed scrutiny "—you saw her car, and you said her front bumper and hood were crumpled, the airbag deployed."

"Yeah?"

"Could she have hit her head, despite the airbag? Do you think she could be disoriented and wandering around that area, injured or concussed? Could she have walked away and be passed out in the hills around the accident site?"

"Anything is possible." Josh twisted his mouth as he thought. "She left without turning off her engine, closing her door or taking her purse with her phone. If she wasn't disoriented by a knock on the head, then she didn't leave willingly. She wouldn't have been that careless with the car, her wallet and phone..."

"Can we assume that the cops investigating the scene at her car will conduct a search of the area along the road if they determine she simply wandered away?" Brady asked.

"Can we?" Zane asked. "I want all bases covered."

"But we're only three people. Granted we have Dave and Helen's help but...we should focus our efforts on what we feel was the most likely and most dangerous scenario." Brady sagged against the side of Josh's truck. He may have been released from the hospital, but lack of sleep and the stress his body had endured the past twenty-four hours had left him bone-tired. Adrenaline, caffeine and concern for Piper were his fuel at this point.

He divided his glance between the twins. "Agreed?"

"Right," Josh said. "Then we need to consider the possibility that whoever has been lashing out at the family with the poison in the pond, the alfalfa fire, and other sabotage around the ranch could be behind this."

"A more personal attack?" Brady weighed that option with a growing pit in his belly.

"Personal, as in plastic stuffed in vent pipes?" Zane said, his arms folded over his chest and his eyebrow arched in query. "The attacks aren't only directed at our family." He angled his head to include Brady. "You and your family were targeted, too."

"Good point," Josh said.

Brady felt a chill unrelated to the weather seep deep to his core. "You think everything that's been happening comes back to *my* family? That someone who wants to hurt *us* is attacking us through the ranch?"

"Expanding *that* theory…" Josh said quietly, "maybe your brother's death wasn't an accident."

Brady whipped his head toward Josh, too stunned to speak.

Zane held up a hand. "Not saying it wasn't, but we have to look at the big picture and consider everything. Turning a blind eye to something as significant as your brother's death doesn't do Piper any favors. And you *are* linked to her by your past relationship." *And by Connor.*

Zane didn't say as much, but it hung in the frosty air like the proverbial elephant in their midst. And he was right. The plastic willfully stuffed in his vent pipe was evidence that someone meant him or his family harm. If the Double M failed and had to sell off the herd and lay off the last employees to pay off debt, he and his father would be unemployed, maybe even homeless. The attacks on the ranch could be indirectly aimed at them, with the McCalls as collateral damage.

"And who would that be? Someone my dad accosted or insulted while on one of his public benders? Seems an extreme form of retaliation. I haven't been a saint, but I haven't wronged anyone I can think of. Last person I punched was in high school, and Gill deserved—" Brady heard himself and swallowed the rest of the sentence.

Josh and Zane both shifted their weight and exchanged a glance.

"You punched Gill in high school?" Josh asked.

"So did you," Brady reminded Josh, "and I didn't start it. He took a swing at me first."

"About?" Zane asked.

Brady's breath stilled. "Piper."

Now he really had the brothers' attention.

"He made a rude comment about Piper, to Piper. I warned him to shut his trap and to apologize, and when he didn't I…" Brady shoved his hands in his pockets and grimaced "…mouthed off about his mother. He took a swing at me, and I decked him. End of fight, 'cause by then there were teachers there, and Piper was pulling me off him."

Zane reached for his truck door handle. "I'll go talk to him. Apparently I'm the only one here who hasn't punched him."

"Wait," Josh said, pointing to a car near the door to the diner. "Isn't that his car? Looks like he's inside having lunch."

Josh started for the restaurant door. "Let's go."

Zane snagged his arm. "Hold up, hothead. Let me go in. We don't want to get him defensive if he thinks we're ganging up on him. I'll call you if I want backup."

Josh shrugged free of Zane's restraining hand. "All right. Then…we'll call her employer in Boston. See if any of her coworkers can tell us anything."

Brady had his phone out looking up the phone number for Piper's CPA firm before Zane could reach the restaurant's sidewalk. "I'm on it."

When the switchboard operator picked up, Brady explained who he was and asked to speak to the head of Piper's department. The operator was silent for a minute, then said, "I think that would be Neil Pluchard, but his line is busy at the moment. Would you like to speak to his assistant?"

"Um, sure." Brady paced the gravel parking lot restlessly and hunched deeper into his coat while he waited to be connected. The misty rain had returned, and he felt the sting of an occasional pellet of sleet.

"Neil Pluchard's office. This is Carol. How can I help you?" a woman's voice asked.

"Um, hi, Carol. I'm a friend of Piper McCall's, and I'm in Boyd Valley, Colorado, with Piper's brothers. We were hoping you could help us with something."

"I'll do my best. Piper is terrific. What, are you planning a surprise for her?" Carol asked.

"Uh, no. Nothing like that, I'm afraid."

"Oh." The one-word reply was rife with disappointment and concern. Carol had clearly heard the grave tone of his reply and sensed the serious nature of the conversation. "What can I do then?" she asked haltingly.

"We need to know if Piper has any enemies in Boston. Are you aware of anyone she's had disagreements with or anyone who could hold a grudge against her?"

"Oh, dear! Has something happened to her?"

"We don't know for sure. She's missing, though, and…" His chest squeezed, making it harder to voice the truth that was so difficult to confront. "We're afraid something bad may have happened to her. We're trying to follow up on any leads that could tell us who might have wanted to hurt her."

"How awful! My goodness, our office has had more than its share of tragedies lately. Now Piper, too! I—I can't think of anyone who'd want to hurt her. We all think she's wonderful."

"No rivals for a promotion? Or…" he took a breath "…ex-boyfriends?"

"I'm sure she has ex-boyfriends. She's a lovely girl, but…she hasn't mentioned any bad breakups. But then she is always the consummate professional. Not one to spread mean gossip or bring her personal issues into the office."

"You're sure there's nothing you can think of? Even if it seems arbitrary or inconsequential, it could help us figure out who has her."

Carol hesitated, stammering, "I… No. Nothing. I'm so sorry. Everyone here loves Piper. In fact, we were saying in the staff meeting this morning how much we miss her." She gave a sad chuckle. "Although that was mostly because we are so shorthanded until she gets back. Not only is she out, but another one of our accountants is taking personal time to be with his sick mother out of state. The work is really piling up."

"Well, if you think of something, will you call me right away? Night or day." He gave her his phone number and disconnected.

Josh gave him an expectant look. "Well?"

"Your sister is universally adored at the office. The boss's assistant had nothing."

While he was glad to hear Piper's colleagues liked and respected her, he was no closer to an answer. Except…

A tingle started at his nape when he thought back on what the woman had said. Frowning, he hit redial and asked to be connected again to the assistant. When Carol answered, he asked without preamble, "What did you mean when you said your office has had more than its share of tragedies?"

"Wha—oh, I just…earlier this year one of our tax attorneys died in a terrible accident at his apartment building. He went over a railing and fell several stories. Then, sweet Sally Henshaw was diagnosed with breast cancer. Now Piper is missing, and Ken's mother is on her deathbed."

"Tell me more about the tax attorney. Was foul play suspected?"

"Foul play?" Carol sounded horrified. "No."

"He just…fell over the railing?" Brady asked, incredulous. "Was he drunk? Were there witnesses?"

"Not that I'm aware of. Do you think his death is related to Piper's disappearance? How could it be? That's crazy!"

His itchy suspicion grew. "How well did Piper know this guy? Were they involved?"

"No. I don't think so, but then… Ron was a real ladies' man. He flirted with all the women in the office. It was innocent, though. Just fun flirtation."

Brady grunted. "And what about Ken? What's his last name?"

"Uh… Grainger," she replied, reluctance coloring her tone.

"He's the one who went out of state?"

"Yes. Why?"

"Where did he go? Did he say?"

"Uh, no. I don't think so. Just that his mother was terribly ill, and he'd be gone for a week or so."

"When did he leave?"

Carol scoffed. "You don't think Ken—"

"When did he leave?" Brady repeated, his tone brooking no resistance.

"Uh…about a week ago." Her voice had begun trembling and getting higher in pitch, reflecting her anxiety with the questions. "The same time…yes, it was the same day Piper left."

Brady muttered a curse word and met Josh's anxious gaze. Alarm bells clanged in his brain, echoing the uneasy suspicions scratching in his brain. He didn't believe in coincidence. Everything in him said this Ken Grainger was their man.

Chapter 16

Brady lowered the phone and tapped a button to put Carol on the speaker setting so Josh could listen.

"I… That has to be a coincidence. Ken would never—"

"Describe him." Brady interrupted.

"What?"

"What does this Ken look like? Age, height, weight, hair color…"

"Uh, I…d-don't…" Carol stuttered, her reluctance to incriminate her coworker obvious.

"Look, if he's innocent, and I'm off base in my assumptions, then no harm, no foul. It will go no further. But if there is even a slight chance that he could be responsible, we need to know who and what to look for. You want to help us find Piper, don't you?"

"Of course. I just…" She paused, and they could hear her nervous sigh. "Ken is about thirty-five. He's average height. Maybe five ten to six feet. A little on the pudgy side but not fat."

"Hair? Eyes? Tattoos?"

"Brown hair. Medium-brown. Not sure about his eyes. Never noticed. No tattoos I know of. But he wears glasses. The kinda squared-off, heavy, black plastic frames that are so popular now. In my day, they were considered nerdy."

"Long hair or short?"

"Longish hair. Not '60s-hippie long, but longer than the more conservative men in the office. And messy. Like he didn't comb his hair in the morning. And my late husband, God rest him, would always say, 'That boy needs a haircut!' when he'd see guys with hair like Ken's, all getting in his eyes." She sighed. "Does that help?"

"Yeah, I get the idea. I don't suppose you have a picture of him you could send to my phone?"

"I don't know. I don't feel right about..."

"If he's not our man, I swear no one will ever know you sent it. If he is, then—"

"He's not. He couldn't be."

"Wouldn't you rather err on the side of caution... for Piper's sake?"

"I'll...see if I have something I can forward to you from our last office party."

"Psst." Josh wiggled his fingers around his chin and lifted his eyebrows in query.

Brady nodded. "That'd be great. Thank you. Meantime, does he have facial hair?"

"Clean-shaven, usually. Sometimes he'd skip shaving and have a stubbly chin, but...no mustache or anything." Carol sighed audibly. "Oh, I feel terrible about this. Ken may be a little odd sometimes, but he's a good guy. Hardworking."

"*Odd* how?"

"No, forget I said that. I... He said he was going to visit his sick mother, and I believe him."

"I'm just trying to cover all the bases. How is he odd?"

"Good luck finding Piper. Please, call me back when you find her. I'm gonna be so worried until I hear back that she's okay."

"What do you mean about Ken being odd?" Brady repeated, but silence answered him. "Hello?"

"She's gone," Josh said, confirming the obvious. "Well, we have a description."

"Shall we start asking around? If this guy did follow Piper here, then maybe someone saw him." Brady hitched his head to the door of the restaurant and stashed his phone in his pocket.

"Right." Josh raised his own phone to his ear. "I'm calling this in. None of this sits well with me. Maybe the cops can issue a BOLO or whatever they call it."

Nodding, Brady blew warmth into his hands, and he prayed that, *if* Piper had wandered away from her car for some reason, she at least was wearing enough warm clothing to protect her against the cold.

Josh twisted his mouth in thought while he waited for his call to be answered. "I'll leave Zoe's to you. I'll start at the Minute Mart."

While Piper's brother, now talking to the emergency dispatcher, headed across the parking lot to the convenience store, Brady stepped into the warmth of the restaurant, where the fragrance of fried food and onions scented the air. Anxiety beat an impatient rhythm in his blood. Time was wasting, and every minute spent searching for Piper was another minute something terrible could happen to her.

Zane was standing beside Gill's table, still engaged in what was obviously a tense conversation.

"I'm not accusing you of anything," Zane said. "But my sister is missing, and I'm asking anyone and everyone what they know about it. I repeat, have you seen her today?"

"Maybe instead of bugging everyone and disturbing their business lunches, you should try calling the police." Gill sat back in his chair and snapped his napkin out before smoothing it in his lap and pulling his chair up to the table. "It's their job to find missing people. Not mine."

"They've been called, but I can't sit by and not do something to help search."

Gill spotted Brady and aimed his fork at him. "That's who you should ask. Word on the street is he's got plenty of reason to be hacked off at your sister. Ask him where she is."

Brady gritted his teeth and swallowed his resentment. Getting into a brawl with Gill wouldn't help find Piper.

Zane glanced back at Brady and shook his head. "No. You're barking up the wrong tree there, Gill. Brady has every reason to want Piper *found*." Zane jerked a nod to Gill and his lunch guest. "If you see or hear anything you think will help us, please call. The bank has our number."

Zane turned to Brady and sighed. "He had nothing."

"And you believe him?" In all honesty, Brady doubted Gill was responsible for Piper's disappearance, but he wondered if the schmuck might withhold information about seeing her out of spite.

Before Zane could answer, the diner's owner called from the bar, "What's going on, Zane? Is there a problem?"

They headed to the polished wood bar, and Zane explained about Piper's abandoned car. "We suspect someone grabbed her, maybe the person she hit, or maybe she was hurt and someone drove her to the hospital, but... We're exploring all options."

Brady added, "We're also looking into the possibility that she could have been followed here from Boston. Have you seen anyone new in town this past week?"

Zane gave Brady a curious look.

"Well," Zoe said, chewing her lip as she scrunched her forehead in thought, "there's been a reporter hanging out here several nights lately."

"A reporter?" Zane shook his head. "I can't imagine he—"

"Describe him." Brady interrupted.

Zane's brow furrowed as Zoe began, "Average height and weight, brown hair, glasses..."

"What kind of glasses?" Brady asked, his pulse spiking. His phone buzzed with an incoming text, and he checked it, praying it was Piper. Instead, it was an unfamiliar number with a Boston area code and a picture attachment. When he opened it, the message said, Ken is on the right.

The photo had two men in a random shot at what was obviously an office birthday party. He zoomed in on the man on the right, then saved the photo to his phone.

"Black frames. Kinda square."

Brady turned his phone to Zoe. "Is this him?"

She squinted at the image, then blinked as she nodded. "Yeah, that's the guy. You know him?"

"No, but Piper does." Brady squelched the roiling anxiety in his gut. "Why do you think he's a reporter?"

"'Cause he's always asking questions about the area. Said he's here researching the wildlife of our area for some science journal. And once, I saw him putting a camera with a huge lens on it into his rental car."

A camera? A sick feeling swamped Brady's stomach, thinking of this guy watching Piper, photographing her, and he met Zane's glower.

"I asked him about the camera," Zoe continued, "and he said he was photographing wildlife for his article. He asked about remote spots where people wouldn't disturb him or scare away the animals."

Remote spots. Fresh floods of acid filled Brady's gut.

Zane dragged a hand down his cheek, groaning. "Did you give him any suggestions?"

"Not really. I told him there were lots of remote areas around here, and he could take his pick."

"Do you have any idea where we can find this guy *now*?" Brady pressed. "We have reason to believe Piper may be with him…and that he means to hurt her."

Zoe's eyes widened in alarm, and Zane's chin shot up. "What the hell? What did you find out about him?"

"I don't have any facts, but I think he's stalking Piper. And there's a chance he may have killed someone from Piper's office a few months back."

Zane plowed a hand through his hair, his expression understandably freaked out, panicked. "What are we standing around here for, then? We have to find this guy! Have you reported this to the cops yet?"

"Josh was calling it in when I left him, but he didn't have this picture." He waved the phone where the photo still glowed.

Zane paced in a tight circle, his movements jerky

and agitated as he tapped the side of his clenched fist to his mouth. Spinning toward the bartender, he barked, "Describe the rental car."

"Um…" Zoe's face grew increasingly pale, and her breath more shallow and rapid. She twisted a towel in her hands and shook her head slowly. "Dark. Blue maybe, or black? Dark gray? No, blue, I think."

"Model? License plate?" Zane prompted, the urgency in his tone clearly flustering the woman.

Brady reached for her hand and gave it a squeeze. "Deep breath. Close your eyes and picture it. How many doors?"

"Two. It was a small sedan. Um… Jackrabbit Rentals. I remember the sticker on the bumper…a bunny with his back feet spinning like he's running really fast."

"Good." Brady nodded calmly, though his heart was racing like the rabbit Zoe described.

"Anything else?" Zane asked, his timbre noticeably more composed, though Brady could see the edgy worry in his friend's eyes. The flustered, raw desperation matched the scrape of nerves in his own belly.

Zoe shook her head. "Sorry."

"Give me your cell number, Zoe." Brady had his phone up, swiping through screens. "I'm going to forward this photo to you. I want you to show it around to people and call me if anyone has information where we can find him."

While Brady finished up with Zoe, Zane hurried out to his truck. He had the engine running, waiting for Brady when he jogged out.

"Now where?" Brady asked.

Josh emerged from the convenience store next door, and Zane blasted the truck's horn and slowed while

Josh swung up into the cab next to Brady. "No luck in there. I'm surprised that mouth-breather behind the counter can operate the cash register."

"We have a lead," Zane said as he pulled onto the road. "Show him."

Brady angled his phone to let Josh see the photo that the secretary at Piper's office had texted him. He tapped the screen. "This is our guy. Zoe saw him and described the car he was in."

"So he *is* here," Josh said, gripping the armrest as Zane sped around a corner too fast. "What's our next move?"

"Motels?" Brady offered while forwarding the picture to both brothers' phones. "The guy's from out of town. He's got to be staying somewhere."

"Good idea," Josh said. "Jeez, how many motels do think there are in the county?"

"Not that many, as it turns out." Zane muttered a curse and braked as a traffic light turned red, halting their progress. "That's one of the things I researched recently when working out the business plan for the adventure ranch. Only four places have more than five rooms for rent."

Josh frowned. "What kind of motel has fewer than five rooms?"

"Bed-and-breakfast inns." Zane twisted his mouth. "Damn it, he could be staying at a B and B. There's probably a dozen of those."

"So, we divide up." Brady glanced to Zane. "Even though it will use time on the front end, it may save us time in the long run for you to take us back to the Double M for more vehicles."

Zane nodded, though he was clearly no more pleased with the delay than Brady.

"Or have someone bring my truck to us." Josh rubbed a hand over his mouth. "Maybe Dave could—"

"Sonofabitch," Zane interrupted. He aimed a finger down the road to the parking lot of the Mountaineer Inn. "Look!"

Brady scanned the property looking for Piper or the creep from her office. "What?"

"The blue car," Zane said. "Zoe said his rental car was a blue two-door. And the back end of that one is crumpled."

Josh sat straighter. "The car she hit. The reason she stopped."

"Bingo." Brady rubbed his hands on his jeans. "So we bang on doors to figure out which room he's in?"

"I'm calling it in now to the cops." Josh had his phone in his hand, his thumb deftly swiping and tapping his screen. "But I don't plan on waiting for them to show. Piper's life could be on the line."

Brady already knew as much, but the reminder of the stakes only spiked his anxiety higher.

Zane grunted. "Didn't you say this cretin has killed before?"

Josh's body jerked in alarm. "Say what?"

Brady nodded. "Suspected. Not confirmed."

"Just the same," Zane said and pulled into the parking lot of the motel and cut the engine. "Charging in before the cops arrive could be unwise."

"But Piper—" Josh started.

"I'm just as worried about Piper as you are. We have to be smart about this. We don't know if he's armed, or on drugs or what his state of mind is."

"I think we've established his state of mind. He's been stalking Piper, right?" Brady said.

"Well…" Josh opened the storage compartment in

the dashboard of the truck and removed the Smith and Wesson .38 Special Zane kept there. "I don't intend to take a knife to a gunfight."

Zane huffed loudly. "Don't be rash, man."

"Just a precaution."

Brady elbowed Josh. "Let me out. The least we can do is show his picture to the desk clerk to be sure we have the right place, then watch his room to make sure he doesn't leave." But Brady wasn't satisfied with doing the *least* he could do.

Though Zane's levelheaded caution made sense, Brady couldn't stand the idea of inaction. Caution was good, yes, but he'd be damned if he'd stand around waiting for the police, while that creep could be doing who knew what to Piper.

He slid out of the truck and motioned to the motel office. "You guys see what the clerk can tell you. I'll watch the back."

And by *watch the back*, he meant snoop from the back. He'd had occasion to use a room at the Mountaineer Inn a couple of times before. Once when his father had been so drunk he'd been called to pick him up from a local bar. Though not legal to drive, a thirteen-year-old Brady, who'd mastered driving on ranch vehicles by age eleven, had driven his father to the motel rather than risk the McCalls seeing how drunk Roy was. The second time had been prom night with Piper. Thanks to those past visits, he knew the rooms each had a window at the back. He intended to look through each window and do a bit of the same spying Piper's stalker had employed on her.

Piper sat on the end of the motel room bed, her hands and feet bound with duct tape. Ken had wrapped the tape exceedingly tight, and her extremities tingled from restricted blood flow. She'd tried a few times to wiggle free of the constraints, but the super sticky binding pulled painfully on her skin if she moved.

Ken was on his cell phone, trying to book them airline tickets to Las Vegas, while he stuffed his clothes back into his suitcase and gathered his toiletries in a rush. "Not good enough. I need something sooner. What do you have going to Reno?"

Piper tried to stay calm. As long as she cooperated with Ken, she could buy time until her family figured out what had happened to her and send help. Surely, by now, someone had discovered her mother's abandoned car.

"In two hours? Two tickets?" He huffed and flung his ratty old underwear into his duffel bag with a grunt of frustration. "Yes, two tickets! Don't you listen? One for me and one for my fiancée."

Piper shuddered at the term *fiancée*, but if marrying Ken, playing along with his delusion, kept her alive until the police tracked them down, so be it. She could file for divorce—or better yet, annulment—later.

Ken scooped several pairs of socks into his arms while he pinned the phone between his shoulder and ear. After dumping the balled socks into his duffel bag, he zipped it shut and tossed the whole bag near the motel room door.

"No, I don't want to take a damn customer service survey!" he growled and snatched the phone from his shoulder pinch and disconnected the call with a mad jab of his finger. "Idiots." He looked up at her and drew a slow breath. "Well, we're all set. Two tickets to Reno are being emailed to me. Supposedly. If the dumbass at the airline can figure out how to do his job." He lifted the corner of his mouth in a half smile that sent a shiver through Piper. "But you're worth the aggravation of dealing with morons."

She returned an anxious smile. *Keep him happy.* She didn't want him to feel pushed to use the gun he'd wielded when he kidnapped her.

"You've gone to a lot of trouble to be here," she said. "I'm...flattered." She almost choked on the word. *Where were the police? Her brothers and parents? Why hadn't anyone come for her yet? When she hadn't arrived at the hospital, what had Brady thought?*

Her throat tightened, thinking of Brady. She'd been so foolish, made so many poor choices regarding him. Over and over, her caution, her reluctance, her attempts to avoid one simple truth had hurt him. She loved him. She would always love him.

"You only know the half of it," Ken said, settling on the bed next to her. He stroked her cheek, and she had to suppress a shudder of revulsion.

"Wh-what do you mean?" she asked.

"Really?" He cocked his head. "You haven't figured it out?"

That you're stalking me? That you somehow knew my business and followed me here from Boston? Yeah, sicko, I've figured that much out, but I've been too worried about staying alive and trying not to set you off to delve any deeper into your twisted brain. "Tell me. I want to hear it from you."

"I've been looking out for you for months. You know, handling the guys that bother you."

She goggled at him, truly stunned. "What men? What do you mean?"

He snorted derisively and narrowed an irritated glare at her. "Don't be obtuse, Piper. I saw that guy bugging you on the subway a few months ago. I gave him a good pounding and told him never to look at you again."

She swallowed hard. She barely remembered some guy flirting with her on her way to work months ago. The weather had just been turning warm. April maybe? Had Ken been stalking her *that long*?

"And Ron. Took care of him when he hit on you."

She blinked at him, stunned as her overwhelmed brain grappled with the depths of Ken's obsession and the horrors he'd committed because of it. "Did you really kill Ron?" she rasped.

"Of course I did. The jerk was all up in your grill at the office. I made sure he left you alone. Permanently." He gave her a gloating smile, and Piper's stomach rebelled.

She forced down the bile that rose in her throat. "You didn't have to k-kill him."

"Yes, I did. He didn't listen when I warned him to stay away from you." Ken rose from the bed and plucked a few more items off the dresser top. His keys, a wallet, a pocketknife. "I tried to take out the cowboy you've been fooling around with, but it didn't work the way I'd planned."

Piper gasped. *"Cowboy,"* she rasped. "You're talking about Brady." A bone-deep chill sank over her. "*You* put that plastic in their vent pipe?"

He sent her a sidelong sneer. "Wasn't Santa Claus."

Rage poured through her like a poison until she shook from it. Bitterness filled her mouth, and she couldn't fight back the snarl that spilled from her. "You almost killed them, you beast! The little boy in that house is *my son*! How *dare* you—"

"Yes!" He whirled toward her, his face red and taut. "I wanted that cowboy dead."

"Even if you killed an innocent little boy in the process? My son!"

Jamming his nose in her face, he roared, "Yes!"

His volume and vitriol shocked her, and she shrank back. Riling him had been a mistake, but her gall at the depths of his depravity had overridden her caution.

"I will eliminate anyone who stands between us! You belong with *me*!" Ken railed. "That kid is a connection to the cowboy, a distraction." He jerked back and began to pace. "Clearly, I need to do something about them before we leave. I can't have you pining over the brat and his father the rest of your life."

"No. Leave them alone," she said, her voice trembling. "I'll go with you. Just don't hurt them."

He grabbed a pack of cinnamon gum from the dresser and unwrapped a stick, tossing the wrapper on the floor. "Humph, it will make us late for our plane, but…" He shoved the gum in his mouth and chewed as he deliberated.

She stared at the gum wrapper, and her gut roiled. Knowing Ken had been on the ranch property, watching her, stalking her, chilled her to the marrow. Because of her, the people she loved had been put in danger. Because of her…

She had to make this right, had to protect her family, no matter what it cost her.

Ken arched an eyebrow and studied her, his eyes narrowing behind his glasses. "I can always come back after I get you settled and take care of unfinished business."

"Ken, if you love me—" she paused to swallow the bile that rose in her throat even speaking the words "—why would you hurt people I love?"

He lifted his chin as if stunned by her question. "I won't share you."

She thought about what he'd said about killing Ron Sandburg, and a new thought came to her. Could Ken be behind all the trouble at the ranch?

"Did you…start the fire in our alfalfa field?"

He snorted. "Me? No. Why would I?"

"I just thought—"

"I saw it, though. Quite the blaze."

She gave him a skeptical look. Did she believe him? He'd confessed readily enough to murder, assault and the sabotage to the Summerses' ventilation. Why would he deny setting the fire if he were responsible?

She sat straighter. "You saw the…? Did you see the person who *did* start it?"

He shrugged. "Maybe. I saw a lot of things. Your ranch is a real soap opera, Piper. You know one of your hands is doing that pretty little cook, right?"

Dave and Helen. Old news.

"Who set the fire? What did they look like?"

He scowled and shrugged again. "I don't know. A cowboy. They all look the same. Dirty jeans and stupid, big hat. What do I care who it was?"

A cowboy? Jeans and a hat? Not much to go on, but it was something. Maybe after the police caught up with them and arrested Ken—*please, God*, let them catch up and arrest Ken—they could press him for more specifics.

Ken returned to his hasty packing, disappearing into the bathroom while muttering, "Your family's problems aren't my concern."

While he was out of sight, Piper tried again to wiggle the tape on her wrists looser. From outside, she heard a car door slam and male voices. Her heart slammed against her ribs. If she screamed, would the men out-side hear her? Did she dare? What would Ken do to her?

Holding her breath, she strained her ears to listen to the voices. She only caught a snatch of conversation before Ken returned with a handful of dirty clothes and his razor and began talking at her again.

But that tiny bit of the mens' voices was enough. Tears stung her eyes, and a tangle of hope and fear twisted in her belly. Her brothers were here.

Chapter 17

"You go talk to the desk clerk," Josh said. "I'm going to check out the car."

Zane grunted and screwed his mouth into a thoughtful moue. "Okay, but don't touch it. The cops may want to get fingerprints from it, and you could smear 'em or something."

Josh raised his hands. "I know. I'll only look through the windows." He flicked a finger toward the motel office door. "Are you going or not?"

Zane spun on the heel of his boot and strode toward the motel's front door. The heat in the cramped office had been turned up full blast, yet the tiny woman who sat behind the counter—Zane thought he remembered her as a substitute teacher he'd had several times during high school—was wearing a thick cardigan.

"Can I help you?" she asked.

"I sure as hell hope so." He bent his head over his phone to retrieve the picture Brady had just texted him.

"No need to cuss, young man. That's what's wrong with today's kids. You don't know enough proper English to express yourself without resorting to foul language." She gave him a sniff of disdain, then shuffled toward the counter.

"Whatever," he muttered, turning his cell to face her. "Have you seen this guy, the one on the right? Is he staying here in one of your rooms?"

She lifted the reading glasses that hung around her neck on a chain and peered at his phone. "Who is he? Why are you looking for him?"

"He's a suspect in a kidnapping."

Her thin eyebrows lifted. "Are you a cop?"

Zane shook his head. "I'm the woman's brother. She went missing today, and we have reason to believe this guy—" he tapped his phone screen "—has been stalking her."

"He hasn't had anyone with him that I saw."

Zane's pulse spiked. "Then you have seen him? Is he in one of your rooms?"

The woman removed her reading glasses and eyed Zane skeptically. "How do I know you don't mean to harm the fella?"

Oh, I do mean to harm the fella if I find Piper with him, he thought. Felony assault was a possibility if the scum had hurt his sister.

"I don't give information out on my customers to just anyone. Privacy laws and all that."

"The cops have already been called. But if he has my sister in one of these rooms, God only knows what the hell the bastard is doing to her!"

She pursed her lips and raised her chin. "What did I

say about cussing? You stop it now, or you can leave my presence, young man." She shook her finger at him—actually shook her finger.

Zane would have laughed if the situation weren't so dire. He sighed and stashed his phone in his back pocket, trying to be patient while everything in him was screaming *Hurry!*

"If the police have been called, then we'll wait for them to arrive." She gave him a look that said *Case closed*, and Zane knew he'd not get anywhere with the woman.

He smacked the counter with the flat of his hand and made a low growling sound under his breath as he turned for the door.

"Young man," the clerk called to him as he headed outside. "If you disturb any of my customers before the police arrive, I will call the authorities on *you* for disturbing the peace."

Zane narrowed his eyes on her and said, "You go right ahead and call them, then, ma'am. Because I will not stand down while my sister is in danger."

"Did you hear me?" Ken asked, stopping in front of her.

Piper jerked her gaze away from the window and worked to school her expression, hide her surprise and hopefulness. She blinked, and one of her tears broke free to roll down her face. With her hands bound, the best she could do was lean her cheek against her shoulder to wipe it away.

Ken glared at her and glanced toward the window. "What's going on? Is somebody out there?"

"No," she replied quickly. Too quickly, damn it.

Suspicion twisted his face, and he sidled over to

the window to part the draperies and peek out. His body stiffened, and he swung his head around to snarl at her. "There's a couple of cowboys out there, sniffing around."

She held her breath, said nothing. She couldn't forget that Ken had that handgun. And that he'd admitted to killing before and attempting to kill Brady and his family. If Ken felt threatened by Josh and Zane, she had no doubt he'd kill them.

Hatred boiled in her gut for her captor at the notion of him harming her brothers. She drew a slow breath, knowing she had to keep him calm and buy time. "I'm sure it's nothing."

"No." He shook his head, echoing his words. "You heard them out there, and it upset you. Why? Who are they?"

"I don't know. This town is full of ranchers."

He took another look, frowning. "Damn it all, it's your brothers." He barked a cuss word, rattling her with the flash of vehemence and anger. He aimed a finger at her and growled, "You stay quiet, or I swear I will kill you and them, too. Got it?"

She bit her bottom lip, and as the acid in her gut grew, she had to swallow hard to keep from vomiting.

"Got it?" he shouted, his chest heaving with rage and frustration.

She nodded and awkwardly rubbed her bound hands, one at a time, on her jeans. She knew she had to stay calm, stay alert, stay ready to act in an instant if the situation deteriorated.

Ken stalked away from the windows and grabbed the handgun from the bag he'd been packing. "We're getting out of here. Now. Before the cops or your brothers come knocking."

Piper sat straighter. "You'll have to cut my feet loose if I'm going to walk. Carrying me out would be slow and attract attention."

He pulled an ugly face as he stuffed the gun in the waistband of his jeans. "Shit! You're right." Ken aimed a finger at her. "But not yet. I'm gonna get the car and pull it around back. Stay quiet, and don't try anything stupid, or I swear I'll shoot first and ask questions later."

With that, he hoisted the duffel and headed for the rear of the room.

Brady edged along the back wall of the motel, keeping low and out of sight. At each window, he rose only high enough to peer inside from a corner. Many rooms had the curtains pulled and the lights out. He kept an ear perked, listening for telltale sounds of a disturbance, either from the motel's front parking lot or inside a room.

The sky remained a dull gray, spitting the occasional drizzling rain, mixed with stinging bits of sleet. A small flock of blackbirds squawked in the field behind the motel, otherwise the only noise was the sound of tires on the wet road in front of the building.

As he eased farther down the wall in a crouch, the screech of stubborn metal stopped him. A window, two rooms down, was forced open, the screen popped out and tossed aside. Rising slowly to his feet, Brady pressed himself against the cold, damp bricks, as far out of the angle of sight as possible. His heartbeat filled his ears with an anxious cadence, but he bided his time, waiting for the moment the person inside emerged. If they emerged. He didn't want to tackle some hapless teenager thinking he needed to flee his girlfriend's father or a cheating spouse fearing he was caught in the act.

But once he knew the person was Ken Grainger, he'd strike.

The window gave another protest as it was forced farther open. A foot came through first, then an arm and head. Medium brown hair and black glasses.

Fueled by a shot of adrenaline, Brady lunged, catching Ken while he was half out the window and off balance. He plowed into him, head down and leading with his shoulder. Grabbing Grainger around the chest to pin his arms down, Brady dragged him out of the window and threw him to the ground.

Grainger recovered remarkably fast, thrashing and struggling against Brady's hold.

"Where's Piper, you sonofabitch?" Brady snarled.

Grainger answered by slamming his head forward into Brady's nose. Brady saw stars, but he didn't release his hold. He felt the man's arm wrench, and belatedly became aware of the hard object that jabbed him in the gut. Grainger wiggled his hand to the object, and Brady loosened his hold on his opponent in order to make a grab for the gun.

His arm freed, Grainger yanked the weapon out, and Brady wrapped both hands around Grainger's wrist. He slammed the man's hand against the brick wall, keeping the gun pointed away from him.

With an earsplitting bang, the gun fired. Through the ringing in his head, Brady heard a woman's scream. Piper!

Grainger stilled momentarily, and Brady seized the opportunity to wrest the firearm away. He flung it with all his strength toward the field where the blackbirds had been scavenging moments earlier.

The shift of his body to rid Grainger of the weapon gave Grainger the leverage to raise a knee. Brady saw the move coming just in time to avoid a direct blow to his groin, but even the glancing hit shot a sharp pain to his gut. He sucked in a breath, grimacing, and Grainger used the moment to twist free of Brady's grasp.

"Josh! Zane!" Brady staggered to his feet, praying the gunshot had already alerted the McCalls. He watched in dismay as Grainger ran toward the end of the building. The bastard was getting away, and Brady summoned all his strength, fighting through the pain gripping him, and ran after Grainger.

Before Grainger could reach the corner of the building, Josh came around from the front. Seeing Josh, Ken skidded to a stop on the wet grass and spun around.

"Brady, are you—?" Zane shouted as he appeared from the other side of the building. Thank God the twins had been smart enough to think about covering both sides.

Grainger hesitated for a moment. Brady read the man's confusion and frustration. He recognized the moment Grainger decided to go find the gun.

Brady staggered toward Ken. As he worked out the ache in his groin, Brady poured on more speed. He had to reach Ken before Ken reached the gun.

Grainger slowed when he got to the general area where the gun had landed. He whirled in a full circle searching for his weapon. And Brady used the delay to pounce. He tackled Ken to the ground and lobbed a punch to the cretin's cheek. With a growl full of hate, Grainger fought back. Brady absorbed a strike to his chin before he could get an angle for another jab with his fist. They rolled, grappling with each other, each trying to acquire the upper hand.

Brady saw another head-butt coming a split second in advance and yanked his head aside just in time. He responded with a similar move that left Grainger's nose bleeding. At some point in the tussle, Ken lost his glasses. Brady prayed that he'd handicap his opponent, but Grainger fought on like a rabid animal.

Extra hands and feet were suddenly part of the equation, and Brady caught a glimpse of Josh as he yanked Grainger to his feet by the back of the man's shirt. Josh snaked an arm around Ken's throat and held fast. "Where's Piper, you piece of garbage?"

Grainger flailed and gasped but said nothing.

Brady aimed a finger at the open window, and Zane took off running, yelling, "Piper!"

Brady panted for a breath and swept a scanning glance around the field until he spotted the handgun a few feet from him. He scrambled on his hands and knees to recover it.

Grainger had regained his wits and was giving Josh a fight. He landed an elbow in Josh's gut and had almost wrenched free.

Brady stumbled over to the struggling men and pressed the muzzle to Grainger's head. "Freeze, Grainger. It's over."

Ken hesitated, swinging his head around to face Brady. His expression showed shock, then fury. "You don't have the guts to shoot me, cowboy."

He made a move toward Brady, and another gun clicked as it was cocked.

"Don't bet on it." Josh aimed the revolver from Zane's truck at Grainger's head. "And if he misses, I guarantee I won't."

With two guns aimed at him, Grainger stood down. Glaring at Brady, he snarled, "You don't deserve Piper.

Leaving you and this stinking cowtown was the smartest move she ever made."

The jibe shouldn't have hurt, considering the source, but it spoke to the deepest fear Brady had concerning Piper. He said nothing, merely holding the man's malevolent stare with one of his own.

But Josh said, "News flash, buddy. She's moving back and going into business with us. Including him." He jerked his head toward Brady and sported a gloating smile. "You're the one who's not good enough for my sister. Brady's a hundred times the man you are."

Grainger clearly took umbrage and puffed his chest up. "He shovels horseshit for a living!"

Josh stepped closer, shoving the gun in Ken's face. "Better to shovel it than to be a shit like you."

"Josh, don't." Brady shook his head. "He's not worth it." Taking a slow breath, he moved closer to Grainger. Pitching his tone low, he grated, "If you hurt Piper in any way, this shit-shoveler will see to it you pay for it every day for the rest of your miserable life."

Josh nodded toward the open back window. "I'll watch him. You go."

Brady didn't need to be told twice.

The gunshot outside had chilled Piper to the marrow. She imagined one of her brothers lying in a pool of his own blood, and grief buried her, suffocated her like an avalanche of thick, wet snow. Losing either one of her brothers was untenable. Whip-smart and caring Zane or risk-taking and loyal Josh. Her heart ached, and every minute she sat, hands and feet bound, not knowing what was transpiring, was torture.

Then she heard another familiar voice shouting her brothers' names. Brady was here. Someone had gotten him from the hospital, and he'd joined the cavalry to find her. A rush of joy flowed through her, followed by a streak of terror. Brady was in the line of Ken's fire along with her brothers. Ken had a particular hatred for Brady.

She squeezed her eyes shut as a sob of dread racked her chest. "No, no, no! Please, God, protect them all."

As much as the thought of her brothers' deaths scared her, life without Brady saddened her more. He was her heart. Her future. The father of her son and the man with whom she hoped to have more children. *Nothing like the prospect of losing someone forever to realize how much they mean to you.*

"Brady!" she called but choked on her tears and only managed a strangled mewl.

Damn it, but she wished she knew what was happening.

She heard more voices, the sounds of struggle through the open window and strained to catch a fragment of what was happening. Then Zane's voice reached her, clear and strong, calling her name.

"In here! Zane!"

"I'm coming! Piper, are you all right?"

She heard the thump and rustle as he climbed through the back window. A fresh flood of tears, happy tears, filled her eyes and made her nose run.

Zane charged into the room, and when he spotted her, his own face reflected the same immense relief that swamped her. On the heels of his gladness, she saw the flash of fury in his eyes when he took in the silver tape cutting into her wrists and binding her ankles.

She shook her head, sniffling. "Doesn't matter now that you're here. I'm okay."

He wrapped her in a bear hug that crushed her ribs.

She could feel shudders race through him as he came down from the adrenaline rush of worry and panic. "Piper, thank God. Are you sure you're not hurt? Did he…do anything to you?"

"Just scared me. I'm fine." She drew a broken breath. "Zane?"

"What?" he asked, still squeezing her tight.

"I'm getting snot on your coat."

A laugh rumbled in his chest. "I don't even care. This one time I will give you a pass."

"Just the same," she said through her sniffling tears. "Would you cut my hands free? They're pretty numb."

He pulled back, swiping suspicious moisture from his own eyes, before pulling a pocketknife from his pocket and slicing through the duct tape. He rubbed her chafed skin and helped her carefully pull the sticky tape off.

She yelped as the adhesive pulled the hair on her arms and as blood rushed back into her hands, causing a painful ache as nerves sparked back to life.

"Sorry," Zane muttered and cringed.

"Don't be. Damn, but I'm glad to see you." She hesitated, then with her heart in her throat asked, "Where's Josh? And did I hear Brady? I know there was a gunshot. Are they—?"

"Fine. They're watching Grainger until the cops get here."

A dizzying second wave of relief flowed through her, just before the thump of boots sounded at the back of the room.

"Piper!" Brady emerged from the bathroom, his face battered and swelling and drawn with worry. He paused to survey the room for mere seconds before crossing to her in three large steps. Zane backed away, allowing

Brady to scoop her into his arms. "Thank God, you're okay," he rasped, hugging her. After a brief embrace he pulled back, eyebrows knitted, and framed her face with his cold hands. "You are all right, aren't you?"

She nodded and touched the edge of his mouth where his lip was split and bleeding. "Better than you, it seems."

He grasped her fingers and kissed them, shaking his head. "It's nothing. I'm just—"

Without finishing his thought, he pulled her close and kissed her. Deeply. Desperately. She tasted his blood, but nothing could have stopped her from returning his kiss. She plowed her still-tingling fingers into his hair and held his head close. She angled her head to seal her lips against his, and a shiver of pleasure and joy raced through her.

"Um…" Zane said, taking a step back and scratching his forehead. "I'll just…go help Josh with…uh, yeah." He headed for the front door of the room. "I think the cops are…"

Needing a breath, Piper broke the kiss but didn't release her grip on Brady. "Zane."

Her brother stopped and pivoted to face her.

"Thank you…for—" Emotion tightened her throat.

When she didn't say more, Zane simply fastened the top button on his coat before he opened the door and winked at her. "Anytime, Pipsqueak."

Chapter 18

"So that was Deputy Ramsey," Piper said two days later, waving her phone as she returned to the dinner table where both the McCall and Summers families sat, waiting for the update from the sheriff's department.

"And?" Michael asked, his expression anxious. "Did Ken Grainger cooperate? They will throw the book at him, won't they?"

"Throw a book at him?" Connor repeated, wrinkling his nose.

"Um, Connor, sweetie," Melissa said, setting her fork down and scooting her chair back. "Why don't we go see what we can find in the kitchen for dessert. I bet we find some homemade cookies in there."

Melissa exchanged a concerned look with Piper, who gave a subtle nod of agreement. Connor didn't need to hear the grim details of Grainger's arrest.

"I'll take him," Brady offered.

Melissa raised a hand to stop him. "No, Brady, you stay. I'll have Michael catch me up later." She held out her hand to Connor with a warm smile. "Come on, little man. I'll show you where I keep my secret stash of chocolate."

Zane's head came up from his rapt attention to his beef and potatoes. "Secret stash? Hey!"

"Easy, bro. I know where it is. I'll show you after dinner," Josh said, sharing a chuckle with Brady.

When Connor and Melissa were out of earshot, Brady returned his gaze to Piper. "Okay, spill. I hope they're putting the cretin away for life."

"Well, they offered him a deal in exchange for information he might have regarding the vandalism around the ranch."

Roy, who'd been released from the hospital with no permanent damage the day after Piper's rescue, scowled. "A deal? That bastard nearly killed my family. He deserves to rot in prison!"

"True," Piper said with a nod, "but any information we can get to help catch the person responsible for the trouble the ranch has been having is welcome in my book."

"What did they offer him? And did he take it?" Brady asked, slipping his hand into Piper's.

"Reduced charges all around. Three counts of attempted second-degree murder, one count of simple kidnapping, with the charges of stalking and trespassing dropped."

"Dropped?" Brady almost came out of his chair. "For invading your privacy and spying on you for months the cretin deserves—"

"The State of Massachusetts can still bring those charges," Piper reminded him.

"Regardless of how many charges and what kind, he's going away for a very long time. That's what matters to me. He can't hurt you or this family again," Michael said, including Brady and his father in that statement with a nod to them.

"I still want five minutes alone with him to…" Josh waved a fist and pinched his mouth in a taut line.

"Get in line," Brady said.

"You already took your swipes," Piper said, touching her fingers gently to the corner of his healing mouth.

"I want another turn. He messed with my woman, and I don't believe in reduced charges." He smoothed a hand down the back of her head and settled his hand at her nape.

"*Your woman*, eh?" Roy said, arching an eyebrow. "Do you two have something you want to tell us?"

"Uh…not at the moment," Piper rushed to say, and she felt the slight tensing of Brady's hand on her neck. "Things have been rather crazy the last couple of days, and our first priority has been making sure Connor was safe and not unduly frightened by the recent events."

She cast a glance to her father whose eyes reflected the same warmth her mother's had for Connor. She'd filled her father in on the whole story and been given the same grace and love her mother had given her. He was thrilled to know he had a grandson.

"What about the fire in the hayfield? Did he do that?" Josh asked.

Piper shook her head. "No evidence of that."

"So what did he tell them about the ranch vandal?" Roy asked. "What did he see?"

"Pitifully little. His ace to get his charges reduced proved to be a much lower card."

Brady huffed his disgust.

Piper continued, "He gave a very generic and un-helpful description of the person he saw in the al-falfa field before the fire started. But he also agreed to take—and passed—a lie detector test regarding *his* involvement with the fire and the poisoning in the pond and so forth. He wasn't responsible for any of the van-dalism."

"He was in Boston stalking Piper when the poison-ing happened," Josh said bitterly.

Brady frowned. "Wait, what about that guy Ron Sandburg? He admitted to you that he killed Ron. He should get first-degree murder for that!"

"The Colorado and Massachusetts DAs are working out his extradition back to Boston for that charge and others," she said. "But the long and short of it is, be-tween the two states, there are plenty enough charges to keep him behind bars."

"And away from you. Permanently. That's what I care about," Brady said, squeezing her hand.

She heaved a sigh and felt most of the tension that had been coiled inside her for days release its grip. Most. She still needed to settle a few things with Brady, and that conversation had her on edge.

"So one menace has been caught and put away, but the bastard who is plaguing our family with crippling assaults on our livelihood is still out there," Zane grum-bled.

Michael nodded grimly. "That's the size of it."

"But…" Josh said, sending his brother a twin-telepathy look, "there is good news to report."

Piper could feel the mood of the room change as ev-eryone cast expectant gazes toward Josh. Clearly, the whole family was ready for some good news to dispel the general gloom of the past few days.

"Zane?" Josh said, waving a hand of deferral to his twin.

Pushing his now-empty plate away, Zane cast a grin to the family. "I put some feelers out last week for the adventures biz and had some interesting responses. Some aren't worth mentioning, but I got an email today from an advertising firm in Denver that is interested in developing a start-up plan with us that will help get the word out. They are reasonably new and looking to expand their client base, so they gave me a great deal for a complete advertising and PR package. Getting the word out is going to be key in the first few months of operation."

"And in order to better assess the adventure ranch and advise us, they plan to send a team to go on a trip with us in the spring. They'll take pictures, get first-hand knowledge, then use their experiences here to work with travel agents to bring us business."

"An advertising agency is bringing a team here this spring?" Brady asked, giving Piper a concerned look. "But that's just four months. Are we ready for that?"

"We will be ready enough for a trial run with them by spring," Zane said. "They need to see the operation to better produce the fliers and website and social-media campaign."

Roy shook his head. "I don't know nothing about social media and all that, but if you want to have a trial run ready by spring, you've got a lot of work cut out for you in the next few months."

Josh nodded. "We know. Can we…count on your help?"

Roy divided a look between the brothers and jerked his chin in agreement.

"Great," Zane said, slapping the foreman on the shoulder.

"And…" Piper said, smiling at Brady before she looked to her brothers, "you can count on me, too. I've decided to take the job as head of finance."

Her brothers grinned and shared celebratory remarks with the rest of the family gathered around the table. Brady turned a beaming smile to her and tugged her close for a quick kiss that made her insides do their own cheer.

The happy noises brought Melissa and Connor, who had a giant, half-eaten cookie in his hand, back into the room.

"What did we miss?" her mother asked.

"The prodigal daughter is coming home!" her father exclaimed.

"Piper is moving back home to be part of the operation of the new adventures business!" Josh said, rising from his chair to pull Piper to her feet and into a firm hug.

Her mother gasped her delight, and with her hands folded under her chin, she said, "Oh, Piper dear, I've waited so long for that news. I'm so happy that our family will be whole again."

Piper gave her mother a teary smile, but her stomach flip-flopped. As Zane shoved his brother out of the way to take his turn giving Piper a bear hug, she sent a side-glance to Brady. The McCall family might be whole again, but what of the family she and Brady might build with Connor? She couldn't put off the question any longer. Before she moved back, she needed to know what her future held with Brady.

* * *

Piper was drying her hands on a dish towel in the kitchen when Brady found her a short while later.

"Can we talk?" he asked, and her heart gave a nervous tremor.

"Mom, do you—" she started, glancing to Melissa who was putting the last of the leftover dinner in the refrigerator.

"Go." Her mother flapped a hand. "I've got the rest of this. Thanks for your help."

Taking a deep breath, she faced Brady. "All right, then." As she followed him out of the kitchen to the mudroom, she asked, "Where's Connor?"

"Playing checkers with Zane in the living room. Roy promised to see that Connor got him to bed on time." He helped her put on her coat and opened the back door.

"Where are we going?" she asked, pulling up her collar against the cold night air.

"Not too far." He motioned toward the stable. "The moon is pretty tonight. Why don't we talk over there?" He laced his fingers with hers and led her to the fence by the main corral.

She tipped her head back to look at the night sky and smiled at the almost-full moon. "It is pretty. And I missed the stars when I was in Boston. The city lights hid all but the brightest ones. Not like here where you can see thousands."

He leaned one hip against the fence as he faced her, capturing her hand between his. "Your family was pretty happy about you moving back."

She smiled. "Yeah." Then her expression sobered seeing his somber look. "But..."

"But...?"

She inhaled and said, "But what about us?"

He twisted his mouth and met her gaze. "Yeah."

In the silvery glow of the moon, she could see the doubt, the pain, the fear in his eyes. Knowing she was responsible for those dark emotions gouged at her heart.

"Well," she started, then paused to clear the thickness from her throat, "we have a son together. We both want what is best for him."

He bobbed his head once, conceding the point. "Let's leave Connor out of this for the moment."

She blinked her surprise. "Leave him out of this? But he's..." She goggled at him, unable to finish her thought.

"He's important, yes." Brady filled in her silence. "But aren't you the one who said you turned down my marriage proposal all those years ago because you didn't want a marriage based on the fact that we were having a baby?"

She swallowed hard. "I was."

He narrowed his green eyes on her. "Has that changed?"

"Well...no. It's just that Connor—"

"No," he interrupted, placing a warm finger against her lips. "We put Connor over here for the moment," he said, patting the air beside him. "Let's talk about *us*. I know I've been thinking long and hard about our relationship and where it might go from here."

The shiver that chased through her was only partly due to the cold. "And?"

He shook his head. "You first. Where do you see us at this point? You've spent the last seven years running from me, and the last several days having everything you believed about our past turned upside down."

She gave a short, humorless laugh. "That's the truth." She pulled her hand from his and turned to prop her arms on the top beam of the fence. "I know I hurt you terribly, Brady. But I hurt myself, too. I let my fears and my selfishness and doubts muddy up what should have been the simplest decision of my life." She cast a glance to him. "And I've been paying for it ever since."

He said nothing, letting her gather her thoughts, obviously wanting her to lay out her feelings before he'd share his.

She took a deep breath before plunging in. "I should have married you when you offered before. I loved you, and I wanted to be with you. I wanted you beside me not just to face parenthood together, but to build a life together. Yet I somehow talked myself into believing that you'd only offered to marry me to be noble. And that the noble and loving thing for me to do was to let you go. To release you from the burden of a wife and child and bills and shattered dreams for an education and…" She paused, fighting back tears. "Anyway… I've spent the last seven years punishing myself for the mistake I made."

He gave a sad-sounding sigh, and his breath formed a gray cloud that wafted through the night air. "Don't do that anymore."

"Then…you forgive me?" she rasped and held her breath while her pulse pounded in her ears.

He squeezed his eyes shut for a moment before turning and pulling her into his arms. "God, yes. Enough is enough, Piper. It's time to stop living in the past and move on."

Her heart slammed to a stop. Move on? What did he mean? Was he saying goodbye?

She clutched the back of his coat as she held on to him, her face buried in his chest. She had to do something, say something before she lost the chance, before she messed up again and lost him for good.

"Brady, I—I never stopped loving you. I never stopped thinking about you or wanting to find our way back to what we had. I only avoided you because I didn't think I deserved a second chance after…after what I did to you. After I gave our baby away."

He tightened his arms around her. "Piper, don't."

"Please, Brady," she said as tears dripped from her eyes. "If you can forgive me, then…can you give me another chance? Can we go back to the way we were?"

His brow dipped, and he scoffed softly. "No, Piper. We can't go back."

Pain lanced her chest, and she took a half step back, her head reeling. She had no one to blame but herself. She'd made bad choices and hurt him so deeply. Perhaps it was karma that he'd reject her now that she knew what she'd tossed away, knew how desperately she wanted him back.

She forced her tight throat to work. "Okay. I…understand." Her voice cracked, and she turned to flee, but he caught her arm.

"No, I don't think you do understand." With a hand on each of her shoulders, he gave her a small shake. "Piper, look at me."

As hard as it was, she raised her gaze to meet his. In his eyes, she saw a fiery passion that made her heart kick.

"We can't go back to the way we were because we are different people now. We've lived through heartache and betrayal and secrets and separation. We've grown and changed and experienced life's ups and downs. You've been off on your own, learning about yourself and gaining independence. I've had to take the helm of my family when my brother died and my dad crawled into a bottle to deal with his grief. Back then, we were starry-eyed kids with idealistic notions of what love was. Maybe your leaving was a good thing."

She jolted. "What?"

"I'm not saying it didn't hurt, but I don't want to re-hash all that has happened. I'm just saying, in hindsight, the last few years have given us both time to…mature. To learn what real love and commitment means."

Her heart throbbed, thrashing painfully against her ribs. "What are you saying?"

"I'm saying our love has stood the test of time and turmoil. I'm saying I'm more sure than ever that you are the one woman I want in my life forever."

She drew a trembling breath. "Brady…"

He dropped to one knee and withdrew a leather pouch from his pocket. "I've been carrying my mother's engagement ring around with me for a couple days now, waiting for the right time."

Tears slipped from her eyes, and a laugh bubbled up from her soul.

"Piper McCall, I've waited a long time for you. Don't make me wait any longer. Please say you'll be my wife."

She fell to her knees and lunged at him, knocking him over as she hugged him, laughing. "Oh, my gosh, yes! Yes, yes, yes!"

She kissed his face, and happy tears dripped onto his cheeks. Or maybe they were his. They shared several deep, hungry kisses before she raised her head and gasped, "Oh, no! What happened to your mother's ring?"

He sat up, mumbling a curse, and they searched the ground for a moment, laughing. When they found it, he fumbled the small solitaire from the pouch and slid it on her shaking hand. She breathed a sigh. "Perfect."

"Well, almost perfect," he said. "There's one more thing." He curled his hand as if grabbing something and brought the invisible item back between them. "Putting Connor back in the mix."

She squeezed Brady's arm. "Right."

"Thing is...even though we are his biological parents, Scott and Pam legally adopted him. So now we have to adopt him to make him legally ours again."

"Then we'll do that. I want us to be a family in every way."

He nodded and smiled. "Equal custody. We raise him together. Our family, the way it was meant to be."

She smiled and kissed his lips softly. "Yes. We were meant to be."

* * * * *

COMING SOON!

We really hope you enjoyed reading this book. If you're looking for more romance, be sure to head to the shops when new books are available on

Thursday
18th October

LET'S TALK
Romance

For exclusive extracts, competitions
and special offers, find us online:

- f facebook.com/millsandboon
- ⃝ @millsandboonuk
- 𝕏 @millsandboon

Or get in touch on 0844 844 1351*

For all the latest titles coming soon, visit
millsandboon.co.uk/nextmonth